MW01148388

Niccolaio Andretti

PARKER S. HUNTINGTON

Niccolaio Andretti

Cover Model: Actor Sebastian Cole

Cover Image: Common Creative License Issued by Unsplash

Kindle ASIN: B072J9RQW9

MORE BOOKS

Asher Black

Niccolaio Andretti

Ranieri Andretti (#2.5)

Bastiano Romano

Damiano De Luca (#3.5)

Renata Vitali (#3.75)

Marco Camerino

Rafaello Rossi

Lucy Black

Asshole. Douchebag. Jerk.

Those are all valid descriptions of me,
especially since fleeing
from Andretti territory.

Angry with the turn my life has taken,
I prefer the silence
and loneliness of my house.
Not only is it the safest place for me
after my brother placed a hit on me,
it is also my sanctuary—
my place to get away from the
bullshit that is people.

Until she comes along—
angry, demanding, and so damn hot.
I hate her immediately.

Bitch. Tramp. Slut.

I've heard it all before.
It doesn't bother me.

I have more important things to deal with—
like graduating from Wilton;
taking care of my little sister;
and yes, finding the next guy to pay for it all.

If I have to sleep around for it? So be it.
If I have to lose the dwindling tethers
of my sanity every day?
So. Be. It.

Nothing fazes me.

Until he comes along—
angry, demanding and so damn hot.
I hate him immediately.

AUTHORS NOTE

Dear Readers,

Firstly, if you're starting this book but have not read *Asher Black*, I recommend that you do so. There's very minimal recapping done, so as not to impede the story's progress. Either way, this novel can also be read as a standalone, so if you don't feel like it, happy reading! At the same time, there will be references to Asher Black that may be spoilers and confusing to those who haven't read it!

That said, I know some of you will hate me for this book. At first, I hated myself for choosing Minka as a love interest for Niccolaio, too. But despite how uncaring Minka is and how mysterious and brooding (and cranky) Niccolaio is, I feel like they both experience pain the same way. Minka's pain cuts her just as deeply as Niccolaio's pain does him, and when I realized that… well, I knew they had to be together.

In fact, that was the lesson I learned whilst writing their love story—everyone is similar in their ability to feel pain. That girl you know in school? The one that wears the expensive clothes and has all the handsome boys wrapped around her finger? She's capable of feeling the same pain you do. That guy at work? The one rising up the ranks in the office and seems to have it all? He, too, is capable of feeling pain.

Some people wear their masks better than others. You just never know when someone is hurting. Some people, and this is so wrong and flawed, wear masks of cruelty. And while it is 100% wrong, it's ve another way pain perpetuates suffering among its victims. Because it doesn't feel good to be mean, and that is something Minka knows all too well.

So, readers, as you sift your way through Minka and Niccolaio's story, I hope these messages impart themselves upon you. Actually, I know they will, because I have the kindest, most empathetic readers out there!

And I love you all for it.

xoxo,

THIS IS
THE SIGN
YOU'VE BEEN
LOOKING FOR

Rossi
Camerino
Romano
De Luca
Andretti
WA
OR
ID
MT
ND
SD
WY
NE
MN
WI
MI
IA
NV
UT
CO
CA
KS
MO
IL
IN
OH
KY
WV
VA
PA
NY
VT
ME
NH
MA
CT
RI
NJ
DE
MD
DC
NC
TN
SC
GA
AL
MS
AR
LA
OK
TX
NM
AZ
FL

MY PROBLEM STEMMED FROM NOT FORGIVING MYSELF.

— SHANNON A. THOMPSON

For L, Chlo & Bau.

Also for my girls—
Carla, Krista, Carrie, and Heidi.

Forgiveness
for·give·ness
/ˌfərˈgivnəs/
Noun
1. the action or process of ceasing to feel angry or resentful toward (someone) for an offense, flaw, or mistake
2. the action or process of ceasing to feel a strong annoyance, displeasure, or hostility toward someone or something

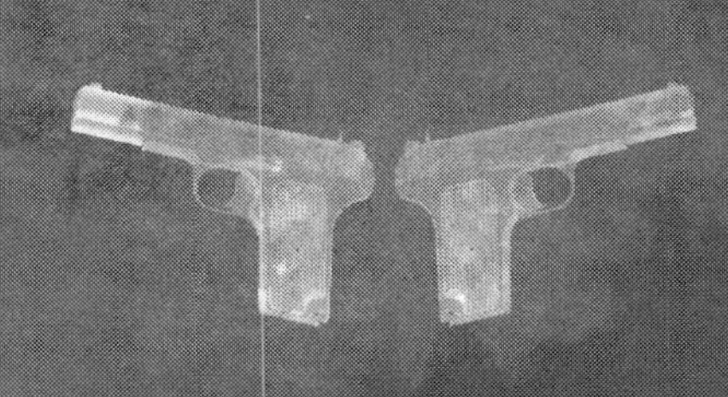

Forgiving others is a difficult decision to make; forgiving yourself, often harder. But when you hold on to those negative emotions, you consume the space positive emotions should occupy.

Forgiving doesn't mean forgetting. It's letting go of hostility—the part of pain and anger that poisons you the most. The part of pain that diminishes happiness.

Liberate that pain. Cleanse yourself. Release those throbbing emotions, and take a step forward in life. Then another. And another. Until you allow yourself to love and be loved.

Because you cannot love if you cannot forgive.

The marks humans leave are too often scars.
John Green

Niccolaio Andretti

Twenty Years Old

There's an eerie stillness to Uncle Luca's mansion as I wander aimlessly through it. He and my brother Ranieri passed out hours ago, and at three in the morning, I should be asleep, too. But whenever I try, I can't seem to shut out the sound of my own thoughts.

Four days have passed since Dad greenlit a hit on Vincent Romano. Four days have passed since our Andretti soldiers failed. And four days have passed in utter silence, the alarming tranquility not unlike the calm before a storm.

When I turn a corner where Giovanni, one of Uncle Luca's guards, should be stationed, I frown at the empty corridor. Gio isn't the most vigilant of our guards, but he knows not to abandon his post, especially not in the wake of a failure this monumental.

Unease seeps into my skin, trickling up and down my spine until I have my gun drawn and eyes alert. I curse myself for leaving my phone in the guest room. This could be nothing, but I'm not about to take any chances with Ranie's life. And if something happens, there will be no way to alert him.

For the first time in twenty years of privileged living, I'm angered by the size of Uncle Luca's place. Two days ago, Dad moved me and Ranie here because the smaller size is easier to fortify than our estate, but it's still an absurdly large monstrosity of marble and gold.

I've never complained about it before, but as I slowly make my way towards Ranie's room on the opposite side of the Floridian compound, I can't help but curse the distance. My foot slips past the marble floor, my socked feet silent after years of training. I stay close to the wall, clearing each corridor I pass, each lonely step more urgent than the last.

I should have passed at least eight guards by now, but I haven't. Whatever threat is here, looming over us, is ghostly, made far more mysterious by the unknown. And it *is* unknown. We still don't know how the Hell the Romano's head of enforcement is alive.

Vincent Romano should be dead. We planned it to a tee. We accounted for all foreseeable variables. Something went wrong, and while we're scrambling to figure out what, everything is silent on the Romano side.

That's almost worse than an all-out declaration of war.

At twenty years old, I'm supposed to take over the Andretti family in the decade to come. I've been trained to handle a gun. I've been trained to strategize a turf war. I've been trained to plan a hit. I've been trained to run a mafia empire.

But this? Waiting idly? I'm not trained for this. Everything in me is anticipating action, stir crazy at the thought of being cooped up in this gilded prison for a second longer. I'm almost grateful for the idea of an impending threat, as long as Ranie isn't the one being threatened.

The restlessness feels weird besides the coiled tension in my body as I clear each hall and room. It's the last hallway leading to Ranie's room that has goosebumps rising out of my tan flesh. Trusting my body's reaction, I stop, pausing behind the bend and extending my hearing as far as it can go.

The silence is there, but in a half beat of a second, I hear the softest of sounds. A slight scuffle that shouldn't be here. And in this world, anything unusual is not to be trusted. That sound, that barest hint of exposure might as well be a slew of war cries.

Someone is going to die tonight, and I'll be damned if it's me or Ranieri.

CHAPTER ONE

A quick temper will make a fool of you soon enough.
Bruce Lee

Niccolaio Andretti

Seven years later...

Lucy is laughing at me.

Why? I don't know, but I do know that Lucy and laughing are never good things—both separately and together. I've only met her once, but I'm pretty sure she's a nutcase, and I'm also pretty sure bad news stalks her like Norman Bates does his mother.

The last time I saw Lucy, I helped her fake fiancé kill nineteen well-armed men, aided in the takedown of a high-ranking board member for a Fortune 500 company, and had to lay low in the fucking boonies for a month.

I just got back from Nowhere, Oklahoma—seriously, that's what it's called. And I don't want to have to go back to Nowhere.

Now, Lucy is standing in my living room, uninvited and unannounced. It's kind of like last time, except Asher isn't with her. Speaking of that dumbass, he wants to marry her for real. So, why is his girl standing in my living room?

And how the fuck does she know where I live?

Last time she was here, I was sure to take precautions to prevent this very situation. I stuck her in a box, and when it was time to move her again, I had one of my men drive us around aimlessly for half an hour.

Yet, here she stands—in the middle of my living room, a disgusted expression on her face as she eyes my overnight bag, which is caked in hardened Nowhere, Oklahoma mud. I have no doubt my tanned skin and dark hair are equally repulsive after a month of unreliable shower water and body wash as shampoo.

She shifts her gaze to my face. "I heard you're back."

There's a tilt to her lips that's more smirk than smile. I'm immediately suspicious.

"...Okay..." It's clear in my tone that I don't know why she's here, and I don't want her here.

In fact, I don't even know *how* she's here in the first place. I have a state of the art security system. Even though my guards have been off-duty given my absence, she still shouldn't have been able to break in. What the fuck is she? Houdini with a nice rack and a homicidal fiancé?

There's that irritating grin again. "I picked your door lock."

"There's no door lock."

To get into my house, you need to bypass the retinal scanner and handprint lock. And on the off chance that happens, there's an alarm that needs to be disarmed with a passcode upon entrance and panels under the floor that measure the gait print of the person walking on them. But you know what there isn't? A door lock. Lucy is up to something. I know it.

Her grin widens. "I know, but you should've seen your face." At my scowl, she laughs. "Relax. Gosh, you're wound up so tightly."

In the backdrop of the wainscoted walls and hardwood floors in my brownstone, Lucy looks like she belongs. Dressed in a white dress that compliments her pale flesh, evergreen eyes, and black hair, I wouldn't guess that she came from the foster care system.

In fact, I only found out after a deep web search I conducted once I learned her real name—Elena Lucy Reeves. Before that, the search I had done towards the end of last September had come up empty.

Nothing. The woman was a ghost. No social media. No employment history. No birth records.

Now, after surviving three very public attempts on her life; setting a wedding date with Asher Black, the Romano family's former fixer and the CEO of Black Enterprises; and publicly humiliating René Toussaint, the former CFO of Black Enterprises, Lucy is one of the most well-known women in the tristate area. Which means she's only making my situation worse by being here.

She needs to get out of here. Now. In fact, I wish she never got in here in the first place, and as soon as she leaves, I plan on rectifying that situation immediately.

"How did you get in?" I repeat, my patience waning.

Well, it was never there in the first place, especially when it comes to this woman. Inherently curious and abnormally intelligent, Lucy isn't someone I have the desire to deal with. How Asher does it is beyond me.

She shrugs. "Asher's company made the security system you used. It wasn't hard to find a master access code at the R&D lab."

That fucker.

I abandon that line of questioning, already planning some upgrades for my security system. "Why are you here?"

"I was in town and wanted a cup of tea with a friend."

See what I mean? Loon. She's an absolute, psychotic loon. Asher is making the biggest mistake of his life, tying himself to this chick. In just three months, too.

She has the audacity to roll her eyes at me, though I haven't said a thing. "I never had a chance to thank you for what you did."

"You could've texted."

Or left me alone entirely.

Again, she rolls her eyes. "Gosh, you're a real piece of work. You know that? Thanking someone for risking their life to help your fiancé isn't exactly something you do over text. I wanted to thank you in person. Plus, I also came to say that, should you ever need a favor, I owe you one."

My arms cross. "What could I possibly want from *you*?"

I know I won't like her answer when she throws her head back and laughs.

Her ever-present grin is troubling, and she has a look on her face, like she knows something I don't. "Here's my favor. A warning—be careful with that one."

And with those puzzling words, she's out of the door.

It's official.

Asher's fiancée is better off in a psych ward than roaming the streets of Manhattan.

CHAPTER TWO

For every minute you remain angry,
you give up sixty seconds of peace of mind.
Ralph Waldo Emerson

Minka Reynolds

One month later...

I **wake up to the cursed** sound of screeching. It's loud and sharp and grates on my delicate ears. It's the sound of metal cutting metal, and I know the source of it immediately. This isn't the first time it has happened since I started sleeping at John's swanky brownstone by Central Park.

Speaking of, John's meaty arm is sprawled across my body, his pudgy fingers gripping onto my tanned flesh. Slowly, I pry his fingers off of my right breast, careful not to wake him up so he doesn't get any ideas. I don't want to be disgusted by him too soon. It would put a damper on my plans.

Because he's *the one*.

The one I'm going to marry.

I've hit the jackpot with this guy. He's in his late fifties, doesn't have any anger issues, has a small sexual appetite, and thankfully wears a condom whenever he actually does slip inside of me.

And at this point in my life, that's all I can hope for.

Carefully, I slither quietly out of the bed and easily slip away from the bedroom door with the practice garnered from years of being the other woman. Sneaking around is a near daily occurrence in this lifestyle, where women rotate in and out of lives quicker than New York City fashion dos become fashion don'ts.

Thankfully, John doesn't have a wife. He only has me. And we're going to get married... He just doesn't know it yet. Figuring how to get from point A—sleeping with him—to point B—a rock the size of my molars—is a problem for a later date.

Right now, I need to deal with the inconsiderate neighbor that thinks it's appropriate to have a construction crew working at this early hour—again. I'm beyond pissed off at the 6 A.M. wakeup call. It's been happening almost every day for the past month, and I can't take it anymore.

It's the weekend. I need my sleep. In fact, I need a lot of it to deal with the headaches I encounter on a daily basis. And this elusive neighbor, whoever he is, is taking that away from me with his nightly construction crew, which works from the late hours of the nighttime into the early hours of the day.

How the rest of the neighborhood—and even John, who is far worse than me when it comes to complaining—hasn't stopped this is beyond me. There are city violations to prevent these sorts of things from happening. I would know, since I'm a pre-law major at Wilton University, an Ivy League school and one of the most prestigious universities in the country.

Once upon a time, the idea of attending Wilton would have been laughably out of reach. Now, it's a necessity—one I can't mess up. Just like my situation with John. I spare another glance behind me, grateful to see the hallway empty before I bound down the stairwell.

When I enter the kitchen, I grab the dress off of the kitchen floor, where John threw it last night after he had stripped me bare, and clothe myself. I grab one of my heels off of the couch and huff in annoyance, searching for my second heel, an unwanted casualty from last night's sexual foray.

When I finally find it, the screeching has stopped, but it doesn't prevent me from marching out there, eyes blazing in fury. My auburn hair is disheveled from sleep, my jade eyes are red from the sudden wakeup call, and my dress is on inside out.

Nevertheless, I proceed.

"This is unacceptable," I growl to the nearest worker.

He looks at me, eyes my heels, dress and bedhead, then shrugs. My mouth gapes open when he picks up his hammer and begins to sink a nail into the wood before him. Unbelievable. This is why I hate people, why I have no tolerance for anyone other than Mina, my little sister.

"Hello?" I wave in front of his face.

He spares another glance at me, shrugs, and continues working. A few feet from him, another worker snorts. I narrow my eyes at him, the anger in me rearing its ugly head tenfold. I've always had a temper, but my inability to get along with others means that very few are ever around for me to target.

But this man?

He's asking for it.

I lean forward and sneer at him. "This. Is. Un. Accept. Able." I make sure to speak slowly, breaking my words into smaller clumps of syllables, so my words can seep through that thick skull of his.

He stares blankly at me.

I try again. "You can't make noise this early. I will report you to the city if this continues. I'll do it, too. You'll lose your license to work. You'll be investigated."

He stares at me with a slight twitch of the lips and lifts his right shoulder in a small shrug.

What is wrong with these people?!

I frown, studying his face. He's older than me by at least twenty years, so probably somewhere in his mid- to late-forties. He doesn't look to be anyone important, yet he's sitting here, amused, like he thinks he's untouchable.

I'll show him untouchable.

I jerk forward, ready to get up in his face and give him the verbal lashing of a lifetime, but I stop when I feel someone approaching us out of my line of sight. Both of the workers widen their eyes before averting them, fearful for the first time.

I frown. They're supposed to fear *me*. I'm the one who's being wronged. I deserve to revel in their fear. Ugh. Life is so unfair sometimes.

"What's going on here?" says a voice from behind me, deep and masculine.

I snap, sick and tired of this morning. I swivel around, ready to give someone—*anyone*—a much-needed verbal lashing, one that I've had coiled and pent up inside of me for weeks now.

But as soon as I see his face, I stop.

Gorgeous dark eyes, tan skin, black hair, and a jawline capable of cutting through glass are introduced to my hungry eyes. And all of that is packaged in a muscular body about half a foot taller than my five feet and eight inches.

The owner of the voice is leaning against the railing to the brownstone, his arms casually crossed and an insouciant expression on his face. And as much as I hate to admit it, I stop and study him.

It's unfair to be that gorgeous and to reek of this much self-assurance and self-confidence on top of that. Especially in the face of my anger, which is a stark contrast from this man's calm, assertive appearance.

Goodness, and *his coldness*.

The overwhelming darkness in his eyes suits the darkness of his expression. And from the prominent display of cheekbones to his sharp jawline and smooth, expressionless features, I wonder briefly if he's even real.

If he's a statue—detached and hardened like stone.

Or perhaps he never smiles.

Then again, who am I to judge?

Smiling is rare for me these days, too.

After looking at him in all of his icy, perfect glory, I'm suddenly overcome with the desire to fix my hair and dress and whatever else I can do to make myself more presentable. The urge takes me by surprise, which of course, is only met with even more anger.

I've never been like this before.

Angry? *Of course.*

Calculated? *Always.*

But lustful? *Never.*

For as long as I can remember, I've always gone after one type of man—wealthy, powerful and usually older. I'm certain this guy isn't old, and I'm unsure if he's wealthy or powerful. Yet, here I am, reacting to the mere sight of this handsome stranger.

And I hate it.

I harden my eyes, forcing a steely glare into them as I strengthen my resolve again.

Lust serves me no purpose.

I'm here to secure a better future for me and my sister, and everything in me is telling me that lusting after this man—this gorgeous, beautiful, indifferent man—will only get in the way.

And I won't let that happen.

CHAPTER THREE

You will not be punished for your anger.
You will be punished by *your anger.*
Buddha

Niccolaio Andretti

It's one of those things you can just tell—the sky is blue, puppies are stupidly cute, and this woman is a raging bitch. With flashing green eyes, vivid red hair, and a curvy figure, she's also every man's wet dream.

But I'll let you in on a little secret—Prince Charming doesn't want to marry a raging bitch.

And judging by the fire in her eyes, the same fire that matches her red-hot hair and the insane amount of sass she's been dealing to my stoned-out-of-their-minds security technicians, she has a bone to pick.

With me.

I look at her, hiding my unease like a seasoned professional. She's a new entity, and new is never good. It occurs to me that this, whatever this is, can be a trap. An elaborate ruse connected to the fucking bounty on my head.

I take a moment to feed on my paranoia, allowing it to fester, build and consume me. After all, it's what has kept me alive this long.

And against ridiculous odds, too.

I hide my suspicion well behind a familiar mask of indifference, and instead, I casually arch my brow as if to say, "Well?"

After all, she still hasn't answered my question.

She juts her hip out and places a slender hand on it, the epitome of sassy. She even manages to look poised while doing so, which tells me all I need to know about this woman. "Who are you to get into my business? Go away. I'm perfectly capable of dealing with this"—she gestures to the guys behind her— "by myself."

Even if I was just a bystander, I would be able to see that the opposite is true. She can't even tell that these guys are acting like this because they're too high to function properly. Luke and Tristan may be the best at installing security systems, but they're also shit at passing up a joint. I've never seen them not high.

I debate whether or not I should be saying something, but I've seen her walking around the neighborhood a few times before. Once is enough to merit my concern, but a few times is disturbing. If I don't treat this situation delicately, it may become a problem for me.

So, remembering to speak tactfully, I say, "You're on my property," which is a Hell of a lot better than "get the fuck out of here."

Her eyes widen, and she shifts her body away from Luke and Tristan, turning her full attention to me. Behind her, they go back to their work, already bored with our conversation. Then again, it may just be me they don't want to look at. Like most people I've met, they've always had trouble making eye contact with me.

"You," she seethes, her venomous voice an invisible but lethal weapon. I can even imagine it slicing through the air.

A lesser man would back down. He would see the craze in her eyes and surrender. I'm many things—an asshole, a jerk, and a douchebag, to name a few—but a lesser man is not one of them. I can't help but rise to the challenge in her voice, something in me wanting to draw nearer and match her anger with my own.

Truthfully, it's not her I'm mad at.

I'm mad I had to spend a month in the middle of Nowhere.

I'm mad at Lucy for breaking in.

I'm mad that I have to revamp my security, installing parts from at least a dozen different companies in the case of another break-in attempt using a master key.

And mostly, I'm mad that my little brother ordered a hit on me after word had gotten out that I had helped Asher raid a warehouse.

These are the things I'm mad at—not this firecracker of a woman. But man, is she an easy target. Huffing and puffing in front of me, I have no doubt she thinks she's the big, bad wolf. Little does she know, I eat wolves for breakfast.

"Me," I mock, my voice cold and belittling.

The condescension in my tone is obvious. After standing upright and taking a step closer, I lean against the railing closer to her and cross my arms casually. My face is the epitome of aloof as I, with careful precision, slowly run my eyes up and down the length of her trim and curvy body.

Anyone can see that, with her clothes on incorrectly and hair disheveled, she's doing the walk of shame right now. I deliberately paste an amused expression on my face, instinctively knowing it'll piss her off.

It does.

She takes a step closer, ballsy for such a little thing, and says, "You've woken me up every darn day for the last month. This is the last straw."

I raise a brow. "Darn?"

She isn't amused. "Yes. Every. *Darn*. Day. But not anymore. I'm reporting you to the city." She frowns at me. "If you were nicer, I would have given you a warning."

"Somehow, I doubt that," I say, unconcerned.

There's a reason it has been a month of nightly noise, and my neighbors on either side of me haven't reported a thing. We—John, Dex and I—have an agreement here. They turn a blind eye, field some questions about the mysterious neighbor, and should the need arise, I do favors for them.

Those favors usually involve bloodshed.

If you ask me, businessmen are worse than mobsters.

And between the three of us, we have enough connections in the city to do whatever the Hell we want. That includes making noise at 6

A.M., though it shouldn't matter. Dex and John are my only neighbors close enough to hear.

They won't say shit.

"B-but yo—"

I cut her off. "Listen, sweetheart," I say, intuitively knowing the pet name will piss her off further, though I'm not sure why I want to. It's probably because I'm an asshole. "You're clearly out of your depth here. I'll save you the trouble and let you leave now, with a quarter of your dignity still intact."

She flounders for a long moment, staring at me with the greenest eyes I've ever seen. She really is beautiful. I'm not surprised to see her lurking around here, given the resident playboy that lives next door.

With a killer body, a light smattering of freckles on the bridge of her nose, and a cocky gleam in her eyes, she looks like an eclectic mix between the Queen Bee and the Girl Next Door. Like she won't hesitate to tear your heart out and feed it to a homeless puppy because he's starving, she feels bad, and she doesn't like you.

She also looks like Dex's type. Any man's type, even, but especially his. Dex is a thirty-years-old, self-made tech millionaire. He's a blue blood through and through, but the money he's made is one hundred percent his own and a byproduct of his technological prowess.

Dex hooked me up with my untraceable home network and surveillance system. He's an average looking guy but an absolute animal when it comes to women, cycling through them quickly, sometimes even multiple times in a day.

I have no doubt that this is one of those girls, though for some reason, she's acting like she's staying around here for much longer. I'm tempted to uncross and re-cross my arms, using my strong build to daunt her, but I figure there's such a thing as too much intimidation. I wouldn't want her to go running off to the damn cops.

She opens her mouth to say something, but after a moment, she closes it again, huffs, and walks away from me. I try not to watch her retreat, but I can't help myself. She has a nice ass, and it's been a while since I've had the opportunity to check out a woman.

But when I turn in the direction of Dex's house, she's not there.

I swivel back, surprised when I see her quietly entering John's brownstone. He doesn't have a family. He doesn't have a wife. He doesn't have a daughter. So why the fuck is she doing her walk of shame to a man almost three times her age?

And why the fuck is it bothering me?

CHAPTER FOUR

Don't get the impression that you arouse my anger. You see, one can only be angry with those he respects.
Richard M. Nixon

Minka Reynolds

I **want to kill that jerk**, but the time it will take to do that equates to less time with Mina. I get two hours with her on Saturdays at her state-run group home.

That's it.

Two hours a week.

Eight-point-six hours a month.

One hundred and four hours a year.

That's less than the number of hours the average person sleeps in two weeks.

The sobering thought only strengthens my resolve to land John. And with that in mind, I swallow down my angry retort and push my way past John's nuisance of a neighbor. Only when I'm past the red brick of the outside steps and through the mahogany doors do I allow myself to take a calming breath.

Rolling my eyes at my attire, I strip myself of everything and grab the button-down John wore yesterday from the couch. I shrug myself into it, buttoning only one button above my belly button and leaving the rest of my toned body on display. I learned weeks ago about this particular preference of his, and I've been greeting him in his button-downs ever since.

I'm nothing if not adaptive.

I order breakfast delivered, paying for it with the black AmEx card John gave me last week. Slamming the door on the delivery kid's face when he gapes at the sight of me in John's button-down, I roll my eyes and carry the bag into the kitchen.

I plate the food onto John's fancy dinnerware, so it looks like I made it. After throwing the empty delivery bag into the trash bin with a bunch of napkins tossed over it for some extra camouflage, I make my way to his bedroom, a convincing smile plastered all over my face.

"Hey, sleepyhead." I wink at him when he groans.

I watch patiently as he makes a show of waking, struggling to lift himself out of the sheets. I can't help but compare John to his jerk of a next-door neighbor, which is how I know I've gone insane.

Nevertheless, I note that John is flabby where his neighbor is hard —which is everywhere. His hands, his stomach, his arms, his face, and even his legs. Something about seeing John, a man I'm sleeping with out of necessity, after seeing his neighbor, a man I'm so attracted to that it's made me momentarily stupid, is so disheartening.

It makes me wonder if this is the life I'll forever be trapped in.

And if so, will I ever be happy?

And does my happiness even matter in the grand scheme of things?

I don't have the answers to these questions, questions I've been able to ignore for quite some time now, so instead, I focus on John and force myself to forget the unforgiving glare of the handsome stranger next door.

He sits up slowly, eyeing my legs and cleavage before settling on the plate in my hand. "You made breakfast again?" he asks, his voice eager.

"Sure did." I give another sweet grin, hoping that I look like every misogynistic man's wet dream—a woman that looks like a Victoria's

Secret angel, cooks like Martha Stewart and spreads her legs quicker than a lady working a street corner.

Yep.

Guys are great, aren't they?

And John is the king of them all.

Last week, he asked me to make him a sandwich. I don't cook. Not even sandwiches. I've burnt water at least a dozen times in the past month. But at least he didn't address me as "woman," like one of the last guys did.

So, I cut my losses and made him a darn sandwich.

It was awful.

Instead of giving it to him, I had Subway delivered. Filthy rich and distantly related to a Rothschild, John never had Subway, nor had he heard of Subway. Naturally, I took credit for the sandwich, too.

When I place the tray beside him, he pats the bed and says, "Come join me."

Giving him a teasing look, I shake my head and walk towards his bathroom. Before I reach the doorway, I turn back to him, and just as I suspected, he's staring at me, a distinct expression of longing in his eyes.

Making sure his eyes remain riveted on me, I unbutton the sole button and allow the fabric to slide slowly off of my shoulders in a teasing movement. With one final wink, I shut the door, cutting off his view of my bare body.

And that is how you gold dig.

Hook.

Line.

And sinker.

But my problem has never been getting men. It's always been reeling them in.

A quick shower later, and I'm heading towards China Town, where my baby sister lives. From the decaying paint to the fishy odor throughout the halls, the building is run down and dilapidated, but it's an upgrade from where we grew up.

When Social Services took Mina away, I was only eighteen. I was too young to get her back, and my incubation pod, who I refuse to address as anything more than the woman who birthed me, didn't bother trying.

Now, four years later, I am twenty-two years old, am on my last year at Wilton, and still haven't gotten my little sister back. As much as I've accomplished by even getting into Wilton, I suspect I'll always feel like a failure. At least until I get custody of Mina.

At twelve years old, it feels like Mina and her childhood is wasting away in this dump of a place. She needs to be around someone who cares about her, someone who loves her. And no matter what her caseworker says, that's with me—not here, at this dreadful place.

The receptionist grins at me when I sign in. I return it, though it's forced. Playing nice has never been my strong suit. I've always found it to be a waste of time, and most of the time, people aren't genuine anyway. But the smile I paste on my face is convincing, because I can't afford to leave a bad impression on someone who possesses the power to revoke my time with Mina.

She matters more to me than anything or anyone else.

And when Mina sees me and smiles, I give the first genuine smile I've given since I saw her last week. With red hair, innocent green eyes, and a bright smile, Mina is the spitting image of me ten years ago. The only difference is her inability to walk.

That only seems to be a problem to her caseworker, Erica. We were fine before they ever visited our place and deemed it unfit to raise a handicapped minor. I had taken care of Mina, and she was loved and cherished, healthy and eating, happy and laughing.

Where was Erica when I was sleeping on the piss-stained carpet most nights? Where was Erica when I was scavenging through empty cabinets for food to eat? Where was Erica when I hadn't a toothbrush to clean my teeth or shampoo to wash my hair?

Nowhere.

It was like I never existed.

Not until I had barely just turned eighteen, and she was there to take away the only person that has ever truly mattered to me.

Shaking the dark thoughts away, I ruffle Mina's hair. "Hey, kiddo."

She groans. "I'm twelve, not six."

"And you'll still be a kiddo when you're thirteen times that age."

Without a second of hesitation, she says, "You'll probably be dead when I'm seventy-eight, and you'll definitely be dead if I ever reach one hundred and fifty-six."

Despite the morbidity of her words, I'm grinning. I take any opportunity to test her mathematical prowess. Mina may not be good at all subjects, but she's a math whiz when it comes to mental math. Fostering that ability of hers is the only silver lining of this forsaken place.

"Seriously, though, how are you doing?"

She rolls her eyes, her pretty green irises vibrant beneath a thick canopy of lashes. "I'm fine. Why do you always ask me that?"

"Because I'm your sister, and I worry." I eye her tiny body and narrow my eyes. "Have you gotten skinnier? Are you eating? Are they feeding you here? Do you have enough food? Are they giving you what you need? Do you fe—"

She holds up a hand to me and laughs, throwing her head back in a beautiful movement. "Minka! Stop! Jeez! I'm *fine*. I promise."

I sigh. "I worry about you."

"I know."

"I love you."

"I know."

"I worry about you."

"You already said that."

"Well, I do, okay?" I take a seat on the plastic chair beside her wheelchair, and the cheap material squeaks beneath my weight. "What do you want to do right now?"

She grins and, in that uber mature way of hers, remarks, "You mean, now that you're done wasting our time asking me if I'm fine?"

"You're such a punk."

"I was fine last week when you asked me, too."

"You suck."

"And I was fine when you asked me the week before that."

"My love is wasted on you."

"And the week before that."

"I will lock the wheels on your wheelchair."

That shuts her up.

She widens her eyes, and then we're laughing, tears trapped in our eyes and hope bourgeoning in my soul.

In moments like this, I forget that I'm not a good person. That I've pissed off and pushed away everyone who's ever talked to me.

In moments like this, I feel like I can move on from who I am, from the person I never wanted to be.

From the person I hate.

CHAPTER FIVE

The truth will set you free, but first it will piss you off.
Joe Klaas

Minka Reynolds

I **focus on the pedestrians** as the Uber I'm in sits behind a red light. Across the street, two men catch my attention. One looks to be in his mid-thirties, and the other can't be any more than a few years older than Mina's twelve years.

My eyes narrow as I watch the older man hand a few bills to the kid. The kid looks at the money for a moment before pocketing the bills, reaching into the brown cardboard box before him, and handing what looks like a foil-wrapped chocolate bar to the man.

To the untrained eye, the whole exchange looks innocent enough—just a poor kid trying to earn some money selling chocolate bars and a wealthy man trying to help. But to my eyes, I see what's really happening.

Actually, I'm *intimately familiar* with what's happening.

After all, I used to be that kid.

I suppress the urge to look around the streets. Somewhere on this street is this kid's boss, be it a parent of his, a neighborhood dealer, or some other scumbag who thinks it's okay to use kids to deal drugs.

A part of me wants to open the door and help the kid out, to get him away from the mess he's in. But I don't. Instead, I sit silently as the Uber driver pulls away from the congested street, because like most things in life, it's too complicated. There are too many variables and way too much uncertainty.

If I helped the kid, I could have done more damage than good. Social Services would come, and who knows? Maybe I'd be separating the kid from an older sibling who's trying her best to get her and her brother out of that mess.

Or maybe I'd be separating the kid from a younger sibling that has yet to be born. Then, I'd be robbing a child of a future protector, and that's the absolute last thing I want to do.

That last thought has me contemplating the next few weeks. My impending graduation looms ahead of me like a lighthouse, but instead of leading me to shore, it's causing my brain to go afloat. The closer and closer I get, the more lost I feel.

Don't get me wrong. I know where I'm going. Before I graduate, I'll find a new place to live, I'll find a part-time job while I study for my LSATs. And if all goes well, I'll apply to and get into Wilton's accelerated law school program for my Juris doctor, which would help me get my law degree in one year instead of two.

Meanwhile, I'll also be working John, and eventually, he'll propose. Once he does, I'll have a stable home environment and the financial means to file for custody of Mina. I'll also be well on my way to achieving a stable career.

That's the plan. It's relatively straightforward, and the steps are quite clear and simple enough to follow...

But the problem is that *I don't want to.*

I don't want to study for my LSATs.

I don't want to get my Juris doctor.

And I certainly don't want to marry John.

Instead, I want to enjoy my youth, to savor it and do the things people my age usually do.

And that makes me feel so *angry* and guilty and lost.

Because I know for a fact that I love Mina, and I truly do want to find a way for us to be together. But if I really wanted that... I wouldn't have any problems with my plans, right? I wouldn't be second guessing myself every other second.

I wouldn't be feeling like *this* right now.

So, with each second closer to graduation, I feel increasingly disoriented. I can see my future, clearer and clearer, and it looks so darn bleak. I want to turn the other way, to take a U-turn and get lost at sea.

Because anything—*anything*—has to be better than pursuing a job I don't want to pursue, than marrying someone I don't want to marry.

That's why, when the Uber driver pulls up to the front of John's brownstone, I stay in the car, my hands shaking and my resolve trembling. I try to take deep breaths in and out, but they do nothing to calm me.

Instead, I can feel the beginnings of a panic attack approaching. Usually, when they happen, I can't stop them. So, I find a quiet place to hide, and I ride them out, feeling each sharp clench of the heart, struggling for each gaping breath.

And afterward?

I'm a nightmare to deal with.

I take out the pain, frustration and anger on anyone near me. I lash out, and I'm cruel to the people around me. It's like the pain pushes aside the little bit of humanity I have left inside of me, and I allow the anger in me to fuel my actions.

I wouldn't wish me post-panic attack on anyone, and I certainly shouldn't be having a panic attack right before entering John's home, where I need to always be on top of my game. Lucky for me, a sharp rapping of a fist on the car door startles me before the panic attack can come to fruition.

Pasting a false smile on my face in case it's John, I turn to the window. When I see who it is, I immediately scowl. After opening the door, I ask, "What do you want?"

John's neighbor ignores my question in favor of his own. "What are you doing here?"

I exit the car, and as soon as the door is shut, the Uber driver smartly hightails it out of here, and I wish I could go with him. But at the same time, I don't, because ~~I don't want to rob my thirsty eyes of an opportunity to drink in this man~~ I have to make an appearance with John tonight.

Once again, I'm startled by my foreign attraction to this stranger. His tall, muscular build is clothed in a black hoodie, black jeans and a black t-shirt. From the all-black ensemble to the black hair and brown eyes, everything about this man should be blending into the darkness of the night, but it's not.

At least not to me.

In fact, he's all that I can see—all that I can focus on.

If there was a fire raging behind him and hungry wolves on the loose around us, I still wouldn't be able to tear my eyes away from him. I hate this man; I'm sure of it. I hate what he represents—all the things in life that I'll never be able to have.

And that alone should be enough for me to loathe looking at him. To turn away from the sight of him and ignore the yearning—the lust—that overcomes me whenever I look his way and catch a glimpse of his intense eyes and chiseled features. Surely, if I can battle through my disgust to be intimate with a mark, I can navigate my way through a foggy cloud of lust and come out on the other side unscathed.

Yet, I can't seem to pull myself away from his magnetism. I'm lost in this odd pull between us, and from the heated look he's giving me, I don't think I'm the only one feeling this. Perhaps I'm romanticizing and exaggerating this attraction because, thanks to a never-ending series of marks after marks, it's been a long time since I've indulged such a thing.

But the small part of me that protests the existence of my vanity wishes that I'm feeling this way for any other reason than he's the only guy that's physically held my attention since my gold digging campaign began.

Am I that shallow? Before now, I thought that, of all my less than perfect qualities, shallowness was one I didn't possess. Being physically attracted to a man has always been a luxury I can't afford, and I never cared for nor indulged it.

Yet, I'm breaking those rules with him, lusting after someone I can't have. It'll do me no good. I'm wasting my time. My resolve to pursue John is waning in his neighbor's presence, in the series of what-ifs it represents.

What if I didn't need the money? What if Mina was never taken away? What if I was a normal girl with normal problems? Would this be something I would indulge? How would it feel? The way my heart clenches painfully at these questions terrifies me.

Which makes me hate him even more.

For being the person to cause such a petrifying, contraband line of self-reflection.

And also, because I need this time alone, and he's invading it and my thoughts. Because the minute of preparation I usually give myself before entering John's is a necessity for my sanity. I use it to steel myself, to remind myself that there's a reason for my madness.

Mina.

And the last thing I need is an interruption, let alone an interruption from a man I'm attracted to.

Correction: a man that's butting into my business.

Reminding myself to hate him, I cross my arms and don't bother hiding the disdain in my eyes and voice when I say, "How's that any of your business?"

He takes in my defensive posturing and takes a step closer. "Some would call what you're doing loitering. Maybe I'm doing my civic duty."

My eyes narrow, and I allow the law student in me to argue, "First off, I'm not loitering. I have a purpose for being here. Secondly, even if I *am* loitering, there's nothing you can do about it. I'm not breaking any laws." I gesture at the *public* sidewalk beneath us. "This is public property." I force a frown on my face when I realize that I'm enjoying arguing with him, that I'm enjoying being around him.

He smirks at me, his stare both menacing and challenging. "Actually, loitering is codified in New York penal law under sections 240.35, 240.36, and 240.37."

His words cause me to frown.

Who is *this man?*

In my experience, the only people who are that familiar with the law have studied law, are breaking it or are defending it. These are people in law school, criminals, or people that have too much time on their hands. I've never been one to stereotype, but he doesn't look like any of the three.

In fact, he looks like a movie star—one of those ruggedly handsome Hollywood A-list celebrity types with haunted eyes, who star in action films until they're Liam Neeson's age and still haven't retired.

I actually wouldn't be surprised to learn that he *is* an actor. I wouldn't know. I don't have much time to watch television, nor do I have the money to go the movies. The guys I date aren't the movie going types either. They're, much to my dismay, usually of the staying-in-bed-naked-all-day variety.

Judging from the slightly pleased look on his face, I've been silent for too long, so I glower and say, "True."

Because he's right. Loitering *is* codified in New York penal law under those sections, but he's also trying to play me, and if it was anyone else standing in from of him, he'd probably be doing a darn good job with that impressive poker face of his.

But it isn't anyone else in front of him. It's me, someone who's spent the past four or so years studying the ins and outs of New York and federal laws. And also, someone who isn't and never has been the type to let things go.

Of course, that's a personal favorite character flaw of mine. It's certainly the most fun. With that in mind, I draw upon my extensive knowledge of New York law. And while the sections he mentioned cover loitering, they don't cover the type of loitering I'm doing.

Obviously, he's trying to intimidate me with vague but true knowledge of the law. Laws that are technically true, but for this purpose, they don't apply. But given my major, he's chosen the wrong subject to talk about, and I'm not about to show him any mercy.

Not with this ridiculous lust coursing through my veins. I need to remind myself—and maybe even him, if he's interested, but why else would he bother approaching me? —how incompatible we are.

I continue, "Except those sections don't apply to me. We're not in a transportation center or on a school campus, and I don't have a mask on my face." When his eyes flicker briefly with shock, I don't stop. "I'm not drug pushing, and I'm not a prostitute."

Not really.

There are differences between prostitution and gold digging, but they're not big enough for me to possess a superiority complex over prostitutes.

"Roosevelt School of Law?" he asks without missing a beat, referring to Wilton's law school and the law school closest to John's neighborhood.

I nod stiffly, not wanting to give away more of myself than necessary. I don't want him to know me. Being strangers is my only defense against my attraction to him.

"That's a good school," he continues, slowly.

"Maybe I'm a smart person. Is that so hard to believe?"

The jerk has the guts to lift a shoulder in a lazy shrug. "A smart person wouldn't be here for John."

Fire flashes through my eyes, and I'm instantly defensive.

Does this guy know that I'm a gold digger?

Either way, I push aside the part of me that enjoys this exchange of wits and snarl at him, "And let me guess... A smart person would be here for *you*."

He lifts his lips in a taunting smile. "No. A smart person would run away from me."

He leans in even closer to me, and darn it, I don't run away, though I know he's right.

I should be running.

From this life.

From John.

From *him*.

Instead, I stay rooted to the ground, my eyes on his and my heart pounding an unsteady rhythm. And when he leaves without another word, leaving me pissed off at the fact that he's getting to me, I don't want to listen to him on principle. But for some reason, I do.

I don't go to John that night.

CHAPTER SIX

Never go to bed mad. Stay up and fight.
Phyllis Diller

Minka Reynolds

A **few nights later, I stumble** down the last step outside of John's home and grasp for the stair's railing, righting myself just before my face hits the unforgiving pavement of the sidewalk.

When I'm upright and balanced again, I look forward and am startled to find a dark figure, looming in the shadows a few feet away from me. I take an immediate step back in the direction of John's home, mentally gauging the distance between me and the door.

Should I run or am I better off screaming at the top of my lungs?

I open my mouth to scream, because honestly, I'm not exactly in the best shape. I may be skinny, but my exercise solely consists of sex with a man I can hardly muster enough enthusiasm for, save for a few fake moans and some hip thrusts here and there, and walking around campus and New York City, but only when I absolutely have to. Which basically means I'm definitely not a runner, let alone a sprinter.

And since John entered my life, I've been letting him pay for my Ubers. Outside of campus, I haven't walked a block for over a month.

The last time I walked, it was to go from my dorm room to the dining hall... to grab a cupcake.

My eyes widen as the figure takes a step closer to me. I open my mouth to scream, but the man speaks first.

"Relax."

I recognize his voice instantly, though I've only heard it twice. It washes over me like a tsunami—deep, dangerous, and all-consuming. John's mysterious neighbor steps out of the shadows and eyes me critically.

Though I recognize him, I don't relax my body. After my last interaction with him, I haven't been able to stop thinking about him lately —and I've tried to stop often. I have my suspicions about him. I saw Lucy letting herself into his brownstone about a month ago. At first, I thought she was cheating on Asher, but then I realized two things.

One, no one in their right mind would cheat on Asher Black. (To be fair, I'm not too sure Lucy is in her right mind. But... she also waved brightly at me from the front steps of John's neighbor's brownstone, which she wouldn't have done if she had something to hide.)

And two, Lucy wasn't accompanied by her bodyguard, the tall, muscled man that usually follows her around everywhere she goes. Since I doubt Asher would let her put herself in danger, I'm betting John's neighbor is safe.

But safe in Asher and Lucy's world is relative.

Because I'm also betting that, like Asher, John's neighbor is somehow related to the mafia. After all, he has more than a working knowledge of the law; I've never seen Lucy hang out with anyone other than Asher and Aimee; and judging by the intensity and intimidation always radiating off of this man in powerful, gushing waves, it's Asher this guy is connected to.

And that suspicion has me on high alert.

I'm not worried about my safety. He's never threatened me, nor has he ever made me feel worried for my physical safety. Plus, growing up in a gang-infested neighborhood afforded me with a pretty good scumbag radar, and I don't think he's one of them. But that doesn't mean I'll let my guard down.

So, I wait patiently and observantly as he takes me in, and I wonder what he's thinking. His eyes are unfriendly and aloof, but he's the one who's approaching me. Not the other way around. What that means, I'm not sure.

But I wait for him anyway, because I can't *not* wait for him.

Again, I'm struck by the realization that everything about this man is magnetic.

His face, his body, his voice, his aura—all of it entices me and draws me in until I'm no longer listening to the voice in my head that's begging me to think of my little sister and her future.

The way I react to this man is pathetic and disgusting, but no matter how hard I try, I can't stop it all the same. Even with the words *Mina, Mina, Mina, Mina, Mina* on repeat in my head, I can't seem to remind myself of how bad it is to lust after him. At the very least, I force myself not to draw my body closer to him, to allow myself to be pulled in by his unreasonable magnetism.

And I just stand here, lacking the willpower to do anything other than watch him watch me, and I hate myself for it.

I hate *him* for it, too.

"What do you want?" I finally ask, breaking the heavy silence.

Like last time we talked, I don't expect an answer to my question.

"John Clinton?" He arches a condescending brow and nods his head in the direction of the brownstone behind me.

"He's a friend." I cross my arms defensively, the movement drawing his attention to my chest. I narrow my eyes in an attempt to convince him—and myself—that I don't like the way he stares at me. And just because I hate the way he has me reacting, I add some extra attitude in my voice when I ask, "What's it to you?"

He smirks, the lift of his lips so beautiful and foreign and *wasted* on such an irritating person. "He's a friend of mine."

I snort, hardly believing it. "John doesn't have friends."

And it's true. As far as I know, John goes to work and stays at home. That's it. And other than that, John's a mystery. Kind of like his neighbor, except I'm actually tempted to unravel the mystery of John's neighbor. Not for the first time, I acknowledge that he'd make a wonderful predator. After all, he was able to make me, a frigid ice queen when it comes to wanting men, flirt. And I realized yesterday that that was what I had been doing. I was flirting with him, showing off my knowledge of the law for no other reason than the fact that I'm attracted to him and wanted to impress him.

God, I'm so stupid.

John's neighbor stalks forward with a predatory grace, each step calculated, methodical, and leisurely, while having the same effect as a swift and ruthless attack would. Though his eyes are on me, he looks vigilant of everything in our surroundings.

Alert.

Aware of everything around us, though somehow most aware of *me*.

"Maybe I'm his only friend." He takes a step closer. "Maybe I'm his best friend." Another step. "Maybe I'm looking out for him."

"And *I'm* the threat?" I look down at my petite body pointedly, but I regret it immediately when his eyes trail the same path down my body.

My breathing hitches, and his eyes flare with lust.

And I recognize that look immediately.

I just never thought I'd see it in someone I'm attracted to.

"You look pretty threatening to me," he says, surprising me.

This man, who has tree trunks for thighs, a chest that spans the distance of the Pacific and arms with crests like hills, thinks *I* look threatening?

What has this world come to?

"You're one to talk," I reply, nodding my head in his direction, at the overwhelming presence that is him.

Surely, he realizes the kind of man he is. The imposing threat his presence alone poses to the world. I would gesture at him, too, but my traitorous hands are shaking from our proximity, so I clench my fists tightly instead and hide the useless things in the deep pockets of my Wilton University Law Review sweater.

I'm distinctly aware of my last name embroidered on the right breast pocket of the sweater. Even though it's unaccompanied by my first name, the idea that he has even the slightest glimpse into my identity is disconcerting.

Not because of his potential mafia connections, but because any knowledge that isn't mutually shared between us affords him a sort of power over me that I'd rather I retained. It's a stupid and childish notion, and I'm probably overthinking things, but can I really be simply imagining this seductive power struggle between us? The way our words are like hands, tugging back and forth on an invisible rope.

I'm telling myself that this is hatred. That hatred is a never-ending game of tug-a-war between two people that are better off leaving things alone but lack the maturity to do so. But I don't particularly see him being immature, and thanks to the metaphorical revolving door my sperm and ovary donors had installed in my childhood apartment, I know what true hatred is, and it isn't this.

This is something else entirely.

"Why are you here?" he asks the same question he asked last time I saw him, and for a split second, I wonder again if he knows that I'm gold digging.

I never said that I was sleeping with John, but it's not a stretch to assume that a woman sneaking out of a man's house around midnight is sleeping with said man. And that's pretty much what just happened, except I left to go get my LSAT study guide and was planning on coming back.

Now? I'm not so sure.

I'm stuck in front of this man, and not because he's not letting me leave. I'm sure if I tried to leave, he wouldn't bother to stop me. He wouldn't care enough to. But I'm stuck in front of him, because *I don't want to leave.*

I want to be here.

I want to see where the intense magnetism between us takes us.

And I don't know why this is happening.

I hate him. From the second I met him, I hated him. Given my body's traitorous response to his presence, I knew he would be trouble for me; for my future; and most importantly, for Mina. Yet, I'm standing in front of him.

And worse—*I want to be here.*

I want the world to pause for just one darn second, so I can stay forever in this moment, where a man I'm attracted to is looking at me like he's attracted to me, too.

Is that too much to ask?

"Why are you here?" he asks again, taking another step toward me. "What's your angle?"

My eyes widen, but I don't take a step back as he invades my personal space. And for a split second, I relish in the proximity, allowing myself to succumb to the bone-deep ache I feel for him. But God help me, I won't let this man see how much of an effect he has on me.

"What?" The word escapes my lips as a whisper, because I have no clue what he's talking about.

My *angle*?

Surely, he's not referring to my gold digging. Because what stranger, even him, would be so forward in such a line of questioning? He may as well have said, *so are you a gold digger or what?* But something tells me that's not what he's asking me, which leaves me with one word—*what?*

"Why are you here?" he repeats slowly, like he thinks little of my intellect despite his knowledge that I attend Wilton for law. "Why are you in this neighborhood?"

I tamper down my racing heart, which is pounding at our proximity. At the fact that, if I breathe too hard, my chest would brush against his body. It takes me a second to register that he repeated himself, and when I do, it takes me another second to realize what he may be talking about.

If he's involved in the mafia, he's likely paranoid. I'm a stranger, an unknown entity, and I'm in his terrain. But... I've been sleeping at John's for about two months now, and he's just now confronting me? That doesn't make sense.

And how have I only just recently met him?

I met Dex my second day sleeping over at John's, yet it took two months to finally meet him. That means he's either never here or always in his home. Either way, he's involved in criminal business, so I shouldn't be indulging him and his invasive questions.

But I do, because I can't stop myself with him, and I don't know why.

I reply, "I'm here for John. I'm *with* John."

I don't know if I'm trying to convince myself or him.

Probably both, because I don't want to be with John, but I can't be with someone like him.

There's a centimeter of space between our bodies, but when he leans forward, he extinguishes it. And that first contact between us has my senses soaring. Waiting. Anticipating. His face slants towards mine. Slowly. Teasingly.

Seconds pass before his lips brush against my jaw, and then he's trailing a teasing path up the sensitive curve of my neck with the very tip of his nose, his touch so, so light but so, so *there*.

And when he finally reaches my ear, he opens his mouth, his lips brushing sensually against my delicate skin, and whispers, "I can feel you reacting to me. I can feel your nipples, stiff against my body. You want *me*. You're not interested in John. I'll figure out why you're really here."

He steps back from me immediately after and walks away.

Even though he's gone, I can still feel him, pressed against me.

And his words?

I have no idea what they mean, but I do know that it doesn't bode well for me.

CHAPTER SEVEN

Anger is one letter short of danger.
Eleanor Roosevelt

Niccolaio Andretti

The darkness is welcome.

It is my freedom.

It is my friend.

It is my family.

When the blackness of night approaches, I greet it with open arms. Already dressed in my uniform of all black, I'm ready to leave the safe confines of my self-made prison. After slipping two guns into the holsters under my hoodie, I exit my brownstone.

Though I'm jogging down the steps, the streets remain silent, oblivious to my presence. My steps are quick yet light, a byproduct of the way I was trained to move. Like a panther, though I'm certainly more lethal.

In New York, people fear the name Asher Black, but they should really fear mine. Haunting and formidable, my name is but a myth, rarely whispered as anything other than the prelude to a merciless death.

In the vigilant presence of daylight, I am Nicholas "Nick" Andrews. Come nighttime, I am Niccolaio Andretti. But the only ones who call me by that name are either ordering death or greeting death.

Both of which occur at my hand.

Tonight is a night for the former, and it will inevitably lead to the latter.

Usually, I take a car to meet Vincent Romano, but for some reason, we're meeting at Central Park tonight. As risky as it is, my mind has been craving open air, and this is as good an excuse as any.

Remaining close to the shadows, I slow my pace, savoring each deep breath of warped freedom.

In.

Out.

In.

Out.

In.

Out.

It's just air I'm breathing in, but it's air a few blocks away from my brownstone. And that little bit of distance from my self-made prison is enough to free the piece of my soul that withers in its cell at the sight of the home.

With each breath I take, I relax.

But with each breath I take, another part of me tenses, always wary and always vigilant.

I eye the street, scanning the trees, the homes, the windows, the cars, the license plates, the scents, and the sounds. I take everything in, analyzing my surroundings in an instant, because if I take a moment longer, I may end up dead.

With a hit on my head, I can never be too safe. Take last night for instance. I saw that girl leaving John's home for the third time in less than a week. Before that, I saw flashes of her in the neighborhood on my security cameras almost half a dozen times since I got back from hiding out in Nowhere.

Something about her and John just isn't sitting right with me, and it's not because I'm attracted to her. That part likely has more to do with not getting laid in a few years than her actual beauty.

Yes, she's fucking gorgeous...

But so are a million other women.

There's just something about her that's instinctively caught my eyes and isn't letting go, and that has me suspicious. That, combined with the hit, has me paranoid as fuck. I almost want to add another damn layer of security to the system the boys finally finished installing, but that would involve putting up with the annoying hesitant stares they give me when they think I'm not looking and the heavy marijuana-scented cloud that travels behind them in their wake. No fucking thanks.

And above all, I need to find out why she's roaming around this neighborhood if I want to sleep at night. No fucking way is it for John. I don't believe that shit. Whatever her reason for being here, I'll find out. I've always been one to trust my instincts, and they're telling me that she's hiding something, and for the life of me (literally), I won't ignore them.

After all, back when I was with the Andretti family, our greatest assassin, Allegra, was a girl. A guy could be ugly as fuck with an even uglier personality, but a few well-placed sultry looks and sweet words from Allegra and the dumb fucks would actually be convinced that she wanted them.

I'm not a dumb fuck, and sultry looks and sweet words do nothing for me. But damn, John's girl has my blood pumping. With a seven-figure hit on my head, the lust she has running through my veins is suspicious enough.

Like I said, you can never be too safe.

When I decide that I'm alone on the street, I continue my movement, crossing the street quickly and quietly until my feet connect with the opposite sidewalk. As soon as it can, my dark figure reunites with the shadows, hiding in the depths of its obscurity.

I quicken my steps when I feel as if I'm being followed. As soon as I reach an opening to Central Park, I take it, swerving silently to the left and dipping into the trees. My feet are light as I walk on the grass, being sure to tread lightly.

No footprint.

No sound.

Nothing.

I was never here.

As soon as I see a tree wide enough, I duck behind it and remain hidden, making sure the wood protects me on all sides against any impending threats. My hands reach beneath my hoodie and lock onto the weapons, but I keep them holstered.

Sometimes, weapons only complicate things.

But as soon as I hear the gentle thud of a shoe kissing the grass, too gentle for the gait of an untrained civilian, my weapons are drawn and pointed in the direction of the sound. Slowly, I emerge from the shadows, never one to kill behind cover.

People call me many things, but a coward will never be one of them.

"Lower your weapons, boy," says a gruff voice in the direction of the sound.

I lower them as soon as I recognize Vincent's voice, but I don't relax my stance. Instead, I do a careful sweep of the area before I dip behind the trees again, nestling myself in the cove of trees, which is surrounded by greenery on all sides except the one I entered through.

"Damn it," Vince says, the annoyance clear in his voice as he shuffles under a particularly low hanging branch. He mutters something that sounds like "fucking paranoid oaf" before he meets me behind the trees. He catches sight of me scanning the darkness behind him and rolls his eyes. "It's clear. My men cleared it."

"You can never be too careful," I reply, keeping my eyes steady on the darkness behind him.

"I trust my men."

"I don't." Satisfied, I return my gaze to his, and I study him.

Though we're unrelated, Vincent Romano has the same eyes as me—dark brown, cold, and calculated. They're usually alert, but right now, they just look tired. In fact, everything about him feels off right now. I don't know what it is exactly, and given the type of man Vincent is, I don't think I'll ever figure it out, but it *is* sounding all sorts of warning bells in my head.

At my words, Vincent sighs, but the sound is light.

Expectant.

As if he expected as much.

As if he knows me, though that's impossible.

I don't even know myself.

"It's good to see you, son," he finally says.

I'm not your son.

"You, too, Vincent."

"Vince."

"Right," I pause, "Vincent."

He grunts again in displeasure, but I ignore it. If I stop drawing the lines between myself and the Romano family, I'll sink myself deeper into this mess. People may think I'm a traitor to the Andretti family, but I'm merely doing what I need to survive.

And when I can, I limit my connection to the Romanos.

Unfortunately, it's not often that I can.

So, I settle on these little moments, where I can do things like refuse to call the Romano's enforcer by his nickname. It's a small action, but it speaks volumes. Sometimes it feels like the smallest victories are greater than the largest feats.

I do another scan of my surroundings, perking my ears up for any signs of threats—aside from the man standing before me.

Finally, I ask, "Why did you call me here?"

I want to ask who he wants me to take out this time, but I refrain myself.

He might be wearing a wire.

He arches a brow. "Hello to you, too."

"Vincent." I cross my arms impatiently.

As much as I like the freedom of the outdoors, we both know that it's a risk for me to be so exposed like this. A risk he has selfishly asked me to take. And as much as I like to deny it, I'm quite aware that some part of Vincent cares about me enough not to ask me to take these sorts of risks.

So, whatever this is, it must be important.

And that has me on edge.

Vincent makes a sweeping gesture with his hand, and I sigh

before spreading my arms and legs out. He uses a device to sweep me, ignoring the sound that emits from the stick when it passes my weapons.

He's not searching for them.

He's searching for bugs.

I don't take offense to it. In fact, I welcome the action wholeheartedly. It's standard protocol. Plus, it's another much-needed line drawn between us. It speaks volumes that he doesn't trust me enough not to scan me.

I'm not his family.

I'm not a Romano.

I'm still an outsider.

And that's as close to being an Andretti as I'll get these days.

When he's done checking me for bugs, he lowers the device to his side and straightens up. "I didn't come here with a kill order."

I nod calmly, though I'm raging inside. If he doesn't need me for a job, he better have a damn good reason for asking me to meet him when there's a one point five million dollar hit on my head.

I'm not an easy man to kill, but I'm certain some talented individual will attempt it for that sum of money.

And so will the low lives. The ones with less finesse.

Those are the ones that are truly dangerous, because they don't care about collateral damage.

They'll bomb a sold out movie theater if I'm in it.

They'll fire shots into a crowd if there's a chance a bullet will reach me.

They'll hurt anyone they need to in order to kill me.

If I had any friends, they would go after them.

If I had any family, they would go after them, too.

It's a good thing I have neither. And my brother doesn't count. Ranieri is the one who ordered the hit in the first place.

I resist the urge to cross my arms, instead tightening my grip on the loaded weapons resting in each palm. "Then why am I here, Vincent?"

"Careful, boy," he warns at the attitude in my voice.

Rightfully so, too.

Sometimes I forget that I'm no longer Niccolaio Andretti.

I'm hardly even Niccolaio.

I'm just Nick.

And being Nick means that I shouldn't mouth off to a *caporegime* for the Romano family.

Even if I really, really want to.

I sigh. "Will do."

"I'm here to help."

That's another frustrating thing about Vincent. He treats me like I'm not expendable. He asks me how I'm doing. He tries to get to know me better. He tries to help. He tells me to be careful out there as if I'm not one of the greatest threats in this city.

I think he's genuine about it, too.

My father tried to kill him, and Vincent Romano still helps me. He keeps me employed. He keeps the cash flowing. He checks up on me. It's a complicated situation, one full of lots of give and take on my part, Asher's and Vincent's.

But that doesn't mean Vincent needs to do this for me.

That doesn't mean what Vincent does for me isn't generous.

He can easily find another fixer. Probably not one as skilled as I am, unless Asher is looking to return to the mafia business. But still. I'm not the only fish in this town. Yet, here Vincent is. In front of me.

And it's not to give me another name, another death.

He's here to help me, and I don't think I'll ever know what to do with that.

I fidget uncomfortably, my regular poise waning. "Why do I need help?" I ask, the words sounding uncannily similar to what I said to Lucy a while back.

"Your brother increased the hit on you. Five million dollars."

And with those words, the violent storm in me thunders until I'm unsure if this anger inside of me is a fleeting occurrence or permanently me—an inevitable explosion.

CHAPTER EIGHT

Darkness cannot drive out darkness;
only light can do that.
Hate cannot drive out hate;
only love can do that.
Martin Luther King Jr.

Niccolaio Andretti

Twenty Years Old

The cock of my gun is unmistakable.

If I could, I'd end this—whatever this is—without bloodshed. I really would. But I'm not naïve. I recognize inevitability, and this is it. Someone is going to die today. There are too many weapons, too much history, and too much anger lurking around in this house to get around the inevitability of death.

The first thing that strikes me as odd is that there are only four men in front of me. Uncle Luca has upwards of thirty defending the compound. Either there are more of these men roaming around the estate, or these men are highly trained, at least better trained than ours.

Either way, the odds are grim for Ranie and me.

The youngest one steps forward, calm despite the weapon pointed at his face. Tall, with eerily blue eyes and dark hair the same shade as mine, he's maybe a few years my junior. But he looks older, like he's seen his fair share of life, and it's aged him greatly.

It's the maturity I see in his eyes that has me warier of him than his three companions, who are at least twice his age and equally formidable in build. I watch carefully as he takes the lead, taking another step closer to me.

I shake my head, indicating for him to stop. Another step closer, and he would have been close enough to disarm me. I have no doubt he would have tried, too. It's what I would do if I was in his position.

He pauses, and I see a fleeting look of understanding cross his eyes. That was a test, and now he knows that I won't be fooled. That the threat I pose isn't just physical but also intellectual. There's a moment of silence, where I wait for him to bargain. That's also what I would do if I had a gun pointed at my head.

And unfortunately, there's a lot for him to bargain with.

After all, my little brother is sleeping in the room behind him. If that wasn't the case, I would have waited. I would have called in back up and waited for more Andretti soldiers to arrive. But I didn't have the time for that.

If I killed these men earlier, hidden safely behind the corner, there still could have been a threat. There might still be more of them. Maybe even already in Ranie's room. How would I know?

I'm in a bind, and I made a choice.

These men? They were about to breach Ranie's room, and I stopped them.

Perhaps at the expense of my life.

But for my little brother, I would risk everything.

At least this way, I have the option to bargain for Ranie's life. To have them call off whoever else may be here with them and stop this before Ranie gets hurt.

"You can't shoot all of us before one of us greets you with a bullet," the leader says.

"I know."

But I can get off a warning shot, loud enough to wake Ranie and give him the slightest chance of escaping. Perhaps even loud enough to alert any remaining Andretti guards. It's not my preferred method of dealing with this, but it's one of the better options.

That's why I took the silencer off of the barrel of my gun.

I wait for this guy to realize this—if he hasn't already.

He nods his head. "This is a suicide mission."

"It is."

"You're Niccolaio Andretti."

"I am."

"And your brother is sleeping in the room behind me."

I nod, because there's no point in lying. "He is."

"He's only fourteen."

It's a test. To see if I'm trustworthy.

Unfortunately, I have to be.

"Eighteen," I reply, forcing my jaw not to clench.

Fourteen would make Ranie untouchable, too young to kill according to the unspoken mafia code of honor. But eighteen makes Ranie a man. It makes Ranie fair game. But I gather this guy already knows this. He knows Ranie's age, and he tested me.

Again, it's what I would do.

When he nods, my suspicions are confirmed. "Still, I would rather not kill him."

The words are welcome. They relieve me greatly, but I don't relax my stance. I don't lower the gun. I keep my weapon level with his head, my arm much steadier, much calmer than my heart.

"And what would you like in return?"

"Your uncle."

I stare at him for a moment, understanding his dilemma. Uncle Luca sleeps behind a door guarded by top-of-the-line technology. His room is essentially a safe, and very few have access to it. Ranie happens to be one of them.

But I happen to be one of them, too.

"What would you have done if you hadn't seen me?" *Or gotten Ranie*, I add in my head, the thought too unthinkable to say aloud.

"Drill into it."

"He would hear that. He would be ready."

"So would we."

I take in the four of them again, dressed in black, bulky bulletproof gear and laden with weapons. I even spot several grenades attached to two of the men. They look like they're prepared for war.

Like they're prepared to die for what they want.

"You're Romanos?" I ask, but it's more like a statement.

Because if nothing else, the Romanos are part hardcore and part batshit crazy. Rumor has it that the batshit crazy is inherited from the men and the women pass down the hardcore, but if that's the case, I'd hate to meet a Romano woman. The men pose enough of a threat.

"We are."

Trust. He's building trust. I gave him mine by revealing Ranie's age. He gave me his by revealing his affiliation. Trust is great in theory, but I know better. It's usually the prelude to betrayal.

Treachery.

Duplicity.

None of those are particularly helpful in this situation, but I have no other choice. I build the bridge and pray to the powers that be that he doesn't stomp on it. Or blow it up like a good Romano soldier would.

"I do this, and Ranie lives?"

"Yes. You will, too."

My eyes widen slightly at the revelation before I tamper my reaction. I didn't even consider that I'd get out of this alive. It's a generous offer, made perfect by the reassurance of Ranie's safety.

"How do I know you won't kill me when it's done? Or Ranie?"

"Trust."

"I don't trust anyone."

He nods. "These three will leave. I'll give them my weapons, too."

One of the three behind him opens his mouth, but he's silenced by a slight shake of the leader's head. It's swift but overwhelmingly full of authority.

He speaks again, "You'll have a gun on me. It'll just be me and you. If anything appears off, you can shoot me and save your brother."

"What's to stop me from taking the gun and shooting you?"

Behind him, all of his companions tense, but I had to ask the question. I could tell that he was waiting for it, and it was a welcome olive branch of trust between the two of us. We both knew I was thinking the question, and by verbalizing that thought, I showed honesty, which can only help in this situation. Even if my particular brand of honesty happens to involve premeditative murder.

He smirks. "If you shoot me and save your brother, you two will be the new targets. Right now, it's Luca Andretti. If I don't return, my men will tell the Romano *caporegimes* what happened. You'll be marked for death." He pauses dramatically. "*Your brother will be marked for death.*"

I don't even have to consider it before I nod. It's a fair offer, fairer than anyone in this household, with the exception of Ranie, deserves. Uncle Luca's life for Ranie's. I'll take it. Hell, if given the choice, I think Uncle Luca would trade his life for Ranie's, too. Either way, it doesn't matter.

I'm the one who's here right now.

I'm the one who has to make this decision, and I'm choosing Ranie.

Always.

"Are you sure you know what you're doing, Asher?" one of the older guys asks the leader.

A flash of irritation, of condescension, flits across the guy's—Asher's—face. He doesn't say anything. He wordlessly takes off his bulletproof gear and the weapons he has on him, even the small knife he has hidden at his ankle. He hands his things to his men, and after a moment, the three guys retreat.

When they're gone, I silently lead Asher a few rooms down, where Uncle Luca's room is. I ignore the burden of my betrayal, which lays heavy against my heart, and focus myself on my objective—saving Ranieri. And somewhere between this second and the last, I've shut myself off from the world, tampering my emotions along with my hope.

I know with absolute certainty that after I open this door nothing in my life will ever be the same again.

Taking a deep breath, I enter the 16-digit passcode and place my palm on the scanner. When the steel door opens with a soft and ominous swish, we're greeted by the sound of Uncle Luca's light snoring.

Perhaps it's the impending death or maybe even the weight of the guilt on my conscience, but the sound sends an unrelenting barrage of memories my way.

Drawing on Uncle Luca's face with a five-year-old Ranie, Uncle Luca's snores drowning out our innocent giggles.

Crawling into Uncle Luca's bed at the tender age of five, because my father was less welcoming, and even my mother believed that men don't cry. Apparently, five year olds were considered to be men.

Clutching Uncle Luca's hand as Ranie and I watched our mother's body get lowered into the ground, her body too riddled with bullet holes for an open casket viewing earlier that day, which was a common occurrence in this lifestyle.

I force myself to tamper down the stem of memories, unwilling to weaken my resolve. *Ranie first.* Ironically, it was Uncle Luca himself who first taught me that. With time, I eventually grew into the role of the protector, but before that happened, it was Uncle Luca who had taught me all I knew about love, family and loyalty.

The same Uncle Luca that Asher is approaching, a gleam of darkness and vengeance in his eyes that has my stomach rolling with unease. And I suspect that, however Asher plans on killing Uncle Luca, it will be slow, and it will be painful.

And Uncle Luca doesn't deserve that.

So, without a moment of hesitation, I raise my gun and pull the trigger.

After the initial boom, there's a moment of silence, where Asher's eyes widen and we stare at one another. I break the eye contact by turning around, forcibly resisting the urge to vomit. I don't look at Uncle Luca's dead body. I don't think I can stomach it.

Instead, I exit the room with Asher close at my heels.

And there, standing alone in the hallway, bleary-eyed and disoriented from sleep, is Ranie. He looks between me and Asher, confused. But then, he does a double take, and I know what he sees.

He sees me.
He sees Asher.
He sees a gun.
And it's in my hands.

CHAPTER NINE

Anger is an acid that can do more harm
to the vessel in which it is stored
than anything on which it is poured.
Baptist Beacon

Minka Reynolds

Present

Time has been slipping past me for a while now. A few weeks ago, I was taking midterms. Now, I've just taken my last final and am a week away from graduating. A week away from participating in my commencement ceremony.

A week away from being kicked out of Vaserley Hall.

I need to find a new place to live and quickly. My best bet? John's brownstone. I've been staying there almost every night anyway. He texts me almost every day, and I'm being honest when I say I'm making progress.

I catch him staring at me when he thinks I'm not looking. There's always a distinct look of longing in his gaze, and it's not just my hope or vanity talking. It's there, and it's strong. Our future together is beginning to feel more and more inevitable, and that only rekindles my hope for me and Mina.

Another month or so, and I'll have a ring on my finger.

I can feel it.

I thank the Uber driver and exit the car, bounding slowly up the stairwell to John's home. I open the door with my spare key, and once I'm in the entry hallway, I lean against the interior of the front door and take a few minutes to breathe, my heart pounding so loudly I can hear it in my ear.

Even though I'm confident about where we are in our relationship, asking to move in this early is a big step.

It's risky, but I don't have much of a choice.

Nella and Lauren, my only two friends from college (and ever), are leaving New York City. Nella is moving back to Arizona, and Lauren is moving back to Canada. Obviously, I can't go with them.

Wherever Mina is, I am.

And that happens to be in one of the most expensive cities in the world.

Go figure.

I straighten my shoulders, fix my hair, and walk up the dark hardwood steps to John's brownstone, adding a sultry sway to my hips as soon as I reach the top of the stairwell. I'm dressed for this mission in heels and skinny jeans, which I know will drive John crazy.

You've got this. This is going to happen. You're going to walk in there, and you're going to suggest you move in. He'll say yes, and the next step after that is marriage. Easy. You've got this, Minka. For Mina.

But even with the mental pep talk, I can't help but second guess myself. I've never asked anyone if I could move in before. It's not often that I'm out of my element, but I certainly am here. I'm not even sure if enough time has passed in our relationship. It's only been about two months, which is a long time to me. But John is so much older than I am, and two months might be nothing to him. Merely a blip on his radar. So much is riding on this, and I'm starting to feel insecure, uncertain if this will work.

And as I silently open the door to John's bedroom and see a redheaded woman bouncing quietly on John's cock, I know for certain this won't work.

My eyes widen as I take in the sight before me.

Middle-aged.

Green eyes.

Freckled face.

Dark red hair.

Full lips.

And a generous chest.

This girl is me.

An older version of me, but me nevertheless.

Except she isn't, because John doesn't have sex with me without a condom on. He doesn't close his eyes and clench his fists when he's inside of me. He doesn't reverently whisper the word "baby" over and over again in my ear.

This version of John before me is foreign. He's worshipping this woman. He's savoring the feel and taste of her, entering her slowly and clutching her body against his like any inch of space between their bodies is an inch too many. And I swear, that look on his face—one that is so unfamiliar to me—might just be love.

I recognize this for what it is immediately.

I'm the replacement.

I'm the woman John calls when he can't have this woman. Whatever history these two have, I'm nothing in comparison. She's the woman he wants when he's with me. She's the reason why he likes me, and she's the reason why he doesn't.

And I know, without a doubt, that I'll never get a ring on my left finger.

Not when that ring belongs on her.

My first thought is *Mina.*

Oh, God, Mina.

I'm homeless after this week. I have nowhere to live. A million questions fly through my head. What will this mean for Mina? What will this mean for us? How will I get my baby sister back if I can't find neither a job nor a place to live?

I feel like I've failed my sister, and all the stupid hope I've gathered from my last visit with her extinguishes under the suffocating weight of my incompetence.

But my second thought is *good for John*.

Because as much as I hate him for this, I can't hate him for feeling something for someone else.

I can hate him for destroying my chances of earning custody of Mina. I can hate him for leading me on. I can hate him for screwing another woman behind my back.

Or was I behind her back?

I don't know.

But either way, I can't hate him for loving her.

The wistful looks he would send my way while we were together, I mistook for infatuation. Now, I know better. They weren't for me. He wanted her, and he settled for me. That's where those looks came from.

I was stupid and arrogant and naïve, thinking that I could waltz into his life and it would be so simple. He's lived far longer than I have, and that affords him more credit than I've ever given him.

And the only thing left to do now is move on.

I've been in the room for less than sixty seconds, and they've been too wrapped up in one another to notice me. So, I slowly back out of the door, focusing my efforts on remaining quiet. On keeping my steps light and my heartbreak silent.

Because if I think of anything else, if I focus on the direness of my situation, the frustration that I've struggled to hold at bay for the last four years will overwhelm me.

However, as I slip past the kitchen and notice that woman's phone on the counter, wrapped in a bright neon green case, the same ridiculous shade of neon green Mina insists is her favorite color, I can't stop the frustration that engulfs me.

But as soon as it comes, it's gone.

Because it's hard to feel anger right now when all my body can process is sadness.

CHAPTER TEN

The weak can never forgive.
Forgiveness is the attribute of the strong.
Mahatma Gandhi

Minka Reynolds

ighteen Years Old

Aaron is an awful kisser.

That's what's on my mind as I exit the musty elevator nto the bleak hallway of my apartment building, where Mina and I ave been living since my biological parents abandoned me. Sometimes the woman who birthed us is there. Sometimes she isn't. But vhat never changes is me and Mina.

It's us against the world.

At eight years old, she's ten years younger than me, but she's still ny best friend. And I'm debating whether or not it's appropriate to ell her that I just had my first kiss when I open the door to the apartment and see a stranger in front of me.

She's short, about half a foot shorter than me. Yet, standing there n her expensive, heeled shoes and fancy white blouse, she intimidates me to the core. My eyes dart to the number on our door, but vhen I read the familiar forty-two painted onto the white-washed wood beside a bold letter D, I know I'm in the right place.

I open my mouth to scream for help before I realize that Mina nd I don't live in the type of building where neighbors would come running for help. Instead, they'd probably lock their doors and hide their drug stash in case the cops are called.

I shut my mouth and warily take a step into the apartment. "Where's my sister?" I ask cautiously, my heart quickening and my eyes scanning every inch of the tiny studio apartment to no avail.

My sister isn't here, but she should be. Mina's school bus should have dropped her off an hour ago. She should be here, doing her homework or watching an old Disney VHS tape on the clunky, 22-inch television set my sperm donor managed to leave behind in his haste to get away from the poison that is Mina's and my mother.

"We've taken her somewhere safe," the woman replies, her tone deceptively gentle.

"Safe," I repeat slowly. I'm trying to process her words, but it's like my brain has produced an impenetrable sludge that blocks any logic.

Safe?

What can be safer than here? With me?

And who is this woman?

Where has she taken my sister?

I'm too scared to panic and too shocked to shake.

I have no idea what's going on, yet I'm too dumbfounded to do anything but stand here dumbly and stare at this elegant woman. At her pretty white blouse, which is nicer than anything I'll ever own; her fitted dress slacks, professional and sleek; her hair, which is pulled into a severe bun; her brown eyes, which are wide and youthful; and her round face, free of wrinkles, except at the corners of her eyes, where they form miniature crinkles.

We stare at one another for a moment, and I know I should say something, but I can't.

Mina. Where is my baby sister?

The thoughts and questions are there, pressing up against my skull right beside my fear, but they don't quite make it past my lips. Instead, there's a loud whimper that slices cleanly through the thick silence. I think it's mine, and it would be embarrassing if I wasn't so preoccupied with worry.

We stand there in silence for a moment, eyeing one another up.

Finally, the woman gestures to the wobbly wooden chair in the kitchen. We don't have a dining room or a table, so I usually just pull the lone chair, a dollar purchase from the Salvation Army, up to the kitchen counter and use the counter as a table, my knees knocking uncomfortably against the cabinet doors.

Mina, on the other hand, has a custom tray that attaches to her wheelchair. I saved up and bought it for her for Christmas last year. She was ecstatic when she got it, which in turn made me ecstatic.

Ever since I can remember, Mina and I have always felt what one another have felt. If she cries, I cry. If she laughs, I laugh. That's just the way Mina and I are, and there's a foreboding feeling in my gut that tells me that, whatever this woman says, this is the end of everything great in my life.

So, instead of sitting, I cross my arms. I try to look intimidating, like putting up a physical front between the two of us will protect me from the harsh reality of her words, but I'm too weakened by the thought of a life without Mina to even bring myself to speak.

She sighs. "My name is Erica Slater. I'm Mina's social worker."

Forcing myself to calm down and think rational thoughts, I narrow my eyes in suspicion. After a shaky breath, I ask, "D-do you have an ID?"

She gives me a gentle smile and nods her head. After digging in her purse, she hands it to me. "I was assigned to your sister after a formal complaint was filed."

I scan her ID with my eyes. It looks legit, though this woman looks too fancy to be a social worker. Her outfit and posture reek of wealth. Not wealth because everything compared to my mangy place looks like The Ritz, but real wealth.

The kind of wealth that speaks of summers in the Hamptons and winters in Athens, of personal drivers and tailored clothing, of menus with items so expensive there's no price on the menu.

The type of wealth I doubt I'll ever see again once she walks out this door.

"A complaint," I say, my voice full of challenge, but in my head, everything in me is deflating.

I knew this was a possibility after Mina's third grade teacher approached me and asked where our parents were. I told her that our mother was working and our Dads were gone. The last part was true, but I doubt the first part was.

With her gone so often, I never really know for sure what Dearest Mother is doing or where she is, for that matter.

Either way, I did my telltale wince when the word "Mom" forcibly slipped past my lips, and Ms. Snow's eyes narrowed. She paid more attention to me and Mina after that. It was just a matter of time. The thing about time, though, is it sneaks up on you no matter how much you prepare yourself for it.

And here I am, staring at something I've been waiting a while for but still so unready.

Because how can I ever be ready for having my baby sister ripped away from me?

The woman sighs, drawing my attention to her. She's scanning the place, and I try to see what she's seeing through her eyes.

Mold on the ceiling.

The faint scent of urine in the air.

A ratty twin-sized air mattress, the hole at the foot of it covered in duct tape.

My sheets on the floor beside it, fashioned into a makeshift bed.

The apartment is ugly and revolting, but it's also the place where I taught Mina to read; where she comforted me when I cried after my first crush broke my heart freshman year, her four-year-old brain too innocent and young to comprehend the source of my tears; and where Mina and I developed our sisterhood, our us against the world motto.

"This place isn't a place an eight-year-old with spina bifida should be raised in."

I open my mouth to argue, but I can't.

She's right.

Deep down, I know Mina deserves more than this. And it's my fault, too. At 18, I'm almost out of high school. I should be working more than a part-time job that barely pays the rent for section 8 housing. Sometimes, Mina and I have to go to the food kitchen, where we wait in line for hours for a decent meal.

But she's never complained.

Doesn't that count for something?

When Erica speaks again, her voice is full of sympathy. "If your circumstances change, you might be able to reunite with your sister. Until then, you're welcome to visit her at her group home in China Town."

She gives me a pitiful smile, unaware of what she just did. She gave me hope. She told me there's a possibility of having Mina again. Of getting my baby sister back.

And in that moment, I promise myself—I promise *Mina*—that I will do *anything* to get her back.

Anything.

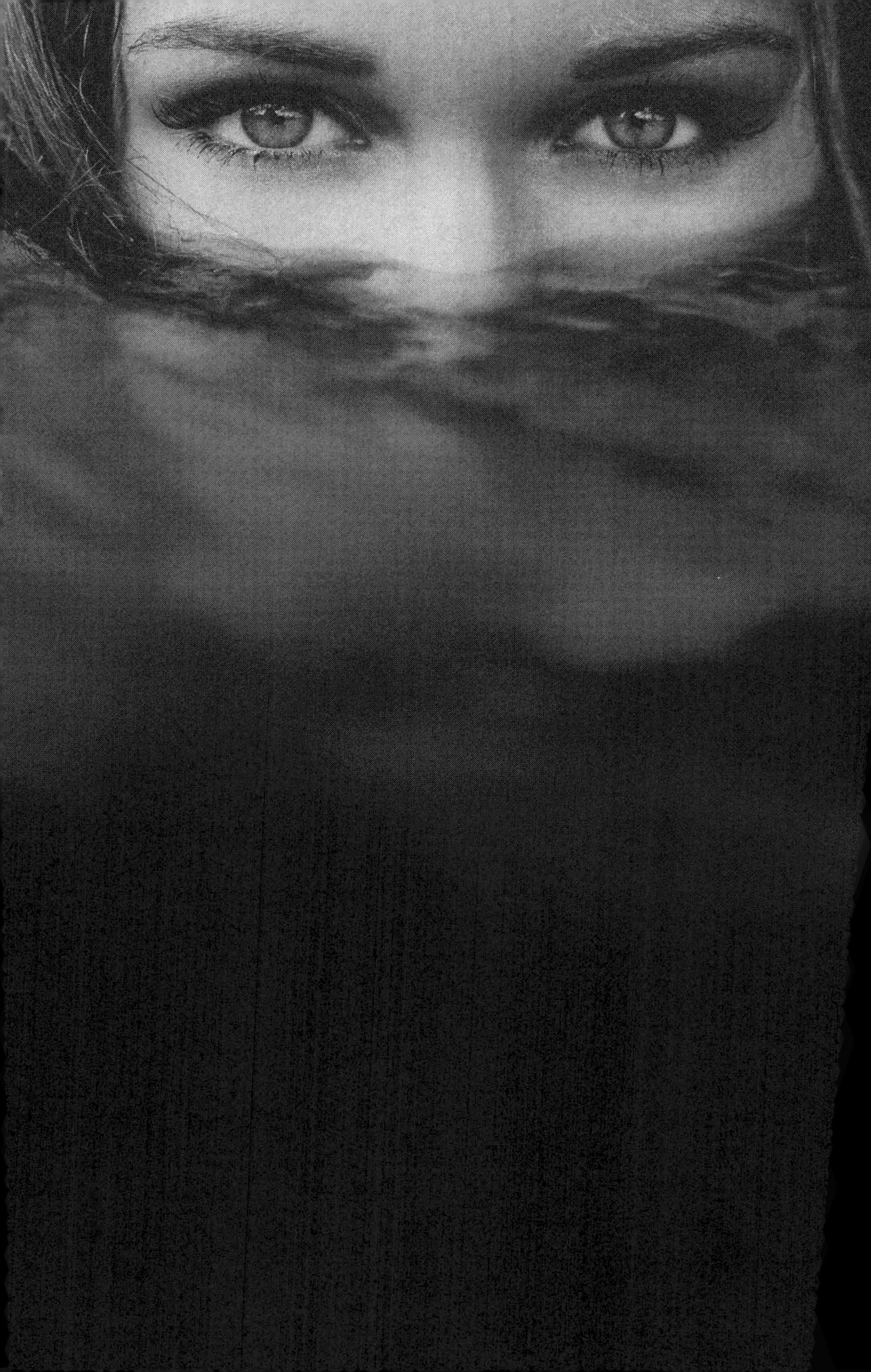

CHAPTER ELEVEN

Forgive your enemies, but never forget their names.
John F. Kennedy

Niccolaio Andretti

Present

For **someone with a five**-million-dollar bounty on his head, my life is pretty damn boring. It's been a week since Vincent informed me of the three-point-five million dollar increase on my hit, and I haven't seen any action yet.

To be fair, I've been camped inside of my brownstone, hiding like a little bitch.

I tell myself that it's because it's not just my life on the line. I have my security guards to think about. Being in public, out in the open, puts them at risk and also the lives of anyone around me.

But a few minutes earlier, when the door of a car slammed shut and I immediately straightened up, I knew I was bullshitting myself.

Who the fuck am I trying to kid?

I had been indoors, doing nothing on a pleasant Saturday afternoon, because I had been waiting for *her* to come back.

And at the sound of her car, I peeked an eye out of my window curtain, catching sight of her dark red hair, the soft curls blowing gently with the wind. I took a moment to consider what I was doing.

I was staring like an awestruck teenage boy.

Was I embarrassed? Absolutely.

Would I stop? Fucking unlikely.

I got another ten seconds of her bouncing up the steps to John's place before she let herself in with a key and was out of my sight. I sighed and returned to my office.

Now, not even a minute later, I'm still sitting idly at my desk, tempted to look her up on the internet.

I don't know her first name, but I caught sight of her last name, Reynolds, on her sweater a short while ago, and years as a killer and recluse have gifted me with the opportunity to develop research talents comparable to the most infamous of stalkers. For a brief moment, I hesitate, my fingers hovering closely above my keyboard.

I can pull up security footage from my cameras outside of my place.

I can grab a still of her face.

I can run it through every facial recognition software known to man.

It would be easy.

I can do all that... but then I would be sinking to a new low.

The truth is, after talking to her a few times, I know deep down that she's not involved in the hit, yet I want a reason to look into her past—*into her*. But...

She's not a target.

She's not marked for death.

She's a nobody.

And I have no fucking clue why I'm so fucking interested.

I sigh, staring at the ceiling, focusing on a smudge, where the corners of the walls intersect. When I painted the walls gray, I accidentally left a light gray dot of paint on the bright white ceilings. I could have fixed it, but at the time, I kind of liked the idea of the imperfect.

It was a tangible, visible flaw, and it was mine.

It was *me*.

But after a while, I started to resent it. I even named it Asshole, because like an asshole, my imperfection mocked me every day when I stared at it with nothing else to do with my life.

Laying low day after day gets boring.

Redundant.

Monotonous.

Wearisome.

Sometimes, when I would get so stir crazy, I would succumb to the insanity tugging at the fringes of my brain, and I'd talk to my Asshole on the ceiling. After the third time or so, I realized that I was talking to an inanimate object, referring to a speck of paint on the ceiling as *my asshole*, and stopped.

At the time, it was an all-time low.

Since then, I've sunk even lower.

Like waiting around all day for a glimpse of fiery hair and a constellation of faded freckles.

Like considering whether or not I should cyberstalk a total stranger.

Like focusing my energy on a random hot chick because I don't want to think about the fact that my little brother, who I still love and would still give my life for, wants me dead so much that he would pay five million dollars for it to happen.

Nope.

Not thinking about it.

I'd rather stare at my Asshole all day.

And I do.

I stare at the damn thing until the grayness of its color blurs into the white, and I'm not sure if what I'm seeing is a color that exists in any color spectrum.

I stare at the damn thing until my neck aches from glancing up at the ceiling, and my shoulders ache from carrying the burden of my neck.

I stare at the damn thing until the tiniest sliver of evening light left outside stretches into an all-consuming darkness, and my boredom doesn't even register in my mind, because my mind has shut down.

Off.

Inoperative.

Out of order.

And when there's a light thud of a door closing on John's side of the street, the subtle noise miraculously registers in my brain, sending me out of my seat and flying toward the door. I shout for my guards to stay behind, assuming they heard me get up.

And for some damn reason, my boredom has reached its limit, and I open the door and ever so eloquently say, "Hi."

I don't even remember the last time I've greeted anyone with anything other than a bullet.

But *hi?*

It's so mundane.

So normal.

So friendly.

In other words, it's the exact opposite of me, and that makes me want to laugh. It's only fitting that a woman that elicits from me a reaction so different than anyone else gets a greeting from me that is equally out of character. And saying hi, like I'm a fucking pre-pubescent teenager that has just barely found the confidence to talk to a girl for the first time after opening his first Playboy magazine or some shit, is most definitely out of character.

She stares at me, her petite face upturned into a pretty scowl. "What do you want?"

It's her go to question, one that she always asks and I never quite seem to answer. And despite the *I don't give a fuck* look I typically have permanently glued onto my face, the corners of my lips turn up into a genuine smile, amused in a way that I've noticed frequently happens when I'm around her. Only this time, I allow myself to show it with a brief smile, because what the Hell. If I'm saying hi like an everyday Joe, I may as well smile, too.

"Nothing," I purposely reply in a tone that says I mean the opposite.

She rolls those emerald green eyes of hers and turns around, giving me her back. It's a nice back, lean and trim, but what it leads to is even nicer. I take a moment to stare at her ass. Round and perky, it's nestled beneath God's gift to men—tight jeans.

Without hesitation, I eye her retreating body and make a dumb decision. Leaning back into my house, I grab two guns off of the entryway table, tuck them into the back waistline of my dark jeans, and chase after her.

The spontaneity feels like freedom amidst my perfectly planned life.

She glares at me, hostility and—dare I say—sadness extending from her in waves. "I'm not in the mood for this. What do you want?"

"I'm bored," I say honestly.

"Bored," she repeats drily. The word sounds foreign on her lips.

"Yep. That's what I said."

"What do you expect me to do about it?"

"You're already doing it."

And she is. Just being here with her, with someone other than myself and the two guards that man my security room, is doing wonders for my brain. Truthfully, it could be anyone, and I would be satisfied.

Seriously.

Anyone.

Except for Asher, Vincent, Lucy, my guards, a Romano, an Andretti, my brothe—

She turns to me, stopping us both, along with my train of thought. "Stop. Whatever you think you're doing, just stop."

"Stop." I play with the foreign word on my tongue, the sound of it unfamiliar to my ears.

I've never been told to stop before.

That's a first.

And it's sexy.

I like the word. I like the sound of it on her pouty lips. I like that she's not giving me the time of day. And I should probably stop talking to her. It'd be for the best. And I will. *One more minute*, I mentally promise myself—and her. I need one more minute of this. I was being honest earlier when I said she was curing my boredom.

The corners of my lips tilt upwards *again* as I wait for her to say something else.

"Yep. That's what I said," she mocks me.

I'm about to reply with something that would have undoubtedly been smart when I hear a familiar clicking sound, and I spur into action, diving over her body and shielding it with my own.

Not even a second later, there's a distinct *whish* sound.

A muffled gunshot.

CHAPTER TWELVE

I was angry with my friend:
I told my wrath, my wrath did end.
I was angry with my foe:
I told it not, my wrath did grow.
William Blake

Minka Reynolds

I lay frozen for a moment.

Shocked.

What just happened?

But before I can articulate my questions—namely, *what the heck?* —John's neighbor is already off of me, whipping two guns out of his pants and into his large palms. They hang loosely at his sides as he casually moves my stunned body behind the cover of a parked car using the lower part of his right leg, yet somehow remaining gentle.

I watch with wide eyes as he pulls the triggers on both of his guns at once. They emit a forced *whish*, quiet in their danger thanks to the silencers fastened on the tips of each barrel. Though I shouldn't, I peek an eye out the side of the car to observe the damage.

On the ground of the empty street lays a man. His eyes are scrunched closed, his lashes resting forcefully against the tops of his cheeks. For some reason, that's the first thing I notice about him.

Not the blood flowing from his hand, which pools around the

fallen gun that lays on the ground beside the twitching tips of his fingers.

Not the crimson liquid seeping through the leg of his jeans, gushing onto the gravel that rests beneath the coarse fabric.

Not the way his mouth is spread open, his tongue pushed slightly past his thin lips as he groans out in pain.

Not the clutch of his uninjured hand against his wounded kneecap as it tries but fails to stop the bleeding.

Those observations come after.

But for the briefest of moments, I focus on his closed eyes, and I see myself in them. I'm there in the way they shut out the world and the pain that comes with it, and I don't know why I'm just seeing this now.

I've done so many things I'm not proud of, and perhaps I've been so driven in my goal of reuniting with Mina that I've blocked out everything.

If I opened my eyes, would I even recognize myself?

And more importantly, do I even want to open my eyes?

I don't allow myself to dwell on these questions any longer than it takes to think them.

Instead, I focus on the sight of John's neighbor as he stalks forward, poised and lethal with the weapons nestled confidently in his hands. His face is an eerily blank mask, void of reaction and the amusement that I saw on it merely seconds ago.

And I don't know which I find more unsettling—his odd bout of amusement earlier or how calm he is in the face of danger.

It's almost as if he's danger himself, and he finds getting shot at nothing more than a cute activity to deal with.

I see it in the way his calculative eyes gleam, dark and anticipatory as he stalks leisurely toward his prey. His peaceful demeanor is disturbing. He reminds me of a panther when he eyes the attacker and slows his approach.

And for a brief moment, I wonder if this man bleeds like the rest of us.

If he feels pain like the rest of us.

If he's even human like the rest of us.

Once bending over and pocketing the attacker's gun, he pats the attacker down, grabs his bad leg and begins to walk, dragging him along the pavement and leaving a long trail of deep crimson liquid behind him.

It doesn't even strike me as odd that I'm not startled by this. Getting shot at? Yeah. That's a first for me, and it was definitely surprising. But watching John's neighbor drag a body behind him, like he's pulling on the handle of a particularly large suitcase? Oddly not disconcerting.

This is why I would make a wonderful lawyer. Most of the things that should bother me don't. Maybe that's messed up. Maybe it's not. Either way, I consider it a survival skill that I'm grateful for.

After taking a few more steps, John's neighbor turns his head over his shoulder and considers me, as if he's just remembering that I'm here. As if I'm merely an afterthought. He makes eye contact with me and evaluates my face before roaming his eyes over my body, cataloging me from head to toe.

I don't think he's checking me out, nor do I think he's checking to make sure I'm okay. He's just staring at me. Studying me. Evaluating me. *Judging* me. And when we make eye contact, there's an unspoken agreement that we won't call the cops.

I know why *I* won't. I can't bring any unfavorable attention to me, not when I'm so close to filing for custody over Mina. Any step backward is a step I can't afford to take.

But I don't know why *he* won't.

After all, he didn't do anything wrong.

This was classic self-defense.

It was hardcore and over the top, but it was self-defense nonetheless. Perhaps his weapons are unregistered? I look at the expensive brownstone homes behind him and immediately dismiss the thought. Possession of unregistered weapons wouldn't be a problem for someone who can afford to live here.

Or perhaps it's the mafia connections I suspect he has. But wouldn't it be better to call the police if nothing shady is going on, rather than hide it and actually break the law and risk garnering the attention of the police?

I wouldn't know, nor do I care.

Because honestly?

His reasoning doesn't matter. As long as the cops don't start paying attention to my life, I'm content. I have enough to deal with when it comes to Social Services, and I suspect this man feels the same, only with the mafia and police.

After a brief moment of contemplative silence, he says, "You can leave if you want, but there may be more of them."

My jaw drops, because there's so much wrong with this situation right now. First, we were shot at. Then, he shot our attacker. Now, he's dragging the guy to his home with one hand, like he's Thor and it's the easiest thing in the world.

He even has his phone out in one hand, casually sending a text.

And on top of that, he just gave me permission to leave.

As if I need it.

If it's even possible, I hate him more.

Yet, I follow after him, because he's right. There may be more attackers, and he looks like he can handle them. Then again, the attacker didn't shoot at me, did he? I wince. He was either shooting at me, or he had really bad aim. It's likely the latter.

Either way, John's neighbor saved me.

So, what should I do?

I was planning on walking back to the dorms. It's a twenty five minute walk, but after what just happened? Fat chance. Instead, I pull out my phone, call an Uber, and continue to follow after John's neighbor.

I pick up my pace and settle beside him, where I plan to be until my Uber arrives and I feel safe. Averting my eyes from the man he's dragging, I focus on my phone. An alert pings, letting me know that the driver is on his way.

I wince when I see the estimated cost of the trip, though my Uber account is still linked to John's black American Express card. I suppose this will be the last time I use it. It's not the first time I've been tempted to book two one-way plane tickets to Fiji and run away with Mina, but I know she deserves better than a life on the run.

I sigh, and for the first time in a while, I wonder if that's me.

If I'm better than what she has right now.

Maybe I'm not.

After all, I just left my sugar daddy's home after catching him having sex with my older look-a-like, and my sugar daddy's hot neighbor followed me outside, saved me from a bullet that was probably meant for him, and is currently dragging a wounded attacker back to his $40 million brownstone.

You can't make this type of crazy up.

And I doubt Social Services would approve of any of this.

"How's your day been?"

I swivel my head to John's neighbor, and my mouth drops in shock. "Are you for real?"

He shrugs and continues to talk in that low and inexpressive voice of his, "When you left John's, you looked upset."

His tone alone is enough to make me want to throw my head back and laugh.

How does he do it?

How does he manage to say something like that, something borderline on caring, and still sound like he couldn't care less about a thing?

Instead of laughing, I let out an unattractive snort. "So, now we're talking about our personal lives?" I pause, before saying in rapid fire, "How much did you make last year? When was the last time you've had sex? Do you like it on top or on the bottom? Have you ever done ana—"

"John's your personal life?" he says, as if we didn't just have this talk recently. He's still adamant that I'm not with John, only this time he's right.

"Not anymore," I mutter.

Between us, the attacker groans out in pain. We ignore him, and a few seconds later, he passes out again from the pain. After another minute of silence, we're almost back to the brownstones. They're within seeing distance when John's neighbor speaks again.

There's a smile in his voice that, per usual, doesn't quite make it to his face when he says, "I like it on top."

I roll my eyes, but I can't help but grin.

But the smile escapes my lips when I see John exit his home, the redhead trailing closely behind him. When she sees me, she narrows her eyes and looks me up and down, a frown tugging at the edges of her lips. She looks even more startled than I was when I noticed how similar we look.

John frowns when he sees me, too. He looks between me and his neighbor, his eyes full of suspicion, before tugging at the redhead's hip and placing her protectively behind him. Making himself a shield between us and the redhead is an oddly alpha male thing to do for someone who gets mani/pedis twice a week.

I smirk at the thought, but once I catch sight of John's neighbor's intelligent eyes, I stiffen. He studies what he can see of the redhead before stealing another glance at me. He's obviously smart, and as I see him piecing everything together, I wait.

I wait for the judgment that everyone else gives me to inevitably come.

But it doesn't.

And darn it, that confuses my heart.

CHAPTER THIRTEEN

Sometimes when I'm angry, I have the right to be angry, but that doesn't give me the right to be cruel.
Unknown

Niccolaio Andretti

Holy fucking shit.

I stare at the woman behind John before glancing back at the woman beside me, stunned by their resemblance. It doesn't take a genius to figure out what's going on. I narrow my eyes at John, who rolls his.

He's fucking doppelgangers now?

And judging by his protective stance over the woman behind him, she's the one he wants. And everything starts to click into place. John fucked Red Junior when he couldn't have Red Senior, and Red Junior…

Young.

Smart.

Gorgeous.

With a man old enough to be her grandfather? A man with no personality other than cranky douche.

And that's coming from a cranky douche.

I've seen this a million times before while living in Andretti territory. Hell, I see this all over New York, too, and I don't even get out much.

Red Junior is a gold digger.

Interesting...

There has to be a story behind that. Any other time, and I would be curious to know. When I want to know something, I don't stop until I figure it out. But right now, I have more important things to deal with.

Namely, the scumbag whose meaty leg I have clutched in my hand.

"John," I greet coldly.

I may use him from time to time, but it doesn't mean I like him.

He eyes Red Junior uneasily before saying, "I got your text. What's up?"

"We're waiting on Dex."

"Cameras?" he asks, referring to the system the three of us have installed all over a five block radius.

I nod, and the four of us sink into silence before a black car turns slowly onto the street. I use my foot to subtly push the attacker onto the ground, behind a parked car and out of view from the driver of the black car.

I keep the bottom of my shoe over the guy's mouth, so he can't speak out. Weakened by the pain and blood loss, he doesn't bother fighting me. I hear a scandalized gasp coming from Red Senior, but everyone ignores her.

I tense the closer the car approaches, my hand automatically reaching for one of the guns tucked into my clothes. But when I see the black and white Uber sticker on the window shield of the car, I relax. Slightly.

"You called an Uber?" I ask Red Junior.

She nods, avoiding eye contact with Red Senior and John. And without a word, she gets into the car as soon as it pulls up in front of us. Less than ten seconds later, she and the car are out of sight.

I lift my foot off of the attacker, who struggles to sit upright but makes no further move beyond that.

"What happened?" asks John, eyeing the attacker on the floor as soon as the car turns the corner.

I stare pointedly at Red Senior behind him and remain silent.

John sighs. "She's cool."

I keep my mouth shut, because he should know me better than that by now.

My caution knows no limits.

They've been with me for more than five years, but I still scan my security guards for wires and bugs whenever they change shifts—not because I don't trust them, but because people are flawed and have weaknesses, and I refuse to let them take me down, too.

To be fair, I'm not an exception to that rule either.

I had a weakness, and his name was Ranie. Back then, if someone held him over my head, I would have been reduced to a pawn, doing anything to assure his safety. Hell, the mess I'm in right now exists for that very reason.

Plus, considering I've been killing people for money for years, I'm probably the most flawed of them all. And worst of all, I'm the type to contemplate about my flaws, and living in hiding means I have a lot of time to do so.

That's why I hate being around Asher. Being around him makes me feel like I'm *too* flawed, like I'm doing life wrong. Asher has lived my life. He's studied under the tutelage of mafia royalty. He's lived the life of a fixer.

These are all things I've done, too. The difference? He came out on top, and I haven't. Perhaps I never will. So yeah, I'll help him out. After all, he's a decent guy, and he's done a lot for me. But I draw the line at hanging out with him, even though he never hesitates to extend an invitation.

Because whenever I look at him, I see what I'm not.

But worst of all?

I see what I can be.

It takes about ten minutes for Dex to get his dick out of some girl and send her on her way.

But until then, John, Red Senior and I wait. And after the first four trying minutes of listening to the asshole on the ground moan out in pain, I clock him roughly on the back of the head with the base of my trusty Smith and Wesson, knocking him out cold.

That earns me a shocked gasp from Red Senior.

John pats her reassuringly on the shoulder, whispers something into her ear that makes her smile, and glares at me. "Did you have to do it like that, Niccolaio?"

"Nick," I correct absentmindedly. I look at my Smith and Wesson with a frown before tucking it back into my jeans, safely positioned beside my beautiful Colt, which has an intricate drawing of a cobra etched into its handle. "And yeah. I didn't want to get his germs on my Colt."

After all, I like the Colt better than the Smithy. I trust it more, and more importantly, it came from better stock.

John rolls his eyes, and the three of us stand together in silence again. I scan the streets, keeping my eye out for any more low lives, while I lightly kick the guy on the ground to see if he's still out.

I wouldn't partner up with this sad sack of shit for a billion dollars, but who knows?

Some idiot might have.

If so, he might still be out there.

And that has me on alert until, finally, Dex emerges from his front door with a tiny brunette stumbling behind him. She's dressed in a slinky dress with one of Dex's suit jackets over her thin shoulders. A few seconds later, a car similar to the one that picked Red Junior up pulls up to the curb.

Dex opens the door for the girl, who leans back to give him a sloppy kiss. He pats her roughly on the ass and shuts the door for her once she slides herself into the backseat of the car. He has a carefree smirk on his face when he casually walks our way.

Once Dex notices that John is out here, too, he asks, "Cameras?"

I nod, and the two of us stare at Red Senior, who stares at John.

Sighing, John says, "Fine. Give us a moment."

I reach down and grab the unconscious guy's leg. Dex and I walk up to my brownstone with the guy dragging on the ground behind us. In the background, we faintly hear Red Senior huff in protest before silently entering John's place.

I wait for John to join us before I press some buttons on the new security system. After a quick retinal and hand scan, the little gadget on the door handle pricks my skin, drawing a drop of blood. After it analyzes it, the door opens on its own, and the three of us step in.

I drop the guy's leg and wave for John and Dex to stay back as I walk down the hall, the floor sensors picking up my gait print, and disarm the security system for John and Dex to follow after me.

Dex eyes the guy on the ground before sighing and reluctantly grabbing his leg. Even with his relatively above average build, Dex struggles to pull the attacker's weight behind him. When he, the attacker and John pass the entry hallway after closing the door, I quickly rearm the security system.

Dex drops the guy's leg beside me. "Overkill," he decides, which is probably saying something, since he lives and breathes tech. He even has a stellar, top-notch security system of his own.

"Necessary," I counter in the same tone, not commenting on the very relevant fact that I have a five million dollar bounty on my head, courtesy of one pissed off, unforgiving and ignorant little brother.

They don't need to know that.

If they find out, they'll probably vote me off the island out of self-preservation.

And then, I'd have to kill them for pissing me off.

And I actually like Dex.

John? Not so much. He kind of just takes up space and air.

"Heads of countries don't even have this level of home security," John adds.

I eye him coldly and deadpan, "Maybe I'm more important."

John remains silent, but Dex snorts, and the three of us head into my security room. I don't even have to say anything, and Emmett and Ryker, the two guards in the room, are already getting up and leaving the room to deal with the unconscious guy laying on the floor of my foyer. I send them a quick text, letting them know to take care of the trail of blood on the street, too.

I sit on the chair before the computer and pull up the software for our street security system. When the three of us had it installed by one of Dex's tech guys, we agreed to have the system operate out of my home.

It's the one least likely to be breached.

The system also only opens up when all three of us enter the password. This is a safety mechanism we added for our privacy and protection, so we don't spy on one another, not that it would stop me. It also guarantees that we only check it when we all agree it's needed.

Having hidden cameras placed all over several blocks of New York City definitely violates a shit ton of federal and state privacy laws, but it's necessary when we live the lives we lead. We all have our own security feeds on the street, but with this system, I'll be able to track where the attacker came from and what he was doing before he reached our street.

The caveat?

Though Dex is hardly innocent, he, of all people, thought it necessary to enact an added layer of protection when he installed the system. Protection *from us*. And that means that every time I need to use it, I have to call these fucks to join me.

I enter my passcode, a series of random numbers, and stand up from my seat for John and Dex to do the same. When they're done, they leave me to work, giving me the power of an all-knowing god.

And for a brief, startling moment, I'm tempted to abuse it.

I'm tempted to use it to learn more about Red Junior, and I have no clue as to why.

Maybe Dex was right.

People need protection from us.

From *me*.

CHAPTER FOURTEEN

We think that hating is a weapon that attacks the person who harmed us. But hatred is a curved blade. And the harm we do, we do to ourselves.
Mitch Alborn

Minka Reynolds

Everyone else is smiling but me.

Well, there's a smile on my face, but it isn't genuine like theirs.

It's fake and ugly and tense.

Usually, I'm a great actress. Just ask my marks. I've pretended to orgasm under the grossest of men—both inside and out—and if you ask them, they would probably tell you that they're the best sex I've ever had.

But the truth is, I've never had good sex.

And that's an odd thing to think about as the Dean of Wilton's Roosevelt School of Law announces my name, my concentration, and the words "Suma Cum Laude."

After taking a deep breath, I plaster the fake smile on my face again and saunter across the long stage, focusing on not falling on my butt and making a fool out of myself in front of potential sugar daddy prospects, employers, professors and coworkers alike.

I keep a sexy sway on my hips as I shake the Dean's hand and wink at the live streaming camera on the side of the stage. There are hundreds of millionaires and billionaires in the crowd right now at Wilton's commencement ceremony for law majors.

It's probably wishful thinking, but a well-placed wink might garner the attention of one of them. Which I desperately need, since I have until tomorrow to move out of Vaserley Hall, and I still haven't found a place to live.

The thought sends another forced edge to my smile, and the Dean whispers out of the corner of his mouth, "Are you feeling okay?"

"Yes," I lie unconvincingly.

He doesn't comment, because let's be real—he doesn't actually care.

No one but Mina does, and that makes the idea of failing to obtain something on my checklist to get her back even more difficult to stomach.

There's not a genuine smile on my face as I pose for one last photo for the commencement photographers positioned at the base of the stage. As soon as the last picture is taken, I wipe the contrived smile off of my face before exiting on the opposite side of the stage and joining the rest of the graduates that have already been called on by the Dean.

I sit down beside a stranger, and after another moment, the next graduate to walk on the stage sits down on the other side of me. She's a stranger, too. And as I sit between them, wedged between two people I don't know on what should be one of the proudest moments of my life, I can't help but feel miserable.

These two probably have family members and friends in the crowd.

Me?

I have no one.

I can't bring Mina without anyone to watch her during the ceremony. I have no idea where my dad is. The woman who birthed me is about as reliable as Dollar Tree condoms. My only friends had their commencement ceremonies yesterday and have already left the state.

That just leaves me.

This is my greatest personal accomplishment, and I'm alone.

How did I get here?

After the commencement ceremony ends, I'm forced to choose between mingling in the crowd of wealthy patrons and honoring an appointment I made with a potential roommate I found on Craigslist two days ago.

The Craigslist post calls for a female roommate to live in an extra room in an apartment on Broadway and White—rent-free in exchange for cleaning services. I would have to clean the entire apartment, wash dishes every day, and cook meals three times a day. The groceries would be paid for by the other roommate/tenant.

If it's just me, this would be a sweet deal.

But it's not.

I have Mina.

And doing this gig means there will be no time to get a full-time job, which I need if I'm going to be able to afford a Social Services approved apartment, earn a stream of income stable enough to support a handicapped preteen, and acquire a steady living environment.

Oh, and pay for a lawyer to file for custody. I would do it myself, but I don't have a J.D yet, which I might need, should I have to sue for custody.

But living at this place will give me time to find a decent job, study for my LSATs, and wait for an affordable apartment to open up.

On one hand, this is the best deal I've found that allows me to live near Mina's state-run group home without having to pay an obnoxious amount of New York City rent.

On the other hand, if this is anything like the last Craigslist post I answered, I'm better off finding a rich man to leech off of in the crowd of wealthy New Yorkers attending the Wilton commencement ceremony today.

But I can't take the risk that I might not find someone, so as soon as I am able to, I race back to my dorm and change into navy blue dress pants and a cute, white blouse. I brush my hair quickly and look in the mirror, satisfied that I look respectable without looking like I have a stick lodged up my butt.

If I was looking for a roommate, this is how I'd want her to look like.

I wince when I look at the time. I don't have enough time to walk to the appointment, so I call an Uber, which is thankfully still connected to John's black AmEx. I slipped the card in John's mailbox the day after the fiasco, but I forgot to delete the card from my Uber account.

I'm thankful for that now when the Uber driver pulls up and gets into the car. I give him the address and spend the car ride thinking about what happened less than a week ago.

Maybe I should have called the cops.

After all, there were guns involved.

But I don't need it on my record that I was involved in something shady when I'm trying to prove to the state that I'm capable of taking care of my little sister. And with that thought, I put my game face on when the driver pulls up to the apartment building.

The receptionist greets me and lets me up when I enter. The building is nice, but it's not as nice as some of the ones I've been in with my marks. Even so, it's far nicer than what I can presently afford, and that lifts my spirits as I enter the elevator and press "6."

But after I exit the elevator on the sixth floor and knock on the right apartment number, I am greeted by a leery-eyed man, and my spirits sink. I immediately feel like a fool, blinded by my desperation.

I saw the sentence, "Seeking a female roommate," on the Craigslist ad and assumed, like many of the other ads, the poster was a girl.

I was so wrong.

Dressed for the roommate interview in a stained wife beater and torn jeans, this guy looks sketchy. When he takes an intrusive step forward, entering my personal bubble without an invitation, I take a hurried step back.

If I'm being honest, I'm desperate. That means, until he invaded my personal space, I was still considering living here. And when he pulls out an itty bitty maid's costume, small enough to fit in his back pocket, I quickly and wordlessly flee for the elevators, knowing I have to get out of here.

I can't get Mina back if I'm dead.

And I definitely think that's a possibility living here.

Because what sane person would start a roommate interview by thrusting a sex costume into his potential roommate's hands?

Then again, I'm not sane either.

Because what sane person wouldn't be suspicious when answering a Craigslist ad that reads:

*Subject: **SEEKING FEMALE ROOMMATE***

I m a twenty year young person looking for a girl roommate around the same age as me, must be willing to clean the apartment every day, must be a good chef and be cook every day three times a day for breakfast lunch and dinner, i will provide the groceries but u must pick them up or order them online, i will give a strict cash allowance for the groceries, again must be young. hurry. this rent FREE gig wont be available long. lots of people in new york city. lots of people want to live here in new recently renovated apartment on broadway.

Grammatical errors and typos aside, this guy is far from twenty, and there are so many red flags in the ad. But this was my last hope, and I was *and am* so desperate, and...

Another idea pops into my head, perhaps more ludicrous than answering this Craigslist ad, but nevertheless, I endeavor to do it.

Like I said, I'm desperate.

And because of that desperation, twenty minutes later, I find myself in front of a familiar brownstone, my finger hovering over a doorbell.

It's stupid.

It's rash.

It's insanity.

But maybe, just maybe, this might just work.

CHAPTER FIFTEEN

You can't shake hands with a clenched fist.
Indira Gandhi

Minka Reynolds

"Someone has been following me."

The lie escapes my lips with ease, my voice an impressive act of anger, fear, annoyance and frustration. Perhaps it's because I actually *am* feeling all of the above right now.

I'm angry at the way I'm spending my commencement day. Everyone else is out celebrating, and I'm here, trying to trick someone who's basically a stranger into allowing me to move in. I'm also trying and failing to trick myself into believing this is a good idea.

You saw Lucy enter this building without her guard a month ago, and Asher wouldn't let Lucy go anywhere dangerous. She knows him. He's safe. Plus, Minka, it's not like you have any other options. Don't be picky. Beggars can't be choosers.

I'm also fearful of what homelessness will mean for Mina's future.

What happens if Social Services asks me where I've been living since graduating?

What would I say that would convince them that Mina won't end up homeless, too, under my care?

Hi, my name is Minka Reynolds. I've been homeless for a bit, but don't worry, guys. As soon as I sleep with the right guy, Mina and I will find a home and live happily ever after. I promise!

I doubt that'd go over well.

I'm also annoyed at my situation. Social Services should have never butt in in the first place; my sperm donor should have never left; Mina's sperm donor, whoever he is, should have never left; and the good for nothing woman who gave birth to us should never have left either.

And some days, I feel like I belong in the category of people who have left.

After all, Mina and I aren't together, and that means I've left her.

Even if it's not of my own volition.

And lastly, I'm frustrated with myself right now. Here I am, on the steps of John's neighbor's brownstone, waiting for his response to my words. Whatever he says may determine my future—it may determine *Mina's* future.

Yet, I can't help but notice the unsympathetic expression in his dark brown eyes and feel winded.

He's just that beautiful.

He's like a precious statue in a museum. One that you can gape at from afar, but you're not allowed to touch or even approach. And it's not because he's fragile. It's because he, in all of his aesthetically perfect, stony glory, is worth more than you can even fathom, let alone ever dream of making in your lifetime.

So, I'm lucky I was able to get the words out before he even opened the door fully. Because one look at him dressed only in sweatpants, the deep grooves of his muscular chest bare for me to see, and I'm stunned into silence.

My brain chooses to replace that silence with memories of his lips against my jaw, his body pressed against mine, and his confusing words whispered into my ear. I try to force the memories out of my head and focus.

I feel vulnerable all of sudden as I wait for him to react.

To tell me to leave or tell me to stay.

And I don't know which answer I would prefer.

After a solid minute of frozen silence, John's neighbor frowns, hovering in front of his doorway, an unflinching boulder as he takes in my words. I watch wordlessly as his cold, brown eyes darken, and both of his brows dip slightly.

Whether it's in disbelief or confusion or shock, I don't know.

He's as unreadable as ever. His expression shifts and moves, reacting to words and things like a normal person would, but unlike a normal person, I can't read him.

I don't know what he's thinking when his full lips form a straight line.

I don't know what he's thinking when he runs his large hand through his thick brown hair.

I don't know what he's thinking when he sighs.

And all of this uncertainty is making me nervous.

It's making me second guess my crazy plan, which I'm already second-guessing enough.

I endeavor to sell the act better, because I need to be on my A-game if I'm going to trick this guy. He's indescribable in ways I've never encountered, and in this moment, the one thing he reminds me most of is a vault.

And you can't trick a vault into giving you its password.

You can't trick a vault into letting you stay at his home.

"This is your fault," I add, making sure to furrow my brows in irritation, my insinuation about that night last week clear.

"Why would they follow you?" he finally asks, and I hate his ability to stand there so composed in the midst of his own silence—and my insinuations and accusations.

"I don't know. I don't even know who *they* are. But what I do know is that, a week ago, I wasn't being followed. But *someone* just had to trail me out of John's home, I was shot at, and now I'm being followed by a big, sketchy man." I cross my arms. "Does that sound familiar?"

He studies me for a moment. "That sounds like *your* problem. What do you want me to do about it?"

My brain feels like it's exploding in the face of his audacity.

"Seriously?! That's all you have to say to me?" And then I pull my biggest trump card, and I put all of my lying skills into selling this bluff. "You know what? Never mind. Forget I asked." I turn around and am halfway down his steps when I mutter softly but just loud enough for him to hear, "I'll just go to the cops for help."

A few seconds pass, and my feet have hit the pavement of the sidewalk by the time he says, "Wait." His voice is cool, like I'm inconveniencing him by merely existing.

I give an exaggerated sigh and cross my arms again before turning to face him. "What now?" I ask, my voice a perfect cocktail of attitude and annoyance.

"Describe him."

I make up a fictitious description without hesitation, describing a younger version of the guy that tried to date rape me months ago. "Tall. Heavyset. Eyes wide apart. Blonde hair. Blue eyes. Falcon-like nose. Maybe in his thirties?"

He nods his head, as if urging me to continue.

I do, pulling ideas from the movies I saw in my Introduction to Entertainment Law elective course last year. "He had a hat pulled low over his eyes. When I saw him the second time, it was a hoodie. Black. After that, he kept wearing the hoodie. Or maybe he changed hoodies, and they just all happened to be black." I shrug, as if that's all I know and I'm sorry if it's not enough.

But in my head, I'm cheering and mentally awarding myself an Oscar. Because, wow, that was a worthy performance.

He crosses his arms, the thick muscles of his biceps bulging and abdominal muscles rippling from the movement, both of which are laid bare for me to see without a shirt getting in the way. "How many times have you seen him?" His voice is all business, but I take it as a good thing.

As a confirmation that he believes me.

I mimic the tone of his voice when I speak, hoping that it'll make him take my lies seriously. "I've caught him five times. Two of the times were in the same day, but except for the hoodie, he was wearing different things both of those times. He could have been following me more often than that, but I don't know. That's how many times I've caught him."

"And what would you do when you'd catch him?"

"The first time I kind of freaked out, but I tried to pretend like I didn't notice him. I was better at it the other times."

He nods in approval, and I consider what to say. I should work in going to the police again, because I suspect he won't like them getting involved in his mess, given the whole mafia thing.

I lower my voice, so it's barely above a whisper, "Well... The first few times, I considered going to the police and filing a report." I take in his dark expression and urgently say, "But I didn't. They'll probably think that I'm crazy. I have no proof of being followed. I should've taken a picture." I add a hint of vulnerability to my voice. "But I was so scared."

I pause deliberately, giving him time to consider his options before I finish, "Maybe if you go with me and tell the police what happened here a week ago, they'll believe me. Actually, what's your name? I can just file my report about that night and have them come here. You won't even have to leave your house. I promise." By the end of my sentence, I'm doing a convincing job of begging.

That's the biggest bluff I've ever made yet. I can't go to the police. I can't involve them in my life when I want to file for custody over Mina. But... he doesn't know that. So, I keep my face straight and my lies convincing.

There's a slight crack in his otherwise undecipherable mask of a face, and he sighs. "We should talk about this in the house."

Playing up my reluctance, I don't budge.

When he adds, "Just in case the guy followed you here," I still don't budge.

I want him to have to work for it. That way, when he eventually suggests that I move in, he'll think everything is his idea—from the moment he had to convince me to step into his home to the moment he has to convince me to stay.

At my silence, the lingering bit of suspicion in his face evaporates, and he looks more human. "I don't bite."

I sigh and add, "Fine. But I still think we should go to the cops."

"Let's talk it out first and see what our best options are."

"Okay," I agree, sighing as if *I'm* doing *him* a favor.

I walk up the steps and past the threshold of his front door, but he stops me with a soft touch of his hand on my shoulder. The contact sends a jolt of thrill down my spine, and I can't help but wonder...

When was the last time I was touched by a man I was attracted to?

Never.

Well, not since *he* touched me last, but that hardly counts. He did that to prove a point. To prove that I was attracted to him and not John. And unfortunately, it did too good of a job at proving his point, and now I'm painfully aware of that each time I'm around him, as I'm helplessly rendered into a mess of confusing hormones just at the sight of him.

Since my gold digging campaign began, I've only once tried to go for a man that I was even remotely attracted to. Once upon a time, I tried to go for Asher, who I was more than attracted to. I saw him in an off-campus bar with Aimee and Lucy and thought he'd be the jackpot. He's young, handsome and more believable than me being with someone like John.

He also has more clout in this city than anyone I've ever met. No way would a custody request from the *Asher Black* be turned down by Social Services.

But Asher shut me down almost as soon as I approached him. He treated me like there was something wrong with me, and maybe there is. Not because of my gold digging. I'm not ashamed—nor will I ever be—of exhausting all options possible to get Mina back.

What I am ashamed of is how I let my anger and jealousy and frustration get the best of me. And how poorly that made me treat Lucy, Aimee, and so many others who have crossed my path.

And for a split second, I indulge my attraction to John's neighbor. I allow myself to wonder what would happen if we were normal, and I was being invited into his house under normal circumstances.

Would he want me?

Would he press me against the wall and kiss me?

Would he lead me upstairs and shower my body with praises, like John did with my lookalike?

"Hold up," he says, giving me an odd look when he catches sight of my expression and, thankfully, shaking away my distracting thoughts.

I watch as he walks to a wall opposite of us and presses a few buttons on what's probably his alarm system.

"Okay. All clear."

I take a few steps forward, and as soon as I do, the door behind me swings shut automatically with a loud *thud*. I hear a few strange sounds, one of which sounds like a hydraulic *whish*, before I can't help but turn around.

I watch as a steel plate, painted to look like a dark wooden door, slides over the outer door, forming a second protective layer. Seconds after, there are three loud clicks that sound like the turning of several locks.

Holy cow.

I knew, walking into his brownstone, that this man probably has ties to the mafia. But this security system? What would necessitate it?

This is crazy.

What have I gotten myself into?

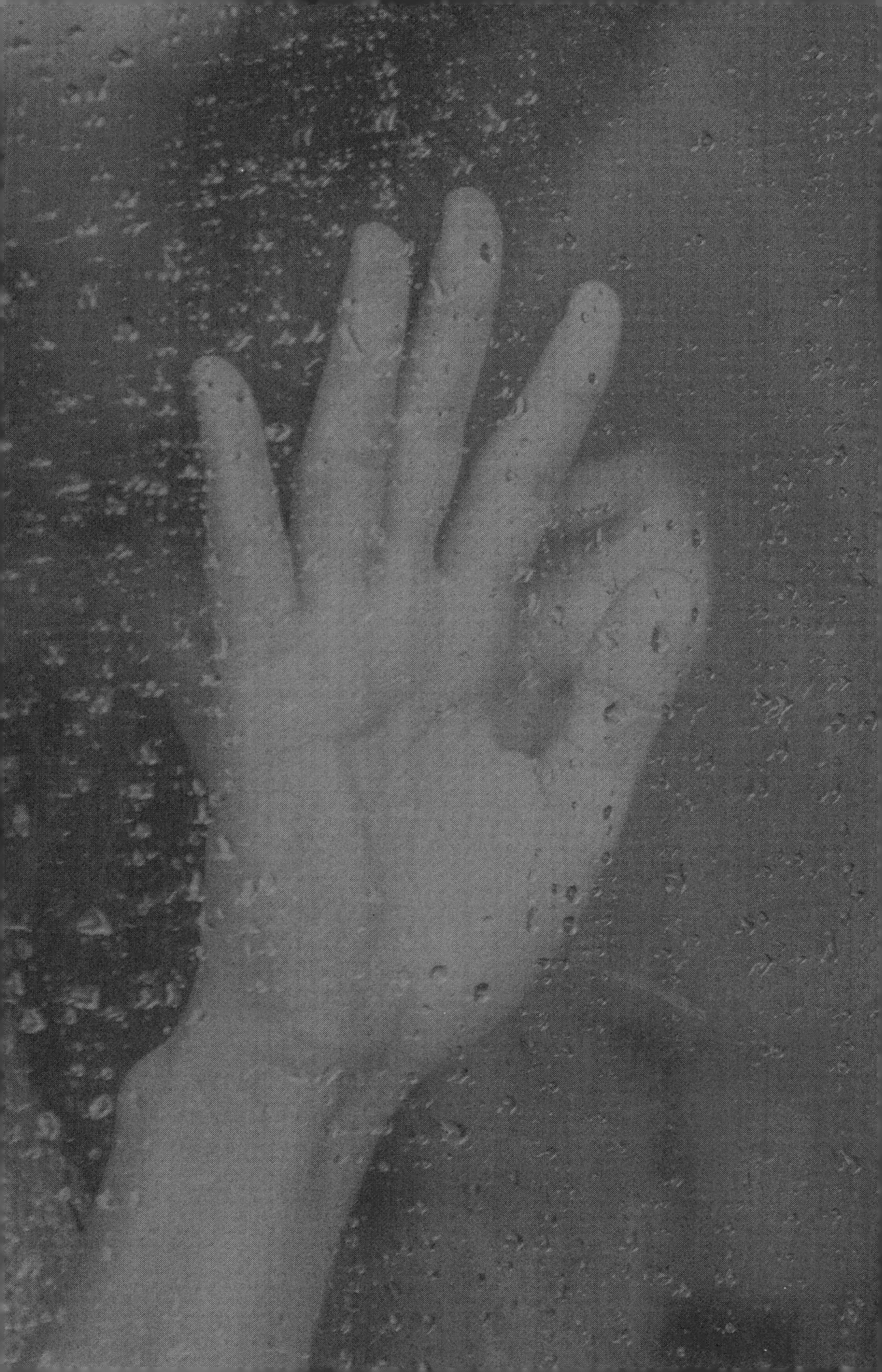

CHAPTER SIXTEEN

Anger is never without a reason, but seldom a good one.
Benjamin Franklin

Niccolaio Andretti

Un. Fucking. Believable.

Someone is following Red Junior, and the fact that she's been able to catch him tells me that it's another talentless hack, trying his hand at the five million dollar hit.

And it's unlikely they would be following her if they didn't see her with me the night of the shooting. Which means Jax, the guy who shot at us that night, was lying to me when he said he didn't have a partner.

I'm actually impressed.

I didn't think he had it in him. When I questioned him that night, he was blabbering like a little boy. By the time I was done questioning him, I had his social security number, the name of the woman who broke his heart, and a promise to name all of his future offspring after me.

I had heartily declined the last offer.

But he just kept going.

T-the first b-boy will be Niccolaio.

The next w-will be Nicholas.

The n-next will be Nico.

The one after th-that will be Nikolaus.

And a-after that, Niklaus.

And if it's a g-girl, I can do Nikki.

Or m-maybe even Nikita.

Nicole is b-beautiful, also...

I'd left my basement, where I was and still am holding him, after he said, "Niccolaio," but I watched him go on for hours on the video footage, stuttering his way through hundreds of variations of my name until he finally fell asleep on the hard floor.

He's still downstairs, and if I walk past the open stairwell to the basement, Red Junior will probably hear him crying, because he does that. He cries a goddamn lot. To the point where I have to wonder if he's got some developmental issues I should be considerate about.

So, I steer clear of the area and take her into the kitchen.

I offer her a bottle of water from the fridge, and we both take seats on the barstools at the end of the kitchen island.

"My name is Minka," she finally says.

I nod my head in acknowledgment.

The name suits her. It's strong but feminine and unique. I've certainly never met anyone like her. One moment, she's an angry ball of fire, and the next moment, she's this woman before me—not quite meek but not quite fearless either.

And I don't know how she can be both.

Things are usually black and white in my life.

I have clear priorities and, for the most part, am able to live my life efficiently, making decisions easily and with little fanfare. Take Uncle Luca's life, for instance. I loved him. I truly did. But I loved Ranieri more, so the choice between Uncle Luca and Ranieri's life was a simple one.

It was easy to make.

And if that decision didn't have me struggling to come to terms with life, acting differently and out of character, like a complex human would, then I don't know what will.

Now, being so near to this woman is almost overwhelming me. She acts so differently each time I see her that I can't help but wonder how she can be so dynamic. How can she be so complex?

Are there this many layers to every person?

I dismiss that thought as soon as it enters my mind, because if I entertain it, it might make my job of killing people harder.

I kill guys who kill.

It's that simple.

Black and white.

No complexity.

No layers.

It's easy, and I like it that way.

"Nick," I say after a long period of silence, giving her the name I give everyone nowadays.

"Nick," she repeats, playing with my name in her mouth, and I can't help but wonder how it'd sound like shouted from her mouth in the midst of an orgasm.

I adjust the baby chub that perks up at the thought, taking note that I need to get laid. I haven't forgotten how fucking turned on I was when I caught her leaving John's, and she'd almost fallen down the steps. She was wearing jeans that showed off her long legs and perfect ass, and her shirt had ridden up as she stumbled, revealing a Hell of a lot of skin.

Maybe she's actually that hot or maybe I really, *really* need to get laid. After all, it's been awhile, since there aren't very many opportunities to do so when you have a hit on your head and stay in your home all day.

I don't even go out to get groceries. I either have one of the guards get them or I have them delivered, switching services randomly and using my fake name, Nick Andrews, for security reasons.

"How about I hire guards for you?" I say, cutting straight to the chase.

"What?" Her eyes widen in surprise, and for some reason, I think I see panic in them.

Perhaps the idea of more men with weapons following her around scares her?

I try to sell it. "You won't even know they're there. My men are well-trained. They can follow you at a distance, where they won't be intrusive. They can stay outside your room at night or even outside your home. Whatever you want. You'll never even have to see them if you don't want to, but they'll be there to protect you, should you need it."

She shakes her head adamantly. "No, I don't want that. Definitely not."

"Well, it's better than going to the cops. At worst, they'll laugh you off. At best, they'll give you a security detail. One guy, who will park outside your apartment or home for two weeks and leave when nothing happens. I'll give you a well-trained security detail for as long as you feel like you need it."

"And what if that's forever?"

"Then, it's forever."

She gives me a disbelieving look.

I gesture around the home, which is clearly a byproduct of wealth. "I'm good for it."

And I am.

Sort of.

I get a healthy amount of money per hit, ranging from two hundred thousand dollars to as much as five million dollars, depending on how difficult the hit is. But on top of that, I managed to empty my portion of my trust fund before Ranie decided to go after my assets.

I may not be Asher Black rich, but I'm easily wealthier than *I'm related to a Rothschild even though it's through a great great great grandfather's cousin eight times removed* John and tech millionaire and blue blood Dex.

The problem, though, is that I can't access that money.

It's hidden in dozens of offshore accounts in case of emergencies. I was stupid when I made the accounts. They're all under my name. My real name. And if I access the money, I'll be telling the Andrettis where my money is, in which case, I might not be able to drain all of the accounts before they access them.

I'd rather not risk it.

As is, Asher was the one who bought this house. In a city I'm allowed to live in because the Romano *capos* allow it. And I'm living off of money I get from hits for the enemy of my family. Hits that Vincent *Romano* generously hires me for. Under a false identity, Nick Andrews, that Asher's techies created for me.

I depend so much on the goodwill of the Romano family, and I still can't help but be amazed by it, given the rough history between the Andretti and Romano families.

But still, I'm good for the deal.

I can't pay for a lifetime of security, but I can call in some favors from friends of my security guys. Or maybe even use this as a training exercise for some trainees from Asher's security company, Black Security.

The offer I'm making is generous.

But for some reason, she gives me a resounding "no."

She doesn't even tell me why.

She just crosses her arms and frowns at me, full of attitude that I've come to realize is just so her. I barely even know her, but in all the times I've met her—literally, every single time—she's been full of attitude. It's the most consistent thing about her.

Is she still pissed about the construction noise?

I narrow my eyes at her. She looks like the type to hold a grudge.

"It's a good deal," I say.

"Well, I don't want it."

"Why the Hell not?"

She cringes at the curse, and I regret saying it. I'm a curser. I swear like a motherfucking sailor. In my mind, aloud, and even in my dreams. And apparently, she's not. I remember what she said when I first met her—*darn*.

She crosses her arms *again*. "I don't want some strange men following me around, going where I go."

I look her up and down. "And where is it that you go?" I can't help but ask, remembering her walk of shame to John's house and my suspicion that she's a gold digger.

Antagonizing her right now probably isn't my greatest decision, but it's not like I judge her for it, since I do some questionable things for money, too. But I want her to say what she is aloud.

For some reason, a reason that likely has more to do with how fucked up I am than what I actually think of her actions, I want to know if she'll own up to it.

I want to see this gorgeous, angry woman tell her truth to me without shame.

But when she doesn't, when she says, "none of your *darn* business," I sag a little in my seat in my seat.

Disappointed.

But I can't blame her.

I don't talk about myself.

I don't talk about my past, present or future.

I don't even let people call me Niccolaio anymore, unless I'm about to kill them or they're too high up in the Romano family for me to correct.

I sigh, because I don't need her to confirm it to know my suspicions are correct. And if she's gold digging, she's probably in need of money.

Money I have but can't access.

Sure, I can dip into my savings from taking out hits, but she can also easily ask for more and more and more once I begin to indulge her.

And it's not like I'm killing enough people to be this woman's sugar daddy.

So, I offer the one thing I think she might accept.

"You can live with me, and I'll protect you."

And damn, I hope I'm not making a fucking mistake.

I've made too many in this life already.

CHAPTER SEVENTEEN

Beware the fury of a patient man.
Publilius Syrus

Niccolaio Andretti

Twenty Years Old

It's cold in Maryland this time of year.

But it's only been a month since I left Florida, and I still haven't gotten used to the change in climate.

And it certainly doesn't help that I'm homeless.

There's a bridge along the Potomac that I sleep under, and for ten dollars a month, I have access to showers and the gym equipment at the nearest Planet Fitness. I spend hours at the gym every day to escape the cold and get a daily shower.

The gym employees think I'm some kind of fitness buff, and I don't correct them. I certainly look and act the part. After a month of daily four hour gym sessions, my body is almost unrecognizable. I was built before, but now, there are muscles on my body in places I didn't know could have muscles.

Usually, the Andretti *capos* like us built but lean. Too many muscles can make you slow. But with the amount and type of training I do, I'm quicker than I've ever been and stronger, too.

It's a shame that I won't ever have the opportunity to use my enhanced skills.

And given where I am, I hope I don't either.

What makes Maryland the perfect place for me to hide out also makes it the worst.

Maryland is a border state for the Romano and Andretti territories. The problem is that the two families have never quite figured out where the border starts and ends. And it doesn't help that, because Maryland is on the fringes of both territories, both families send the nobody *tenentes*—lieutenants—to control the area.

These are men and women that don't mean shit to either family but are still Hell bent on trying to prove their worth.

Damaged egos are a dangerous weapon.

And in the border, a damaged ego causes the *tens* to do crazy shit.

Like start border wars in a never-ending pissing contest of Whose Penis is Bigger?

But despite how dangerous living in a border area is, it's also safe because it's on the outskirts. I know firsthand that my dad doesn't give a damn about this area, and he's the head of the Andretti family.

If the head doesn't give a damn, no one else gives a damn.

And that makes this the perfect place to lay low.

Plus, it's not like I can go anywhere else. When I left Uncle Luca's, I ran. I didn't stop to get money or my passport. All I had was the money in my wallet and cards that had already been canceled.

I couldn't flee the country, and I still can't now. I don't have the connections to get a new passport with a new identity. And I sure as Hell don't want to leave Andretti territory, given the other threats out there for someone who bleeds Andretti blood.

The United States and parts of Canada are split into five territories, each controlled by one of the five syndicates—the De Luca family, the Camerino family, the Rossi family, the Romano family, and the Andretti family.

My family's territory is in the South. Aside from the Romanos, we're pretty much left alone. Obviously, the Romanos are out of the question. The Romano family has been our enemy for hundreds of years, and I'm as good as dead if I step into their territory.

Even if I finished out a hit on my own uncle.

I may not be welcome by the Andretti family anymore, but I still have the Andretti last name and Andretti blood still runs through my veins. And that means I'll always be the greatest enemy of the Romano family.

Some prejudices are too strong to overcome.

I can't go into Rossi territory either. Their territory is on the West coast, so I've never had to deal with them. That means I have no fucking clue how they run, which makes it a bad idea to enter their territory without adequate intel.

And the De Luca territory? That's not even an option. The De Lucas are fucking batshit. They'll kill you first and ask questions later. They're the only family of the five syndicates that have abandoned the original mafia code—innocent women and children are off limits.

To them, innocents are fair game.

Fuck that shit.

I can't live somewhere like that.

And while the Camerino family isn't as bad as the De Luca family, there's too much going on in their politics for me to risk being seen there right now. They're at war with the Rossi family, and not the passive war the Romanos and Andrettis are engaged in, where no one really remembers why we're mad at each other.

Their war is fresh and angry and unrelenting.

So, here I am.

Homeless in Maryland during the fucking cold ass winter.

I sigh when my break ends, and I reluctantly enter Phantom, the club where I bartend every night. I make a fair amount of money here, but it's better for me to save it in case I need it on the run.

I made a mistake by transferring all of my money into an offshore bank account under my real name, but I was in a rush, didn't have an alternate identity set up, and wasn't thinking straight, having just killed my uncle.

Now, I'm paying for that mistake with every dollar I choose to save instead of spend on a warm bed. I'm not sure how much longer I can take this. Living on the run is against every instinct of mine.

I was born to fight and live the mafia lifestyle.

Being idle and on the run is my worst nightmare.

But it's also my only hope of survival.

Which is why, when I hear a clank in the alley I just left and open the back door of Phantom a bit to investigate, I wince at the familiar site of crazed blue eyes and scruffy brown hair. There, standing in the dark alleyway with a man I don't know, is one of my former friends, Ignazio Colombo.

And in a car that just blocked off the exit to the alley is someone I've only met once but would recognize anywhere.

Asher Black.

"We're gonna fucking be legends," Naz says to the guy beside him, his voice splicing the silence.

I groan in my head, because anything Naz thinks is a good idea is one hundred percent bound to be a horrible idea.

Naz is a reckless idiot. He's a total, complete, unbelievably dimwitted idiot that is, without a doubt, about to get himself into trouble right about now. And I may be Andretti enemy number one right now, but he's still an old friend of mine.

Naz used to work in Florida with me—until he shot an innocent civilian who he thought looked like a Romano *caporegime*, because in his idiotic mind, it was logical for a Romano *caporegime* to be entering a goddamn Baby Gap in the heart of Andretti territory out of the fucking blue.

The civilian survived Naz's piss poor aim, lots of men in blue were paid off, and Naz was sent to the border, where he'd be someone else's problem.

And right now?

That someone is me.

CHAPTER EIGHTEEN

Holding on to anger is like grasping a hot coal
with the intent of throwing it at someone else;
you are the one who gets burned.
Buddha

Niccolaio Andretti

Twenty Years Old

Naz pulls a shiny Smith and Wesson out from the waistband of his jeans, while the other guy pulls out a Colt with the outline of a snake etched into the base.

Turning to the guy beside him, Naz says, "Watch and learn, man. Watch and learn. They'll be begging me to come back to Florida after this. I'll be a fucking legend, dude."

Man, don't fucking do it, Naz, I beg in my head, still hidden from view.

And he does it.

I watch as he eyes the guy beside him and gives him a smirk before lifting his gun in Asher's direction. Already, three Romano men have joined Asher and another is exiting the car. If Naz does this, he'll die.

He thinks he can take on this many men, because he's seen me do it.

But he isn't me, and he doesn't know what Asher is capable of. Up until a month ago, Asher was virtually an unknown entity in the mafia world. He came out of nowhere, and if Naz has even a semblance of a brain in his head, that should tell him all he needs to know about Asher. But of course, it would be asking too much to ask Naz to think things through.

So, before I can second guess myself, I pull the gun I used to kill Uncle Luca out of the holster hidden underneath my hoodie. I shoot to kill the guy beside Naz, then I shoot Naz's hand, the one holding the gun.

Asher turns to us, and the guys behind him pull out their weapons.

But Asher holds up a fist when he sees me, and his companions lower their guns.

"Niccolaio?!" Naz exclaims, clutching his injured hand tightly. His eyes are trained on mine, equal parts vehemence and disbelief in them.

If I look closely, I suspect I'd see the betrayal in them, too, which is why I don't look too closely. Instead, I quickly reassess the situation and make a decision. The gun lays on the ground beside Naz. I ignore him, reach down and grab his Smith and Wesson and his friend's Colt, too. I pocket them both in the waistband of my pants, keeping my gun in my right hand but loosely at my side.

Asher approaches us. When he looks at the dead guy on the ground, I shake my head, indicating that he's no longer alive. Asher nods and turns his attention to Naz, who—like the idiot he is—is trying to get up.

I use my left foot and push Naz back down, knowing if he gets up, he'll only make things worse for himself.

"Fucking traitor scum. You don't deserve the Andretti name," Naz spits out.

I don't say anything, because I was expecting the insults the moment Naz spit out my name like it was an incurable disease. Instead of rising to the bait, I keep my mouth shut and wait to see what Asher will do.

He gives me a look that brings me back to the night I killed Uncle Luca, when he gave me that same look. We had just escaped the compound after Ranieri took one look at me exiting Uncle Luca's room with Asher and ran into his bedroom for a weapon.

I had no doubt that he called Dad after that, and we were now targets in Andretti territory. I had to get out of there, and I didn't know what to do. Asher stared at me, gave me this odd look like I surprised him, and then he just left.

And I was on my own.

Now, a month later, I can't exactly say that I've been doing very well on my own.

But I'm alive, and that's gotta count for something.

From beneath my foot, Naz snarls, "What the fuck is wrong with you, Niccolaio? Ya know, I didn't believe them when they said you killed Luca. But I should have known you were scum. Do you know who this man is? Asher fucking Black. How much is he paying you?" He shakes his head in disbelief. "First you take Luca's life, and now you save *his* life?"

Asher arches his brow as if to say, *yeah, why'd you save my life*?

But the truth is, I didn't save Asher's life.

I saved Naz's.

The ungrateful shit just doesn't realize it.

But if I let him kill Asher, Asher's men would have mowed him down. He was outnumbered, and there was a good reason why Naz had been sent to the border. He isn't like me or Asher. He's like one of those five pound Chihuahuas that thinks that he's a German Shepherd or some shit. The only reason he's under the protection of the Andretti family is because his dad is cool with mine.

Other than that, he's pretty much good for nothing. But still, once upon a time, he was my friend. And for some reason, that still matters to me, so I did what I could. I saved him, and in doing so, I happened to save Asher.

Now, I'm standing silently, waiting to see what the consequences of that are. I know Asher will piece together why I did this—if he hasn't already. It's just a matter of time. And once he does, I wonder what he'll do to me.

After all, I was still born an Andretti.

"Angelo?" Naz calls out pitifully, turning his head in the direction of his companion.

I sigh and gentle my voice when I say, "He's dead."

Naz's eyes flash, and they're full of fury. "He was one of ours," he seethes.

"I didn't recognize him."

"You've been gone for a while."

"I've been gone for a month."

"A lot can happen in a month."

He's right.

A lot can happen in a month. In many ways, I'm a different person than I was a month ago. Physically, I'm stronger and quicker. Inside, I'm colder. Hardened by my uncle's murder at my own hands.

But in some ways, I haven't changed.

A month ago, I would have tried to save Naz. And as it turns out, a few minutes ago, I was still willing to do the same. Even if Naz is an ignorant, ungrateful ass. And unfortunately, both Naz and Angelo had guns.

And I only had one.

I couldn't risk Angelo getting a shot off while I disarmed Naz, so I killed him. It was easier that way.

Did it suck that I had such a disregard for life?

Of course.

But even I recognized that, in a weird way, I also had a reverence for life, too.

I valued Naz's life. It just happened to be at the expense of Angelo's. Just like I valued Ranieri's at the expense of Uncle Luca's. It's a disgusting ability to be able to look at lives and prioritize. To say which one is worth more.

But as the Andretti heir, that's what I was taught by my own father to do.

But judging by Naz's reaction to seeing me, none of the Andrettis see what I did this way.

And that means I'm still on the run. That perhaps I'll always be on the run.

But then, Asher turns to me and gives me an offer that changes everything.

He offers me asylum in Romano territory, and damn it, I accept it.

And because I've hated living on the run and the Andrettis already hate me, I don't even consider that it might be a mistake when I accept Asher's offer.

That, once I do this, there's no turning back.

CHAPTER NINETEEN

Anger is a wind which blows out the lamp of the mind.
Robert Green Ingersoll

Minka Reynolds

Present

L**ucy smashes into me** as I open the door into the hallway leading to my dorm room in Vaserley Hall. The movement causes the medium-sized moving box I'm holding to crash onto the floor, and the clothes in it spill out onto the carpet.

She doesn't do it on purpose, but it annoys me nevertheless.

"Sorry," she says with a smile and reaches down to pick my things up.

I like it better when she avoided me. When she didn't talk to me at all costs. A few months ago, if she accidentally bumped into me, she would have passive-aggressively stared at me and turned the other way.

(And I probably would have sent a scathing remark her way.)

Now, she's apologizing. With a *smile* on her face.

And I'm standing silently. Staring at her with an insult at the tip of my tongue that evaporates before I can speak it. For some reason, I just don't have it in me to be mean to her. Yet, at the beginning of the school year, I couldn't stand her and Aimee.

Aimee was competition. I had my eyes set on the Dean of Wilton's

Jefferson School of Business, and he had his eyes set on Aimee. He's wealthy, from old money, and he runs several successful businesses. It doesn't hurt that he's easy on the eyes.

And I was acting like *that* girl. The one that's catty to someone for no other reason than she's jealous and threatened. And as Aimee's best friend, Lucy got caught in the crossfire. It was wrong of me. I know that. Heck, I knew that from the moment I started the stupid feud, but I did it anyway.

But something about the way the two of them are together reminded me—and still reminds me—of how Mina and I used to be together before Social Services took her away from me. I remember seeing them the first time, when we moved into Vaserley Hall, and thinking, *how dare they be so carefree and full of life when my sister is trapped in an awful, rundown building in China Town?*

And I reacted.

I was jealous, and I lashed out.

The first thing I said to Aimee was, "Ew. What are you wearing, Hill Billy?"

She had on ripped jeans and trendy, worn out cowboy boots that were, honestly, nicer than anything I could afford without the help of one of my marks. And Lucy stood there, gaping as Aimee gave me a smart, sarcastic remark.

It was war after that, and it didn't help that the next day I saw Aimee talking on campus with the Dean of Jefferson, his eyes glancing down every few seconds to the generous swells of her breasts, the lust clear in his eyes.

Looking back now, I realize that I was being stupid. Like it often does, my anger had gotten the best of me, and what's worse is I wasn't even angry at Aimee or Lucy.

I was angry at the world.

I still am.

And it's worse that Lucy turned out to be a good person.

And right now, even as I'm trying to change, she's still being a better person than I am.

This isn't the first time she has been friendly with me since I let her hide out in my dorm room. For instance, about a month ago, she greeted me cheerily when she caught me leaving John's place. Come to think of it, it's probably a good idea to ask her why she was entering John's neighbor's brownstone in the first place.

Nick's brownstone.

My eyes narrow at her, ignoring the way her bodyguard hovers protectively behind her at the movement. "Who lives in that brownstone I saw you entering a month ago? The one by Central Park."

There's a flash of a smirk on her face before it evaporates, and she gives me an innocent expression. "I don't know what you're talking about."

Behind her, her bodyguard snorts. She turns to glare at him, but the glare is playful and silly on her delicate features, and the bodyguard's snort turns into full-blown laughter. She watches, a soft smile of endearment on her face, as his giant, muscular frame shakes with laughter.

I clear my throat to regain her attention. "Yes, you do." I take a step closer. "How do you know him?"

I curse myself for letting her know that I know the neighbor is a he.

Lucy, of course, catches on. Her eyes widen at my slip, and she doesn't even bother holding back her full-blown smile. "So, you've met Nick?"

Nick.

Yesterday, he told me his name is Nick, but I still don't think it suits him. It's just so normal when he's anything but. His name is so average that learning it was almost anticlimactic. I liked it better when he was a nameless entity in my head.

I mentally force out those thoughts that have been taking so much real estate in my head. He shouldn't even be mentioned in the same sentence as the word "like," unless I'm talking about how much I *dis*like him. Even if he is doing me a solid by letting me stay with him.

Though to be fair, I kind of backed him into a wall in that regard.

"Do you want to go to my wedding?" Lucy asks, interrupting my thoughts and taking me completely by surprise.

"What?" I parrot idiotically.

Because, really...

What?

Has she forgotten what I did to her? That I tormented her for months when she hadn't even done anything other than befriend someone I was threatened by. I avert my eyes guiltily, remembering how, despite the way I had treated her, she saved me from being drugged and date raped by one of my marks.

Lucy is a good person. That's something I'm not and will never be. It's too late for me, but I'm glad I'm still able to recognize her goodness. That it's at least not so foreign of a concept that I can't see it for what it is.

"My wedding," she repeats slowly, and I get the feeling that she's laughing at me in her head.

Because as good of a person as Lucy is, she's also weird.

And maybe even crazy.

One time, I was about to exit my dorm room when I caught sight of her beside her bodyguard, the one with her now. She was staring at a few of the girls in our hall and mouthing some pretty bizarre things, possibly something about Switzerland. Maybe even cheese.

As soon as I saw her, I pivoted and returned to my room, not down to deal with her craziness that day.

Staring hard at her now, I let out a pent-up breath. "No, I heard you. I just don't know why you're inviting me." I fidget from foot to foot, uncomfortable with the direction this conversation is heading.

"Because you helped me out."

And there it is. I knew she would bring it up, but I'm still not prepared to hear it. Because if I'm being honest, I helped her out of guilt. She helped me out, and even I knew that it was messed up not to do the same. But also, I thought that maybe if I helped her out I would find some sort of redemption. A way to end the guilt and the cycle of lashing out in anger.

I didn't. Her presence annoyed me every second she stayed in my dorm room. So much so that Nella and I crashed at Lauren's dorm room. And when it was over, I still didn't feel like a better person.

Baby steps.

I cross my arms over my chest, as if the barrier will protect me from how uncomfortable this conversation is making me. "You helped me out first."

She sighs. "Is that really how you want to live your life? An eye for an eye? Expecting everything to be reciprocated?"

I shrug, the movement awkward on my crossed arms. "Why not?"

It's only fair.

"Because expecting something in return for everything you do is calculated, and that's a shitty way to live life."

I sigh, wincing automatically at the s-h-i-t word. "Why are we even having this conversation? Shouldn't you be mad at me?"

"Why would I be mad at you?"

"Because I was mean to you."

"You're right. You *were* mean to me, but you're not anymore."

"And you forgive me? Just like that?"

"Why not? I helped you. You helped me. And you haven't been mean to me ever since. I don't think you will be in the future either. So, what's the point of us hating each other? It kind of drained my energy avoiding you back then."

I snort, because she may have avoided me, but I avoided her, too.

And she's right.

She has a point, but at the same time, extending an invitation to her wedding goes beyond the call of civility. We can be friendly without the wedding invitation.

In fact...

"We can be nice without being friends."

She laughs. "Minka, just accept the damn offer of friendship. If you haven't noticed, Nella and what's her face are gone. You probably will never see them again. And honestly, I don't think you're as bad as you think you are, nor as bad as you pretend to be. Anyone can see that you're just lonely. Just accept the friendship and think about the wedding invitation. I've forgiven you. I promise."

And when she leaves, I press my back against the hallway wall and stare up at the ceiling.

Conflicted.

Lucy has forgiven me, but can I forgive myself?

CHAPTER TWENTY

There are two things a person should never be angry at, what they can help, and what they cannot.
Plato

Minka Reynolds

Eighteen Years Old

As he trails sloppy kisses down my body, I wonder again if what I'm doing is the right thing to do.

But then I remember all the money he has and what tying myself to him can do for me and Mina. I think of last Saturday, when I saw Mina's heartbroken face, her eyes streaming with tears when the time came that I had to leave her after seeing her for the first time since she was taken from me.

And with that shattering image freshly etched into my brain, I know without a doubt that I have to do this.

So, I steel myself, and I let out a convincing moan when he touches me in a way that would make me lose control if I was even a little physically or mentally attracted to him.

But since I'm not, I cringe in my head, struggling to keep the disgust at bay.

I'm not one of those girls that cares about her virginity, but it still kind of sucks that this is the way I'm losing it. With the life I've lived and the people I grew up around, I never expected to have candles and rose petals scattered across the floor of some fancy hotel I'm staying in when a man enters me for the first time...

But I also didn't expect to be underneath a man three times my age as I let him paw ravenously at my virgin flesh.

Yet, here I am, and that's exactly what's happening.

He takes his plump right hand and drags it slowly and firmly across the inside of my right thigh, and I whimper. I feel him grin against my neck, probably assuming that the sound was one of pleasure not anguish.

And for the rest of the night, that's exactly how I feel.

Anguish at each touch.

Anguish at each lick.

Anguish at each thrust.

But somehow, in the midst of it all, that anguish turns into anger.

And I feel better.

I find refuge.

"Minka."

"Huh?"

"Well?"

"Sorry. What did you say, Mina?"

Mina groans, her cheeks puffing out in a way that makes her look younger than her eight years. "Stop ignoring me!"

"I'm not ignoring you." I hold up some fingers. "Scout's honor."

"What's scout's honor?"

"Never mind," I say, my mind already straying.

I eye the giant bottle of Costco Kirkland hand sanitizer, sitting next to the sink that's behind Mina. I wonder what would happen if I steal it. Would they catch me? Would I even care if they catch me?

Last night, after losing my virginity and being told immediately after that I was no longer wanted, that I had been played, I went home and showered.

But when that one shower wasn't enough, I showered again.

And again.

And again.

And again.

And again.

I showered thirteen times, and I still felt dirty.

No matter how many times I scrubbed my body raw or how many times I scoured shampoo through my hair, I didn't feel clean. I could still feel the bruising touch of his hands on my skin and his breath against my neck. No amount of soap and water was going to wash the dirtiness of it off.

And finally, I had to stop.

After all, I couldn't afford to take that many showers.

Thanks to the millions of showers I took yesterday, I'll have to use less soap and take shorter showers for the next three months to make up for all the shampoo, body soap and water I wasted last night. Maybe I'll even have to pick up a few extra shifts at the diner I work at full-time to pay for the bump in the utilities bill.

But still, I have to do something.

My skin feels itchy and gross, even though I know in my head that it's clean.

I eye the hand sanitizer yet again and wonder if I can fit it in my little bag. It's a big bottle, probably the height of my forearm and double the width. So, I doubt it would fit... but man, do I want to take it home with me, pour it in the bathtub, and lay in it for days and days until I feel cleansed.

"MINKA!!!" Mina says again, shouting directly in my ear this time.

I wince and recoil from her. "Jesus! WHAT? What do you want?" I ask, sharply.

As soon as I say it, I regret the words, but I can't take them back.

Mina—my beautiful, innocent, incredible baby sister—shatters before me, and I feel like the biggest monster on the entire planet for doing this to her. I've never been like this before. Ever. Sure, I have a short temper—the shortest. You would, too, if you had my sperm and egg donors as parents.

But I've never snapped at Mina.

Never.

Not even once.

Yet, here I am, watching my baby sister splinter before my eyes.

And *I* did this.

I'm breaking her.

I should have protected her better.

I should have dropped out of high school and gotten my GED years ago.

I'm smart enough to have done that. But I was delusional. I thought that maybe, if I finished high school, I could go to a community college for a couple of years while working and caring for Mina. Then, I'd transfer to a good school in the area, like NYU or Columbia or maybe even Wilton.

Then, I'd be able to get a good job, and we'd be able to live better.

It was a pipe dream, and I risked everything for it.

I risked *Mina* for it.

I should have gotten my GED. I should have spent the extra time out of school homeschooling Mina and taking extra shifts at the diner. It wouldn't have been the life I wanted for myself, but I would still have Mina, and I would have made sure that she had a better future than me.

But I chose not to do that.

Instead, I chose to be selfish.

I decided that I deserved to finish high school and go to college when I should have been focusing on Mina and her future. I should have been making decisions that were best for her, not us. Not me.

And now, Mina is suffering because of my actions.

She's here because of me. Because I didn't hide our situation well enough.

She doesn't need this. She doesn't need to bear the brunt of my anger and heartbreak and despondency from last night. Not now, when she's staying here, at a strange place, under the care of total strangers.

I shouldn't be taking what happened out on her.

"Hey," I say gently to Mina, grateful when her tears slow and she turns to face me again. "I'm sorry, Mina. I didn't mean that. I'm just tired. I love you, okay?"

She nods her head, and despite her tears, a tiny smile lifts at the corner of her lips. "I love you, too." And then, her lower lip trembles, and she says, her voice so full of vehemence for such an innocent, little thing, "I hate it here. I hate it here so much! I wish I could go home with you, Minka."

I reach forward and cradle her head against my chest. "I know, Mina. I wish you could, too." And then I whisper, my lips pressed against the crown of her head, "We'll be together again. I promise."

And when the time comes to leave her again, I no longer feel dirty. I let the pain inside me darken to anger, embracing the familiarity of it. And I let that fury fuel my resolve.

I can do this.

I have to.

For Mina.

I just hope I don't lose myself along the way.

CHAPTER TWENTY-ONE

The sharpest sword is a word spoken in wrath.
Gautama Buddha

Niccolaio Andretti

Present

When Minka moves in, it's almost pitiful how few things she brings with her.

There's one small box of clothes, about the size of a carry-on luggage; an even smaller box full of knickknacks, a couple of textbooks and some romance novels, which I find completely out of character from what I've seen of her; and a medium-sized purse that looks like it's on its deathbed, and judging from the two sole items in it, Minka doesn't trust it to carry anything heavier than a wallet and keys either.

I can't help but let a bit of the old Niccolaio out as I stack the boxes on top of one another, throw the bag on top, and lift the three things easily at once. "Damn. We should have hired a moving crew," I joke, out of character and feeling like my old self in that moment.

She scowls at me, the irritation in her eyes familiar. "Are you making fun of my poverty?" She looks around at my place from our spot in the grand foyer, slowly taking everything in. Everything is nice, shiny, and sparkly, but that's how having money works. "Not everyone is as privileged as you are."

I shrug, because if you don't include the bloodshed and being disowned by my family, she's right. For the most part, I've lived a pretty damn privileged life. Even though the past seven years have been spent in hiding, for most of it, I've lived in luxury, except for that one cold ass month when I was homeless and living under a goddamn bridge for a bit.

"You're shameless," she mutters, though it sounds deflated.

In fact, she doesn't seem like her sassy self. Sure, she's not exactly meek. But over the past twenty-four hours or so since I offered to let her move in, I was preparing myself for a spitfire. For a sassy hellion. For battle after battle with her sharp tongue.

And the woman before me isn't the woman I was expecting.

She looks almost... contemplative.

Like she's somehow gone from a woman who knows who she is to a woman who's still trying to figure it out.

For some reason, that disturbs me deeply.

I think I like her better when she's angry at the world and especially me.

What's wrong with me, I'll never know. Call it boredom or call it attraction, but her typical sass excites me. Seeing her like this, though, is almost draining. I resist the urge to press her body against the wall and watch her eyes flare with excitement and lust, anything other than the despondency I'm witnessing right now.

"Where's my room?" she asks, and I'm grateful for the opportunity to drop her off and rid myself of her in this odd state of hers.

I lead her upstairs to the bedroom across from mine. It's a generously sized room with a queen-sized bed, a flat screen television mounted to the wall, a large bathroom, and a walk-in closet capable of holding ten thousand times the amount of clothes she actually owns.

I place the boxes on the floor by the opened door. "Want a tour of the place?" I ask, because I don't want her wandering where she doesn't belong later.

When she nods, I lead her around the brownstone, pointing out some spare bedrooms, my room, the office, the library, the gym, the theater, living room, and the security room, which is empty, since I already sent everyone home for the day.

Judging by her reaction when I suggested hiring personal security for her, I thought it might be safer not to risk freaking her out. As I lead her toward the kitchen, I hear a loud groan coming from the stairwell.

The one leading to the basement.

The basement where I'm illegally holding the guy who shot at us prisoner.

I hope she didn't hear that.

"What was that?" she asks.

Fucking Hell.

"Nothing," I reply casually, hoping my prisoner stops acting like a little bitch.

"It didn't sound like nothing."

"Don't," I say, but she's already heading towards the stairwell.

And honestly, other than that halfhearted "don't," I don't bother stopping her. Because she'll figure it out eventually when she sees me bringing food and water down to him. It would be exhausting hiding him from her for the duration of her entire stay.

Plus, maybe she can help me change out his pissing bucket every now and then.

Then again, probably not.

I eye her and roll my eyes at the way she walks. She has her chin held up and her back prim and straight, walking like she's the Queen of fucking England or some shit. I don't know where she learned to do that, but it's at odds with what she insinuated to me about her upbringing.

Her "poverty," as she called it.

When we round the corner to where I'm holding Jax, I study her, waiting to see how she reacts, knowing that I'll be learning a lot about her from her reaction. And damn, if I'm not a little curious to learn more about her.

And at the last second, I force myself to turn away.

Because what the Hell kind of thought is that?

She's not here for me to learn more about her, like we're on a fucking dating show or whatever. She's here because she threatened to call the cops on me, and I'm not shitty enough of a person to kill an innocent civilian just to keep them quiet.

That's all.

A gasp leaves her lips, and I see her stopping beside me from my peripherals.

"Why is he here?" she asks, her voice calm and not even a little incensed.

And honestly, that takes me by surprise, because it's a far tamer reaction than I expected.

This girl's got spunk. Any other girl, and I can guarantee there would have been screaming. Maybe even some crying. Because Jax's face is a fucking mess, caked in dried blood and ugly green and purple bruises.

Both of his bullet wounds were clean shots, through and through, so I sewed him up, and that's about all the upkeep he's gotten from me since.

He hasn't even showered.

In my defense, I spray some Febreeze on his skin every now and then when the stink gets to be too much.

Good as new.

I turn to her. "You're not angry? Disgusted?"

She shrugs. "He shot at me."

"Fair enough," I say, but my mind is reeling.

Because this chick is badass.

"He's here because I've still got questions for him," I continue, answering her earlier question. I kick at his feet, ignoring his whimpers that are loud despite the tape on his mouth. "Jax, here, is a liar." I turn towards him and look him in the eye. "Aren't you?"

He mumbles something unintelligible through the tape, and I tear it from his mouth, unfazed by his screams at the tape ripping from his skin. He has got to be the biggest baby I have ever met. If I even step in his direction, he'll shriek. I'm almost offended that he thought he could kill me.

I've seen ex-girlfriends sit through Brazilian waxes with sultry smiles and bedroom eyes on their faces.

In fact, the girl beside me seems like someone who can take pain like a champ.

At that thought, the part of me that hasn't gotten laid in too long wonders how rough she likes sex.

"I'm not a liar," Jax groans, drawing my attention back to him.

I turn to Minka. "He told me that he doesn't have a partner. He claims he only works alone." I shift my attention back to Jax and say, "But Minka told me that someone's been following her. Who am I supposed to believe? You, an F grade, bottom of the barrel, wannabe hitman, or Minka?" I lower my voice to a false whisper, "I'll give you a hint—I'm more inclined to believe her."

My voice returns to a normal volume, and when I turn to Minka to ask if she wants to have a go at questioning him, I see something in her eyes that confuses me.

I see guilt.

CHAPTER TWENTY-TWO

Not the fastest horse can catch a word spoken in anger.
Chinese Proverb

Minka Reynolds

"You lied to me," **Nick says,** turning his body away from the sorry shell of a man tied to the floor beside him.

"What are you talking about?" I laugh out convincingly, like I think what he's saying is ridiculous.

But inside, I'm staggered, a frantic mess.

I know he's smart. I knew that from the moment I saw him. It was something I could just tell. No matter what he's saying or doing, pure intelligence seeps out of his eyes and through his mannerisms.

But still...

How did he figure me out already?

I've been here for less than half an hour, and my gig is already up.

"You lied to me," he repeats, his already callous eyes darkening and something in his voice akin to disbelief.

Maybe he's even impressed.

Like the fact that I was bold enough to try to trick him and able to do so, even if it was only for a brief amount of time, is the most fascinating thing in the world.

"I don't know what you're talking about," I deny, my mind racing, wondering how I can spin this in my favor.

I've been in a lot of bad spots over the years, but I've never been homeless. I've been lucky to have a full scholarship at Wilton that paid for tuition along with room and board, but now I have to get back to the real world.

Where I can be booted onto the street, and literally no one but Mina would care.

Least of all the indifferent man before me.

He takes a step forward, and I stand still for a moment, enjoying our proximity before I instinctively take a step back, fully aware that I should have done so in the first place. From behind him, Jax watches us, still whimpering intermittently.

"I'm not going to hurt you," he says. "I'm impressed. And curious." He pauses and opens his mouth to say something, but when the doorbell rings, his open mouth shifts into a frown. His eyes flash in annoyance, presumably at the interruption and hopefully not at me. "That's probably the deliveryman for the groceries. We'll finish this later," he says and heads toward the staircase without a goodbye or an invitation to follow him.

I follow him up anyway, not wanting to be alone down here with Jax. It smells absolutely disgusting in the basement. Like someone dumped a few dozen bottles of Febreeze down a sewer and thought it'd take care of the stench.

It didn't.

I trail behind Nick and follow him into the foyer, because it'd be weird being alone in a room in his house. Even though I should get used to it if I'm going to be staying here for however long it takes for me to get back on my feet.

Once we reach the door, Nick presses a button on a panel beside it, and the screen shows a man outside. His head is down, and since the angle is from above, we can't see any part of his face past his baseball cap, which has the logo of the grocery store on it. His muscular arms are holding a large box, and in it are several bags full of food items.

Nick presses a button, and the inner door slides open, followed by the outer door. When the doors open, the guy lifts his head and studies me for a split second before turning to Nick. The box in his hand drops, revealing the gun in his right hand, a silencer attached to the end.

My eyes widen, but Nick is already grabbing my arm and jerking my body behind his, moving both of us away from the door right before the gun emits a muffled *whish*. Nick pushes me to the side and lifts himself off of me, his body still mostly shielding mine.

When he grabs two guns from the entryway table, the fake deliveryman widens his eyes, gapes, and shouts, "Motherfucker! You kept our guns?!"

Ruthlessly and without hesitation, Nick shoots them both, ruthlessly lodging two bullets into the intruder in quick succession.

One in the middle of his head.

One in the middle of his chest.

I watch as the deliveryman sinks slowly to the ground, his gun falling from his grip onto the floor with a softer thud than I expected. In fact, aside from the deliveryman's odd last words, the whole ordeal was silent, thanks to the silencers attached on his gun and Nick's.

"Huh," Nick says, his dark eyes on mine, casually observing me as if there's not a dead body on the floor in front of us.

As if he didn't just shoot that guy in the head and chest.

As if this is just a normal day for him.

And perhaps it is.

Though if that's the case, he should probably move.

These people coming after him already know where he lives.

"Huh?"

"You didn't scream."

"I grew up in the Bronx."

In an apartment complex full of crack addicts, pimps, whores, and drug dealers. Some of whom were all four. They've knocked the building down since then, but the memories of living there are still intact.

This isn't the first shooting I've witnessed.

It isn't even the first shooting involving Nick that I've witnessed.

Nick nods his head thoughtfully before leaning down. I watch as he picks the dead guy's gun up and grips his shirt with a large fist.

When he nonchalantly straightens and begins to drag the guy's body, I almost laugh.

The image is so similar to what happened last time, it's almost laughable how crazy this is. The other shootings I've witnessed involved domestic abuse, drugs, or gangs. They had no finesse and were disgustingly sloppy.

Given my suspicions about his mafia ties, I have a feeling this is none of the above.

Nick turns his head over his shoulder and says, "Bag up the groceries, will you? I don't want to have to wait for another delivery."

I open my mouth to protest, but he's already turned around and is beginning to walk again. Sighing, I drop to my knees and pick up a few random items that fell out of the box when the deliveryman/assassin dropped it, and I'm thankful to see that there isn't blood on anything.

I pick up the heavy box and walk in the direction of the kitchen, ignoring the moans coming from Nick's prisoner in the basement. Nick is already down there, presumably dropping off the dead guy's body.

When Nick joins me, I gesture to the box of groceries I dropped onto the kitchen island and point out, "They could be poisoned."

"He's not smart enough for that."

I narrow my eyes. "You know him?"

He nods, but he doesn't add anything else.

I sigh, eyeing the clock. "You know what? I don't have time for this. I have somewhere to be."

Specifically, Mina's. My visit with her starts forty-five minutes from now, and I have to get there on foot. I already removed John's credit card from my Uber account, and I don't really have the funds to pay for a ride.

"You're not going anywhere."

"Ha. Ha. Funny," I say, brushing past him.

"He saw your face."

"He's dead."

"He had a getaway driver."

"I didn't see one."

"You weren't looking."

"It's not me he's after."

"You're right. It's me. And now that he's seen you in my home, he'll think getting to you will be getting to me. Go ahead and leave if you want, but I can't guarantee that you'll be alive to come back."

"Gosh, I hate you so much right now."

"You're not exactly a Georgia peach yourself."

I bite my tongue to refrain from growling. "I have somewhere to be."

"Not my problem."

"Are you always such a jerk?"

"Again, not my problem."

I study his rugged face, annoyed beyond belief at him. Then, I stomp away and head to the door, which is still unarmed and unlocked.

And I leave.

CHAPTER TWENTY-THREE

At the core of all anger is a need that is not being fulfilled.
Marshall B. Rosenberg

Niccolaio Andretti

I **figure I've got maybe ten** or fifteen minutes before she stomps her way back here, realizing that I wasn't lying.

Someone was out there, watching.

And while I'm pretty damn good at my job, I can't outrun a car on foot. So, I didn't even bother trying.

I eye the digital clock on the microwave oven and walk to my office, ignoring Jax's moans from downstairs. The man is impervious to everything I've tried.

Tape doesn't shut him up.

The man, and I use that term loosely, can moan his way through cloth tied around his mouth, too.

And sleeping pills only keep him unconscious for so long until he's up and fucking moaning around again. I'm also running out of liquid sedatives to inject him with, so I'm saving that for when I really need it.

I make a mental note to purchase a ball and gag set online from the BDSM shop Dex frequents.

I didn't even have to hack him to figure that out.

The guy advertises his sex life every chance he gets, and though I rarely am out of my brownstone to see him, I've unfortunately run into him enough in the past seven or so years to know his kinks.

He's that bad at keeping his mouth shut.

Once I'm at my desktop, I pull up Wilton University's internal database, which I hacked into a while back when I did a background check on Lucy for Asher. I type in Minka's first and last name, Minka Reynolds, which she had written on the moving boxes I carried to the guestroom.

Her file pops up, and I click on it. Looking through her transcripts, I see that she's got straight As, and there's nothing weird about it to merit interest or any further investigation.

Instead, I look at the background information the school's got on her:

Financial and academic based scholarship.

So, she's poor and smart, but I already knew that.

Boring.

Next.

I scroll through several of her admissions essays until I find one that catches my eye.

ADMISSION'S ESSAY #4

Question: In four hundred words or less, explain what has been the most significant day of your life and how it altered (and continues to alter) your perception of your future.

It's a Dream
by Minka Reynolds

Everything that's gone wrong in my life can be narrowed down to one day. Isn't that sad? I have just one day that I can play on repeat in my mind, over and over again.

And it does just that, forever taunting me. I don't even have the luxury of a movie reel, playing multiple scenes in my mind, because they don't exist.

There's. Just. One. Damn. Day.

You may be asking yourself why I'd rather have multiple bad days than just one. Because I'd rather have a variety of nightmares than the same one—over and over and over again.

You'd feel the same way, too, if your sister was ripped away from you, and you have to see her drowning in her tears once a week.

And the most messed up part?

I *want* to see her cry more than once a week.

Because that would mean that I get to see her more often than Saturdays from noon to two. If you offered me the opportunity of being there for my sister's tears twenty-four hours a day, seven days a week, I would take it without a second thought.

Is that messed up that I'm so desperate to have more time with my sister that I'd happily accept her tears?

I don't know.

But I do know that the most significant day of my life also happens to be the worst day of my life—when Mina was taken from me. And everything I've done ever since—juggling a full-time job and high school, craving a college degree, searching for a better future—has been for her.

You asked for four hundred words. I could give you four hundred thousand. But at the end of the day, my drive boils down to four—I love my sister.

And because of that, I know there will only be one bad day in my life, for I can't afford any more. I'll get the degree I need, and I'll do it with perfect grades. I'll get an amazing job, and I'll do wonderful things with my future. Most importantly, I'll get Mina back and provide for her the future she deserves.

And in ten years, when it's my sister's turn to write this essay, she'll be able to tell you that the most significant day in her life isn't a nightmare.

It's a dream.

NOTES FROM THE ADMISSION'S OFFICER:

While the student's essay does not focus entirely on herself, she does show a selfless devotion to her sister that I believe will make her a successful student at Wilton. After all, we seek students with a natural drive and inclination for success, and in spite of her adversity, this student appears to have it in droves.

Furthermore, the student shows a level of self-awareness unusual for students her age. She questions the ethics of wanting to see her sister so badly that she'd be willing to do so—even if it means that her sister suffers in pain.

Most importantly, she's honest with herself—and us—about these feelings (and flaws) and is able to channel them as motivation.

My only concern is that she, in living her life for her sister, may begin to lose herself. In the end, she cares so much about another being that she is willing to put that person before her. But is that not what we'd want in a lawyer?

Oh, my God.

Is she...?

This woman, who I referred to as a raging bitch the first time I met her, is gold digging to support her little sister. It's noble. It's unexpected. And it's so, so stupid that I have the strongest, inexplicable urge to put a stop to it.

I started the search looking for something to use against Minka, and I found it. She has a sister under state care, and she'd like to get her back. That means she can't afford any scandals. She can't afford to go to the police and has been bluffing this whole time.

But I also found something I didn't expect.

Common ground.

Everything Minka wrote in that essay, I've felt before.

I know what it's like to have a younger sibling. What it feels like to put him before me and get burned by doing so. With Ranieri and even Naz, who now lays dead in my basement, I've gladly put them before me at one point in my life.

Also like Minka, the most significant day of my life can be boiled down to one day. The day I killed my Uncle Luca. And everything after that, every day I have lived from there on, has been a result of that fucking day.

By the time I'm done reading Minka's essay, I'm staggered that this woman I've been giving a hard time—this woman whose life I've been making harder for no other reason than she entered my life uninvited and fate keeps bringing us together—is someone I can relate to.

Before reading this, I was going to kick her out.

I was going to blackmail her into shutting her mouth and leaving my life for good.

But now?

I don't think I can.

And fuck, a roommate—correction: a roommate that I'm attracted to physically *and* mentally—is the last thing I need right now.

CHAPTER TWENTY-FOUR

Angry people are not always wise.
Jane Austen

Minka Reynolds

I make it a few blocks before I start to second guess myself. Aside from my short temper, I'm usually a levelheaded person, but when it comes to anything involving Mina, rationality flies out of the door, and I'm one hundred percent emotion.

I can't help it.

That's what happens when you love someone.

You think with your heart and not with your head.

Sure, sometimes I think I'm being rational, but after a bit of time, I'll usually realize that I'm not.

This time around, that took about five minutes, and now, I'm walking back to Nick's brownstone, feeling like a total idiot. I can't go to Mina's on the off chance someone actually does come after me. I'm not about to risk bringing killers to her doorstep.

Plus, I still need a place to live, and until I find another one, Nick's is all I have. So, when I walk through his door, which he even arrogantly left unlocked and unarmed for me, I'm ready to beg him to let me stay, to apologize for leaving or whatever else he wants to hear from me.

Which is why I'm surprised when I enter the kitchen and he looks up at me with that expressionless face of his and asks, "How are you so calm about all of this? And don't give me that bullshit 'I grew up in the Bronx' excuse. Yeah, that'll probably make you tougher than some suburban princess, but not to this extent."

He gestures to me and continues, "You're not shaking; you didn't blink an eye when I killed someone earlier; and down in the basement, you saw a guy tied up and gasped. *Softly*. I've heard people whisper in movie theaters louder than your gasp. So, spill."

I glare at him, my attempts at acquiescence forgotten, because this is the one topic I don't want to talk about.

Ever.

I force myself to sound bored when I say, "None of this bothers me. The guns, the violence, and your broody cloak and dagger routine? It's not impressive. It doesn't bother me. That's it. There's no story. I just don't give a darn."

He scoffs and leans back against the backrest of his seat at the kitchen island. "You expect me to believe that someone who says, 'I just don't give a darn' is also someone unfazed by killing?" His eyes narrow, and he shoots me a sinister look that's both alarmingly handsome and alarmingly disconcerting. "Get real."

I cross my arms over my chest defensively. "Why should I say anything to you? You're being a jerk."

"Fine, don't say anything." He gestures towards the foyer. "The door's that way."

"So, if I don't talk about my personal life, I have to leave?"

He nods.

My fists clench tightly, and my eyes flash in anger. So much for begging him to let me stay. I refuse to talk about this, so I pull my trump card. "What's to stop me from leaving and calling the cops?"

The corners of his lips lift in a beautiful, wicked smile, full of threats and promise. I instinctively take a step back. He responds by standing from his seat and approaching my spot on the other side of the island. I stand my ground, unwilling to relent on this. No way am I indulging him with my past. There's just absolutely no way that I'll do it.

Standing in front of me, he places an arm on the counter on

either side of my body, effectively trapping me in, yet not touching me.

His smile widens as he says, "You wouldn't call the cops."

I scoff, forcing myself not to react to his proximity. "Because you know me so well?"

He shrugs, causing his arm to brush up against mine. "Go ahead and call the cops. Tell them all about me and how you witnessed me shoot a guy in the leg and imprison him in my basement." The smile turns into a menacing smirk. "Then, how about you tell the cops about how you agreed to move into my home? How you stood there, uncaring and nonchalant, in front of a tied up man? How you watched me kill someone without screaming? And maybe we'll see how Social Services likes that."

I stiffen, everything in me becoming completely rigid at this revelation. "What... what did you just say?"

He leans in closer and whispers, "Mina" into my ear, like someone would whisper, *Boo!*

It's a taunt.

It's an *evil* taunt.

I succumb to his earlier demand, because if there's one person I'll suck it up and do anything for, it's Mina.

And darn him, he's figured this out.

Looking him dead in the eye, I glare at him and begin with a voice full of hatred, "My biological father used to supply the woman who birthed me with drugs in exchange for sex. He left for a while after I was born, so he wouldn't have to take care of me, and by the time I was five and he came back, my," I wince, "*mom* had dropped me off at a neighbor's—Mrs. Rosario's—years ago.

"When he came back, though, he brought my mom with him, and they took me from the neighbor, who actually did a decent job of raising me. Her daughter died young, and she was lonely. I think she actually wanted to keep me, but she wasn't going to go after my biological parents for custody."

I shrug. "Mrs. Rosario didn't have the money for it. So, the three of us—my biological mother, father and I—moved to another apartment building, where they decided I was old enough to run drugs for *Daddy*," I say the title bitterly. "After all, who would arrest a five year old selling chocolate bars for money? Except they weren't chocolate bars."

Nick nods slightly in understanding, like he knows the con, which wouldn't surprise me given his background. Not that I think my "dad's" set up would be done by someone affiliated with the mafia. Someone like Nick.

My dad was small time. A tadpole in an infinite ocean. Nick, on the other hand, strikes me as the type to dominate whatever pool he's swimming in. And that probably means knowing all of the cons, all of the games, out there. Like the one my dad used to have me run.

I continue despite Nick's familiarity with the gig, for some reason needing to talk about this, "They were just drugs wrapped in gold foil, and it worked. I was running drugs for Daddy dearest until my mother got pregnant with Mina by another man. My father left after that, but I was already exposed to the guns and violence and killing that came with drug dealing."

Nick studies me, and I'm actually pleased to see no sympathy in his eyes. They're just blank. The exact opposite of what I expected. I've only told one other person this, and she started crying and tried to suffocate me with hugs.

I was at an alumni admissions interview for Wilton University. The alumna interviewing me was a philanthropic woman, who was wealthy from old money. I knew that if I aced my interview, she would put in a good word for me, and it'd hold a lot of clout in the acceptance process.

So, I sucked it up and told her my sob story. I gave her the Hillary Swank, Oscar-winning, tearjerker truth about how my parents never wanted me; my dad had me running drugs at five years old; and my mom just up and left me with a baby to take care of when I was eight years old, had no clue what I was doing, and had to beg the drug-addicted woman next door for some help.

Then, I told the story of how, despite it all, I had straight As in high school, a full-time job, an Ivy league dream, stars in my eyes and all the other redemptive, inner-city kid goes to college, becomes the president of the world or whatever fantastical, uplifting story elements she wanted to hear.

I gave her the inspiring story at the end, and I told her everything I was doing was for Mina, which was the biggest truth of them all, and the lady just bawled.

She straight up bawled into my shoulder, and I had to comfort her for the greater part of half an hour until she straightened up and said, "I'm so sorry that happened to you, honey. You're so strong to have survived all of that."

And her eyes?

They were so full of pity, I wanted to vomit. To scrub it off of my skin and scream, "I don't need your pity. I just need Mina!"

Yeah, it was great that she cared enough to cry for me, but that wasn't what I needed or wanted. I was a kid making decisions on behalf of another kid, and never for a second did I ever feel like I knew what I was doing.

I wanted someone to tell me what to do. I needed confirmation that the path I was taking was the right one. I didn't get that confirmation, but I did get her pity and, later, an acceptance into Wilton.

And after that, I've never wanted to tell anyone about this again. But when I look at Nick and the way he takes in my words without judgment or even a reaction, I feel like my pain and my past are completely normal. Nothing worth reacting over.

I don't feel like the fragile doll the Wilton alumna made me out to be, nor do I feel like the villain I often convince myself that I am. I just feel... normal. And despite my initial reluctance, I realize that I don't actually mind talking about my past. It's almost cathartic.

Even if I was pressured into revealing everything.

Nick angles his head slightly to the side and studies me. "Trafficking drugs is dangerous. How the Hell are you still alive?"

"A lot of it is luck. But my dad also sent me to his longtime clients, who, for the most part, never gave him trouble in the past and were unlikely to do so in the future. Most of the clients just left me alone, because the system was working and I was just a kid at the time. So long as I was alive, their supply wasn't getting cut off."

He nods, and I expect him to make a comment about what I said when he admits, "I already decided that I was going to let you stay before you walked through the door."

My jaw drops. "Then why did I have to tell you all of this?"

He shrugs casually, as if I didn't just bare myself to him for no reason. "I wanted you to know that I know about Mina, and I wanted to know more about you."

My lips part in surprise, and I don't reply to his words, because I don't even know what to make of them. The second half would almost be cute if it wasn't preceded by a vague—perhaps threatening—comment about the person I love most in this world.

And the saddest part?

With his arms on either side of me, his face close to mine, and the scent of his masculinity wrapped around me, that's the most romantic thing anyone has ever said to me.

CHAPTER TWENTY-FIVE

Bitterness is like cancer. It eats upon the host.
But anger is like fire. It burns it all clean.
Maya Angelou

Minka Reynolds

"We're leaving," Nick says suddenly after removing his hands from the kitchen island counter and standing upright.

"Where are we going?" I ask.

He turns back and stares at me. After a while, he finally says, "You'll see when we get there."

I reach out for his arm, stopping his movement but also nearly stopping my heart at the same time. He stares at my fingers and the way they firmly grip the massive bulk of his impressive biceps before I quickly pull them back, as if they've been scorched by the contact.

And they may as well have been.

I can still feel the heat from his body—from the attraction pulsing between us—against my fingertips.

"Just tell me where we're going," I say, shaking the aftereffects of the brief contact out of my head, hating myself for being so affected by him. I take a deep breath and take a risk, because he hasn't killed me yet, so I figure he won't. "I know you're involved in the mafia."

I sort of expected him to look startled, but he doesn't.

He takes the revelation in stride, his eyes level on mine as he asks calmly, "How?"

"I saw Lucy Ives come in here a month ago. She used to live in my dorm hall, and she waved at me while letting herself into your home."

He shakes his head slightly and mumbles something like, "So you're the warning," but it's cryptic and not what I want to know.

I understand why we need to go. Obviously, this place has been compromised. But wherever we go, I need it to be near Mina. So, even though I want to ask what he means by that, I redirect my words to more important things.

"I asked Lucy who you were when I picked up my things at Vaserley, and she was helping her friend move out of the dorms, too."

"What did she tell you?" There's interest in his eyes.

"Nothing. But it's obvious you're involved in mob activity. Lucy only hangs out with Asher, her guards, Asher's family, and Aimee. And I think Lucy would have let me know if Aimee claimed you, so that leaves Asher. You could be one of his legitimate business contacts, but with all the bullets flying when you're around, I'm betting that you're someone from his mafia past."

"Alleged," Nick says, though there's a look of amusement on his face.

I roll my eyes. "*Alleged* mafia past," I correct myself. "I don't care about the legalities. You know about my illegal past, and you have Mina to hang over my head, so just do me a favor and tell me where we're going."

"I'm already doing you a favor by taking you with me."

"Fine. Then, do me another favor."

He takes a moment to study me, and I guess whatever he finds satisfies him, because he answers, "We're going to a safe house. I texted Vincent Romano, Asher's... dad of sorts. He set one up for us to stay in for as long as we need."

"And where is this safe house?"

"Hell's Kitchen."

I give myself a moment to consider the distance. That's about a three dollars and nine minutes subway trip to Mina's group home. I can live with that, so I nod my head without further argument and take off to gather the few things I own from the beautiful room I never had a chance to stay in.

When I exit Nick's brownstone to place my belongings in Nick's trunk, I see a quick flicker of movement coming from the curtains in John's bedroom. I roll my eyes at John's nosiness, but I expect nothing less.

I've seen him obsessively checking his security feed from his phone before. One time, I watched him listen in on a bunch of blue blood moms gossip about their children's upcoming cotillion while stretching across the street.

I didn't even want to think about how he got audio over there.

In the back of my mind, I wonder if John is bothered by this. By my involvement, however odd it is, with Nick. After all, John and I were sort of together. Not exclusively or officially but together nevertheless.

At the same time, given that I saw my doppelganger earlier outside of John's home, John is the one who's actually with *with* someone else. Even though I shouldn't be worried, I can't help but be a little concerned.

If John is angry at me, he might take it out on me or Nick. I don't think he knows about Mina, since we share different last names and I never talked about her when we were together, but John does know Nick.

John's a powerful guy, and if he wants to, he can probably give Nick a hard time. At the same time, I can't picture anyone going up against Nick. Not even Asher Black. So, I shake the dark thoughts out of my head and enter the brownstone, ignoring the ominously prophetic feeling of my suspicions.

And when I meet Nick in the basement and watch him inject a syringe full of sedatives into his prisoner's neck, I groan, wondering how I went from being John's gold digging girlfriend to Nick's partner in crime.

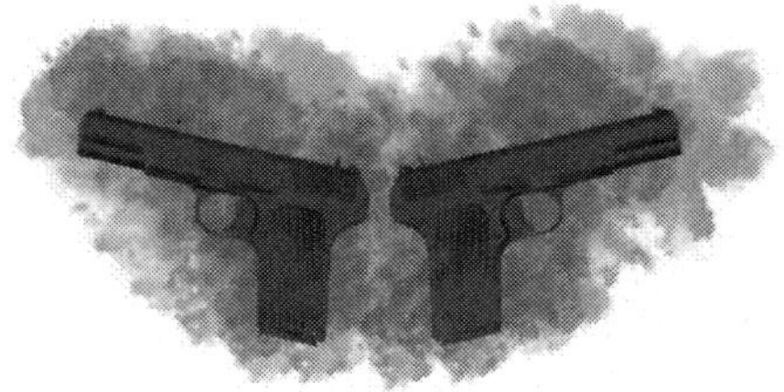

It's quiet on the drive to the safe house. Jax is laying unobtrusively in the back seat, knocked out and silent, thanks to the drugs Nick injected him with. Upon my insistence, his arms and limbs were bound earlier, and in addition to the gray duct tape over his mouth, he has one of my ratty scarves wrapped tightly around his eyes, several times over.

Nick says there's no chance he'll wake up from the strong sedatives, but this is my first time in a situation even remotely like this one, and I'd rather not take any chances. And given the fact that this is my first time, I feel as if I should be panicked, concerned, shocked, or *anything* other than the calm I'm feeling right now.

Until now, I didn't realize how unfazed I am by things that should trouble me. Even at a young age, I remember people commenting on this trait of mine, but it's been some time since I've done anything quite so discerning.

Unless you count gold digging, which tore me apart, but I've long since gotten used to it. Heck, even then, it only took me one day to get used to gold digging. Whenever the feelings and panic threaten to overcome me, all I have to do is think of Mina, and I conquer the wave of emotions.

When my mom first left me, I used to cry every night. And each time, Mrs. Rosario, the woman who raised me for a bit after my biological parents pawned me off onto her, would tell me to picture a bunch of waves. Each wave was an emotion that I could surf over until there were no emotions, no pain left. It worked—and still works—like a charm.

Back then, I was always going on and on about how I wanted to be a lawyer like Mrs. Rosario's dead son. So, Mrs. Rosario would tell me that I was fearless and that, because of it, I'd make a good lawyer one day.

Father dearest, on the other hand, told me I had the makings of a good whore—quiet and discreet.

Given my life choices, I guess they were both somewhat right.

I'm not a prostitute, but I may as well be. I sleep with men; they lavish me with expensive jewelry and clothes; and by the time they've moved onto the next girl, I've sold it all. I'm also on track to becoming a lawyer.

Go figure.

At the same time, it's odd that I'm okay with this situation with Nick, almost comforted by the familiarity of crime, yet I have to smother my panic at the idea of having to sleep with John or another mark once more. So, maybe Daddy Dearest was wrong.

I take more comfort than I should in that thought.

"What are you thinking about?" Nick asks, his eyes glancing from the car's rearview mirror to the side mirror.

We've been driving in random paths around town for the past hour. I think this is Nick's way of getting rid of tails, but other than his bodyguards following in the car behind us and the millions of taxicabs that look identical, I haven't recognized a single car.

This man brings a new meaning to paranoid.

Then again, I suppose I have my moments, too. I glance at Jax, sedated, gagged, blindfolded, and tied up in the back seat.

I return my gaze to Nick. "I'm thinking of Mina," I say, not quite lying but not quite telling the truth either.

Truthfully, if Mina's not in the forefront of my mind, she's always in the back of my mind. So, technically, I'm always thinking about her.

Nick spares a moment to glance at me, and I think I'm hallucinating when I see a spark of concern in his usually impassive demeanor. "What about Mina?"

"I was supposed to visit her today. Saturdays are my days with Mina."

"And you couldn't because of this," he finishes for me.

I nod. "When do you think I can?"

He hesitates, which immediately causes me to stiffen. "Honestly... not for some time. It's not safe for you. Or her."

I want to argue, but I don't. If he thinks I shouldn't, I should listen to him. I'll never forgive myself if I bring Mina into this mess and she somehow gets hurt, and above all, Mina's safety is the most important thing to me.

But at the same time, I need to make sure things are okay with Mina at the group home. I usually get my reports on Mina's wellbeing from Erica, Mina's social worker, on Saturdays, and without those, I can't make sure she's being fed well, happy or doing well in school.

I'm not happy about this, and I find myself—thankfully—resenting Nick again. I allow my familiar annoyance at him to settle against my chest, making sure to lock the sentiment there. I can't allow myself to forget that I dislike him, because after all of this is over, I have to go back to my normal life, where rent and school and gold digging are my reality.

Just because I was able to talk about my past with him doesn't mean that we're friends or will ever be friends. This man is connected to the mafia, and I'm trying to keep a clean record to get my sister back. It's a convincing argument for why I should distance myself from this man, but my body just isn't agreeing with my mind.

My body still wants him, and my brain wants to throttle my body.

"You're mad at me," he says.

I nod, not bothering to deny it. I'm not just mad at him. I don't like him. I *can't* like him. We're probably equally to blame for me being in this mess, along with whoever wants to kill Nick...

But I just don't feel like accepting the blame for forcing my way into Nick's life, so I let him take the blame. After all, I need to continue to hate him. It's the only way I'll get through living with someone I'm so attracted to with my resolve to gold dig intact.

At the same time, I'm smart enough to realize that I shouldn't antagonize someone I'll be living with. So, when he doesn't respond to my affirmation of anger, I let it go.

Behind us, the guards' car turns left while we turn right, but I don't question it. I trust Nick—at least with my safety. So, I allow us to simmer in silence, because it's easier that way. Given how hectic my life is, easy is a victory.

Pretty soon, we pull up to a warehouse in a lesser populated area of Hell's Kitchen. Nick drops me and Jax's body off at the alleyway entrance of the warehouse. Then, he goes to find parking without any issues. A few minutes later, he's back and opening up the place for us.

The warehouse is set up like a decent-sized, expensive New York studio and doesn't actually look like a warehouse inside. There are security cameras set up around the warehouse. Nick also has me configure my eye and palm for the subtly-placed scanners at the entrance.

The floor plan is open, with the custom closet, kitchen, bedroom and living room all in one room. It's a bit of a tight fit, but it's enough for two people and a captive, which Nick tells me is all the place needs to fit, since his guards will be covering another empty safe house to deflect attention from us.

And honestly, the place is really, really nice...

But that's not the problem.

The problem is there's only one bed.

CHAPTER TWENTY-SIX

Speak when you are angry and you will make the best speech you will ever regret.
Ambrose Bierce

Minka Reynolds

Even though Nick lets me take the bed while he takes the small couch, his presence still bothers me enough to affect my sleep. Tossing and turning all night, I barely sleep, and when I finally do, my eyes are only closed for a few hours before I'm waking up again, courtesy of a groaning Jax.

"Can you shut him the heck up?" I politely ask Nick, who's laying on the couch, playing Angry Birds on his phone while Jax's musical of groans is getting louder by the second.

I take one of the extra pillows on the bed and throw it at the couch. It bounces off Nick's head and onto the floor. He grabs it and tucks it under his head, using it as a pillow, which makes me realize that last night, he slept without a blanket and a pillow.

Now, I feel even guiltier because Nick barely fits on the couch. His long legs hang over the edge, and the width of his strong body barely fits this narrow couch. In fact, there's more of his body off of the couch than on it.

I remind myself that it doesn't matter if he sleeps uncomfortably, because 1) I'm *not supposed* to like him, 2) I *don't* like him and 3) I'll *never* like him. But… I can't help the twinge of guilt that envelops my body, so I endeavor not to argue too much with him this morning to make up for it.

"I tried. The *man*," Nick says, emphasizing the word in a way that makes me suspect that he thinks the term is hardly appropriate, "can moan his way through anything."

I sigh and get up. The clock on the wall reads twelve past six in the morning, which basically means that I have a long day ahead of me. And I don't want to spend it listening to Jax complaining all day. So, I enter the kitchen, grab a nice-sized nectarine from the fruit bowl and walk over to Jax.

He eyes me warily and with good reason.

I lift the nectarine in front of his face and say in a tone I would use on a toddler, "This is to stay in your mouth until you can prove to me that you can be quiet. Okay?"

He shakes his head furiously, but I don't care. Behind me, Nick lets out a sexy laugh that sends a series of chills up and down my spine. I ignore the feeling and continue on with my plan, shoving the nectarine into Jax's reluctant mouth while being careful not to actually touch the guy.

I turn to Nick. "He smells."

Nick gets up and grabs a bottle on the floor behind him. It's Febreeze. I roll my eyes as I watch him spray it all over Jax, and now the disgusting stench smells like a disgusting stench mixed with Febreeze.

I walk towards the bathroom, and over my shoulder, I say, "I'm going to shower. You know, how normal people get clean."

I close the door before I can hear Nick's response. After stripping out of my clothes and throwing them into a hamper in the bathroom, I wait for the water to warm up before getting in the marble shower.

Not even five minutes later, I hear the door opening. Alarmed, I peak my head out of the curtain, only to find Nick with a toothbrush in hand. Facing the mirror, he's not even looking at me and is acting as if being in the bathroom while I'm naked is no big deal.

"What are you doing?" I ask.

If I was the cursing type, I would have said, *what the fucking fuck do you fucking think you're fucking doing?* But I haven't cursed since I made a promise to mold myself into the model parent after Mina was taken away. Plus, I don't think four variations of "fuck" are enough to express my alarm. I need at least a baker's dozen.

"I'm hungry," he says.

My eyes widen in disbelief. "Okay... go eat."

"I need to brush my teeth first, and who knows how long you'll take in here. I didn't want to wait."

I roll my eyes but close the curtain and try to shower. But I can't. All I can think of is how naked I am and how close to me he is. My nipples harden at the thought, and goosebumps rise all over my flesh despite the heat of the water.

I eye the shower curtain, knowing that neither of us can see through it, but needing to check nevertheless. Closing my eyes, I allow myself to focus on the proximity between Nick and my naked body, and I let my hands drift lower down my body until my fingers brush against my clit. Startled, I jolt at the sensation, not use to ever enjoying touching myself. It usually feels awkward and uncomfortable, but this... This was magic.

From the other side of the curtain, I hear Nick mutter something that sounds like "everything okay?" with a mouth full of toothpaste.

"Yep! Dropped the soap," I lie and force myself to behave.

I stand under the showerhead, waiting for him to leave and trying to focus on anything other than how embarrassingly affected I am from being naked in his proximity, even though there's nothing remotely sexual about this situation aside from the naughty thoughts I shouldn't be entertaining.

A few minutes later, I hear Nick turn on the sink and spit toothpaste out of his mouth. I expect him to leave, but he doesn't.

Instead, he says, "How are you feeling?"

Still behind the curtain, I answer, "This is hardly the appropriate place to be having this conversation."

"Do you want me to leave?" There's amusement in his tone. "So you can touch yourself in peace?"

My jaw drops and cheeks heat in embarrassment. "I wasn't—" I begin to protest before cutting myself off, deciding that he'd see past any lie I'd tell anyway. I sigh. "I don't care. Do what you want," I say, because I don't want him to think his presence here is bothering me, even though it *is* getting me hot and bothered. And apparently, we're both already too aware of that. I hope to distract from what just happened by answering his other question, "I'm feeling... as good as I can feel given the circumstances."

After a few seconds of silence, he says, all traces of humor gone from his voice, "I'm sorry that you couldn't see Mina."

And darn it, his genuine tone has the anger and embarrassment in me receding.

I don't reply to that, because there's nothing I can say to it. While playing the blame game is fruitless, I still feel as if he's partially to blame for this mess. And it's not okay that I couldn't see Mina, but I don't want to talk about it.

I am, however, willing to talk about some aspects of yesterday. "What happened to the guy you killed yesterday?"

I'm not sure if he'll answer my questions, since I'm pretty sure whatever happened yesterday isn't legal, but I wait anyway. It's not like I'll tell anyone. I'm not innocent in all of this. When I brought in the groceries yesterday, I was contaminating the crime scene. I don't even have to be a law student to realize that.

He surprises me by answering me truthfully. "There was a cleaning crew that came to deal with it while we were asleep."

"Won't people ask questions when they realize he's missing?"

"Probably," he says, which should concern me, but the indifference in his tone eases my worries of getting caught. "But he's not from around here, so it won't be the first place the police will look. And that's *if* they are alerted."

He sounds so certain that they won't be alerted that I let it go.

"You said yesterday that you know him... How?"

He sighs. "I go by Nick now, but I was born Niccolaio Cristiano Andretti."

I still at his words.

He's an *Andretti?!*

I did some mafia research after I got on Asher's bad side over the school year. There are whole websites dedicated to the five American syndicates, kind of like a Wikipedia for the mob. And in every single post that mentions the Romano and Andretti families together, there's always mention of the longstanding feud between the two families. A longstanding and *bloody* feud.

The Andrettis and Romanos are like the Capulets and Montagues, only dangerous. I don't know why they hate each other, but I do know that the hatred is strong. And an Andretti being in Romano territory should be tantamount to war...

Yet, Niccolaio isn't just in Romano territory. He's embedded in it. From what I've seen and gathered, he's friends with Asher, and he mentioned that Vincent Romano helped acquire this safe house for us.

There's a story behind this, and even though I'm dying to know, I don't ask, because I don't allow myself to stroke the flame of my curiosity regarding Niccolaio. I suspect that getting to know Niccolaio won't help keep my lust at bay.

And *his name*. I knew that Nick doesn't suit him. It's too plain and ordinary, but Niccolaio Cristiano Andretti... It's exotic and sexy and everything that I've come to realize ~~Nick~~ *Niccolaio* is.

He continues, "I lived in Andretti territory until I was twenty and had to leave. While I lived in Florida, I was friends with this guy named Ignazio. *Naz*. He's the one I shot yesterday. Anyway, his dad was a friend of my dad, so we pretty much grew up together. A few years before I left Florida, Naz accidentally shot a civilian and got sent to Maryland, a border territory state.

"When I left Florida, I lived in Maryland for a little, and while I was there, I was working at a club. I was outside taking a break when I saw Naz. He and a friend of his had their guns out, and they were going to shoot Asher."

When I gasp, he ignores it and continues, "He was going to kill Asher, but if he did that, the people with Asher would have killed him... So, I stepped in. I killed Naz's friend, because I didn't want him to risk getting a shot at Asher while I took care of Naz. Naz never forgave me for that."

He lowers his voice, and I think he says, "And other things," but at that low volume, I can't hear him over the sound of the showerhead.

"You saved Asher Black," I say, wonder in my voice.

My words hang silently and boldly in the air, and we let them simmer in the stillness as I try to absorb the profundity of my statement. He saved Asher Black, one of the most powerful men in the world, let alone this city.

That's *huge*.

After a few more minutes of silence, I take a deep breath before asking the real question I've been wanting to ask, "Why are people trying to kill you?"

"There's a hit out on me."

"A hit?!" The disbelief in my voice is clear.

"Five million dollars."

And for a disgusting second, my mind wonders what I can do with five million dollars.

I can find a home.

I can hire a lawyer.

I can file for custody of Mina.

Five million dollars would solve all of my problems, except I can't kill this man.

I may not be the best person in the world, but I'm certainly not a killer. Not only can I not hurt this man, but *I also don't want to*.

I've finally found a line I'd draw in what I thought was an infinite list of things I'd do for Mina... and I hate Niccolaio for being it.

CHAPTER TWENTY-SEVEN

When angry, count to four. When very angry, swear.
Mark Twain

Minka Reynolds

Even though I feel bad about Niccolaio sleeping on the couch, I don't do anything about it. I hate to highlight any of his good attributes, but I have to admit that he's gentlemanly enough to insist that he sleep anywhere other than the bed.

And I'm not about to invite him to join me.

But it's only been seven days of hiding out, and my resolve is already wavering. I'm not sure how I feel about this. After all, Jax sleeps slouched against the wall, and I don't feel an ounce of guilt about that.

At the same time, Jax shot a bullet at me. Well, it was at Niccolaio, but with his terrible aim, I ended up in its projectile. So, I have a good reason not to feel guilty about Jax's treatment. On the other hand, if Niccolaio hadn't followed me out of John's brownstone, I wouldn't be in this mess.

But... I also wouldn't have a place to stay while I study for my LSATs.

My brain continues to go back and forth between the reasons to and not to allow Niccolaio on the bed when the man in question enters the warehouse, casually whistling an unfamiliar tune. My giant LSAT practice book is on the bed in front of me, and I quickly flip to the next page to hide the list I've drawn in the margins:

To (Literally) Sleep with Niccolaio or Not To?

PROS

1. I'll stop feeling guilty about him sleeping on the bed.

2. He saved me from bullets (twice), is giving me a place to live, and has been a complete gentleman.

3. I'd end up jumping his bones.

CONS

1. He's the reason I can't visit Mina.

2. He was the reason I needed saving from bullets (twice), is the reason I'm living in a safehouse and blackmailed me into revealing my past.

3. I'd end up jumping his bones.

I stare purposefully at the new LSAT practice page in front of me, but the words end up blurring together. I closed the book with a resigned sigh, since I haven't glanced at it once in the past three hours anyway.

Instead, I've been stuck in my head, juggling my confusion about whether I like or dislike Niccolaio and my anger and frustration at not being able to see Mina. My worry for Mina has been lodged in the back of my mind for the past week, but today it's at the forefront of my concern.

I was supposed to visit Mina today, but for the second week in a row, I couldn't. The worst part is I haven't been able to tell her why I can't visit her. I just left, like a ghost. Like her mother, her father, and now me. She's either out of her mind in worry, feeling abandoned, or both.

And that's killing me.

It's that thought that reinforces my resolve to stay angry at Niccolaio. Plus, it's better for everyone if I keep my distance emotionally.

So, when Niccolaio approaches me and opens his mouth to speak,

I cut him off with an appropriate amount of attitude, "What do you want? I'm studying."

"I ha—"

I lift up my book, shake it and interrupt, "Studying."

"Minka," he says, firmly this time.

The demanding way he says my name sends shivers down my spine.

I make a production of sighing, pushing away my book, and crossing my arms. I arch a perfectly shaped brow. "Yes?"

"I have something for you."

"Oh."

"Oh," he mocks, a smirk on his face.

I roll my eyes and accept the small box he hands me. Inside of it is a tablet from Black Enterprises.

"What's this for?" I ask, my eyes widening as I open the box.

"Turn it on."

I narrow my eyes at him in suspicion before cautiously pressing the "on" button. Niccolaio takes a seat next to me on the bed. I let him grab the tablet from me as soon as it powers on. He presses something on the screen, and a few moments later, Mina's beautiful face appears on the screen.

My jaw drops. "Mina?!" I turn to Niccolaio. "How?!"

Mina answers for him, her voice an excited screech, "I got a tablet, Minka! A *tablet*! Can you believe it?"

"No," I answer honestly, because I *can't* believe it.

Tablets are a luxurious expense Mina's group home can't afford. I've thought of saving up to buy her one before, so we could video chat, but that idea was vetoed immediately by Erica. Apparently, it would be cruel for only one child to have one and not the rest.

While I agreed with Erica that it would be cruel, I hated that it meant I couldn't talk to Mina on a daily basis. Yet, Mina has a tablet right now, and I know the group home wouldn't approve of it, which brings me to my earlier question.

"How?" I ask Niccolaio again.

Mina happily interjects, "He got us all tablets! *Everyone*!"

"All of them?!" My eyes widen, and the stare I give Niccolaio is equal parts disbelief and confusion.

I should be grateful.

Actually, I *am* grateful.

But I'm also confused.

Why would he do this for me and Mina?

He shrugs casually, as if he's playing it off. "It's not a big deal. Asher's company donated them."

"It *is* a big deal. This wouldn't have happened without you," I insist. Remembering our situation, I put the video chat on mute and say, "What about the hit on you? Don't the people after you know that you're connected to Asher Black? Isn't it risky for Asher to suddenly donate a bunch of tablets to a random group home?"

"It would be," Niccolaio agrees, and I tense. "That's why he donated tablets to every group home in the city."

My jaw drops. "What?! Every single one?! That must have cost him a fortune! Why would he do that?"

Niccolaio shrugs and doesn't answer me. And even though I want to know, I don't press him. I'm too happy to care. So, when the urge to hug Niccolaio grips me by the throat, I don't fight it. I lean forward and wrap my arms tightly around his broad torso, soaking myself in the seductive scent of sandalwood, musk and Niccolaio.

"I don't know how you got Asher to do this, but thank you," I whisper into his ear.

Even though I should let go, I keep myself pressed against Niccolaio. After a few awkward seconds, he wraps his arms around my body, returning the hug. It occurs to me that this is the first hug I've ever received from anyone other than Mina and Mrs. Rosario.

I don't care that it's in front of Jax, who is staring at us from the other side of the room with a brand new nectarine lodged in his mouth.

I don't care that it's in front of Mina, who is surprisingly quiet on the other end of the video chat.

I don't care that it's with someone I keep telling myself I'm supposed to hate.

All I care about right now is how ecstatic I am, the fact that someone would do something for me without expecting anything in return and the incredible way his arms feel wrapped around my body.

Like bliss.

"Pssttt!" Mina's youthful voice comes from the tablet in a loud whisper. Her voice is clear when she whisper-shouts, "Is he your boyfriend?"

I jump back from Niccolaio's body, untangling myself from him when I realize the tablet is facing us and Mina can see everything. I unmute the video chat, trying to will away the redness on my cheeks.

Niccolaio sends me a knowing look and gets up, stretching his body even though he was only sitting for a few minutes. I appreciate it when he gives me and Mina privacy, entering the bathroom and turning on the shower.

When he shuts the door behind him, I finally answer Mina's question, "No, he's not my boyfriend. And he heard that, Mina!"

Mina shrugs innocently. "I whispered," she says, as if it excuses mortifying me. She gives me a no-nonsense look. "He's sooo cute. You should date him."

I groan. "I don't choose to date guys just because they look nice, Mina."

"Then, how else do you choose guys to date?"

I choose them based on how big their bank accounts are and how easy of a mark I think they'll be.

Of course, I don't say that.

I'm silent for a moment, contemplating my words before I finally reply, "When you're old enough to date, choose a guy that makes you feel amazing. Someone who does things for you when you ask and even when you don't. Someone who makes you feel safe. Someone who gives you butterflies but also makes you feel calm."

"What you're describing doesn't sound human," she says, no doubt thinking about the pre-teen boys in her class, boys that she's frequently compared to ogres during some of my visits to her.

I laugh and agree. "Nope. Not in the slightest." My face turns serious. "But you're an amazing person, Mina, and if it's up to me, you'll never settle for less than you deserve, which is absolutely everything."

She's silent for a moment before she says, "You're an amazing person, too, Minka."

And darn it, my heart swells ten times its size, and I wish I could agree.

Instead, I paste a smile on my face and nod my head. "Thanks, Mina."

"Are you going to tell me why you haven't come to visit me?"

I hesitate, pondering what I should and shouldn't tell her. "I can't come visit you for a while, but I'll try as soon as I can. I promise. Just... there are people after Niccolaio and maybe me right now."

She takes in my words, her eyes widening in concern, but she doesn't voice it. That's the somber reality of our lives. I can't remember a time when one of us hasn't been at risk in one way or another, whether it be from one of our parents, eviction, starvation, Social Services, and so on.

"Minka, do you feel safe right now?"

I nod my head emphatically. "Yes."

That's not a lie, either. Even though some ridiculous things have happened to me lately, I do feel safe. I have a roof over my head, food to eat, and free time to study for my LSATs. And as reluctant as I am to admit it, I trust Niccolaio to keep us both safe.

"Do you feel calm right now?"

I give her a weird look. "Yes..."

"Did you ask Niccolaio to get us tablets?"

"No, he did that on his own."

"And when you hugged him, did you feel butterflies?"

Yes. "Mina, what are you going on about? You're being weird."

"How are my questions weird? It's *your* checklist."

My jaw drops, because she's right.

Holy cow. Niccolaio checks off every box on my list.

And I don't know how I feel about that.

CHAPTER TWENTY-EIGHT

Always forgive your enemies;
nothing annoys them so much.
Oscar Wilde

Minka Reynolds

"**Attention! Attention!** I ate ants for breakfast!"

At my words, Mina breaks out into the cutest fit of giggles.

"Your turn!" I remind her.

"I-I c-can't. Can't. S-stop. Laughing," she gasps between bursts of sweet, innocent laughter.

I accidentally drop my tablet onto the mattress when I hear a deep voice mock, "You ate your aunts for breakfast?! My love, aunts should only be eaten at dinner time. Uncles are for breakfast!"

"I gotta go," I say to Mina while she bursts into another fit of laughter.

"Bye, Minka!" She shouts, "Bye, Niccolaio!"

After Niccolaio says bye to her, I end the video chat and turn off the television. For the seventh time since Niccolaio gave me the tablet, Mina and I were watching French daytime soaps together.

Instead of subtitles, we decided the first time we did this that it would be more fun to guess what the actors were saying. Guessing turned into making random and ridiculous things up, and now this is a fun game I look forward to every day.

I was surprised when Niccolaio joined in for the first time a few days ago. Now, I'm used to it, but I still don't understand why he's doing all of this. I've been pushing it out of my mind, because it's easier not to think about it, to continue to villainize him.

Instead, I've been focusing my attention on studying for my LSAT and talking to Mina every day. Sometimes, I'll get Jax something to eat, but Niccolaio usually deals with him, which I'm thankful for. That basically means that, for the first time in a long time, I can relax and take some much-needed time to gather my sanity again.

And in the back of my mind, I know that I owe this opportunity to Niccolaio.

It'd be so much easier if he gave me more reasons to hate him. Yeah, he still speaks with way more assertiveness than I'm used to, but I've come to realize that it's part of his charm. And yes—Niccolaio is charming.

Dangerously so.

Which is why, as he loosens his tie and approaches me, looking way more attractive in a tailored suit than should be legal, I make sure I have my defenses up.

I clear the lust out of my throat and say, "I didn't hear you enter."

He smirks and arches a brow as if to say, *duh*.

I roll my eyes. "Did you find Naz's getaway driver?"

He shakes his head. "From the video footage we got from street cameras, we traced his car back to a building in Brooklyn, but we didn't get any decent resolution images of his face. I sat with a Romano sketch artist today to do a mockup of his face."

"And then what?"

"Vince is distributing the sketch to all of his contacts by the end of the week. Hopefully, it'll turn up some new leads. Either way, it doesn't really matter. It's safe to assume the driver is just one of many people after me."

I nod. "But he's the only one who we know for certain knows about me."

His eyes darken, and his voice is serious when he says, "I won't let anything happen to you or Mina."

My breath catches in my throat at the simmering promise in his words, and I don't know what to make of them. He doesn't have to protect me. He owes me nothing. Nothing that happened is technically his fault, yet... I'm starting to think Niccolaio is a decent guy under all that bark—and bite—of his.

So, I stare him right in the eyes and say, "I believe you."

And I do.

Truly.

The storm in his eyes clears at my words, and he takes a seat on the bed beside me. "I have a favor to ask."

My brows raise. "From me?"

"No, from Jax."

I snort unattractively, and we both turn towards Jax, who is—finally—passed out on the floor. Aside from when I get to talk to Mina, my favorite time of day is when Jax is asleep. Unfortunately, the guy has more energy than the Energizer bunny. He sleeps just four hours a day and is up the other twenty.

It's exhausting to deal with.

I wish we could get rid of him—and quickly.

But I don't want to kill him, and Niccolaio doesn't want him free to try to kill us again.

That means the only thing left to do is pawn him off on someone else to watch, which Niccolaio refuses to do since he trusts no one, or continue to look after him until Niccolaio no longer has a hit on his head, which is starting to feel like never.

"Seriously, though... Can we get rid of him?"

"Honestly, probably not for a while."

I sigh and, remembering the favor, gesture for him to continue.

He does. "Lucy's wedding is coming up."

"I know. She invited me."

"Perfect."

I narrow my eyes. "I wasn't planning on going."

"Unfortunately, I don't have much of a choice. Will you go with me?"

I have to force my jaw to stay in place. "What? Why?"

"Firstly, Asher donated tablets to every state-run group home in the city, including your sister's."

That's a good enough reason to go. He could have stopped at that, and I would have agreed, but he doesn't.

Instead, he continues, "Secondly, the safe house we're staying in has been provided to us by the Romano family. Asher may not work for a Romano anymore, but he practically is one still, so it'd be ungrateful to decline his invitation."

Another valid reason. I should tell him to stop, but I don't. And that's a massive mistake, because his last reason absolutely guts me, sending me completely off kilter.

"And lastly, because I want you to."

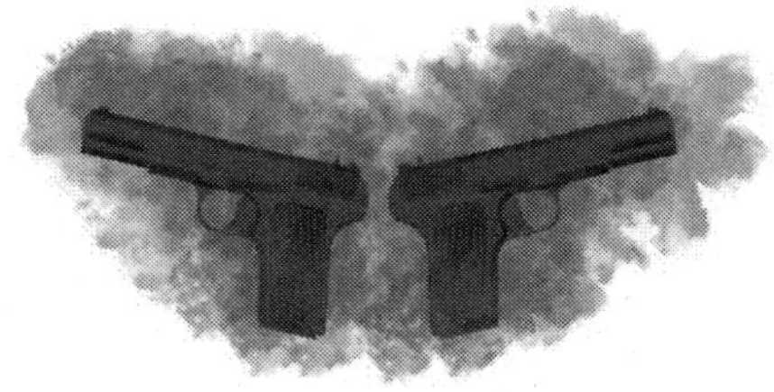

My finger eagerly swipes at the tablet, and it moves onto the next page of the book. A Charleigh Rose erotica romance novel. My obsession started out as means of sex research for my gold digging, but after a while, I started to enjoy these types of books. Now, I'm hooked and read them for fun.

It still blows my mind that these women enjoy sex. That they lust for it, wish for it, and think of it all day long. I've never been like that. Before Mina was taken, I was too young to pursue it and too busy working to be interested in it. After Mina was taken, it became a means to an end, one of many steps to get Mina back.

Now, I'm more open to learning where these women are coming from. I've felt the lust they describe around Niccolaio, so maybe I'd be able to feel like the— I glance hesitantly around the safe house instinctively, though I know it's empty.

I put Jax in the bathroom earlier, bound, gagged and blindfolded with a clunky set of Beats headphones blasting music in his ears. It's probably overkill, but I wanted the extra privacy. The idea of reading erotica around other people makes me uncomfortable.

I can't help but wonder what it would feel like to touch myself and feel good doing it. Satisfied that I'm alone, I allow my fingers to drift below the skirt of my sundress and into my panties, pressing against my clit in soft, lazy circles as I read the words in the novel.

"Good girl."

Only thing is... I'm not good. And I'm about to become even worse than he had ever imagined, because this—right here—his compassion, is driving me nuts. Without thinking about the consequences—something I never do when I'm around him—I push him to the chair in front of me and hop on the wooden counter of the small kitchenette. I part my thighs, ever so slightly. Pretend to check the bloody wound.

He swallows hard, and my eyes catch the movement in his throat. His eyes drop—finally, finally*—between my legs as he takes another swig.* Victory.

I swallow at the words, my fingers dipping lower, slowly traveling the short length of my slit. I picture Niccolaio as the Mr. James to my Remington Stringer, and I'm startled when I feel a gush of moisture on the very tips of my fingers.

My heart is doing cartwheels in my chest, and even though he hasn't so much as touched me, I feel myself growing slick. His eyes stay fixed on me, and it gives me the courage to take it a little further. I slide my fingers up toward my plain white bikini underwear and graze my clit over the fabric. For half a second, I'm insecure about my less than sexy undergarments, but the look in his eyes—a little pissed off and a lot horny—squashes that thought.

I can see it in my head, Niccolaio every bit fulfilling my naughty teacher fantasy, taking me onto *his* boat and watching with thinly veiled lust as I come apart in front of him. Closing my eyes, I let the tablet slip from my fingers and onto the soft mattress. With my now free hand, I pull the hem of my dress up and over my head.

I allow my right hand to trail a path around my nipple, causing the small bud to pebble painfully. With my eyes still closed, my other hand drifts past the lips of my pussy and slips easily inside of me, and I'm amazed when I realize how wet I am—wetter than I've ever been in my life just at touching myself to the image of Niccolaio in my head.

I've read this book a million times, since I've never had the money to buy new books often. But these words have never affected me as much as they do now, when I have the image of Niccolaio in my mind to accompany the words.

Removing my fingers from my pussy, I open my eyes to stare at them, to witness the foreign wetness soaking them with my own eyes. But when my eyes open, I find Niccolaio staring at me from the edge of the bed, his intense eyes roaming the length of my body before they stop on my wet fingers.

I try to process this—him being here. Even in his suit, I can see the hardness of his muscles, muscles that are tense right now, accompanied by clenched fists, a widened stance and crossed arms. His eyes take in the scene before they land on the tablet beside me, and I think I see the faintest glimpse of a smile on his face before it's gone.

"A-are you going to just stand there?" I ask, putting much effort into maintaining an adequate level of sass in my voice.

In only my panties, I feel vulnerable so naked beneath his gaze, but I can still feel the wetness on my fingertips, and I realize that perhaps this is what I want. To let someone—to let *him* —consume me.

So, I plead, "H-help me."

His nostrils flare, and for a brief moment, I think he's going to say yes, but instead, the jerk says, "No."

My jaw drops, but he's already reaching forward for the tablet, his eyes skimming through the passage on the screen. "*Misbehaved*?" he says, amusement in his voice as he reads the title of the book. His lips finally curve up into a sexy smirk, and he reads, "*I'm afraid he's going to turn me down again.*" He laughs out loud at the coincidence, the seductive sound a soothing balm on the fresh wounds his denial has inflicted upon me.

"*Tell me to stop. Throw me in the fucking lake, I don't know. But he doesn't do any of those things. Instead, he stands and grabs a beer—once more—then returns to the booth,*" Niccolaio's voice trails off as he enters the kitchen himself to grab a glass bottle of beer, and oh, God, I see where this is going.

He takes a seat on the bar stool, legs spread apart, his elbows on his knees, and an open bottle of beer in one hand and the tablet in the other. "*This is the last thing I should be thinking about doing after tonight, but this is the first time he hasn't shut me down, and I need to know I'm not the only one feeling this. I need to know I affect him as much as he affects me. He sits forward, with his elbows on his knees, the bottle dangling between two fingers as he studies me.*

"He wants to watch.

"*I lean back on my elbows and bring my knees up so my feet are resting on the edge of the counter. Now my legs are spread wide.*"

My heart racing, I back myself up, so my back is resting against the headboard of the bed, tilting my body to give myself a clear view of Niccolaio, thanks to the open floor plan of the studio safe house. Spreading my legs, I allow him to see the wetness staining my drenched white panties.

"*If anyone walked in right now, he'd appear to be disinterested.*"

And Niccolaio, bless him, makes the perfect Mr. James, his features impassive, except for the distinct clench of his impressive jawline. I dart my tongue out, trailing a path across my lips, imagining that I'm trailing a path along his jawline instead. His eyes follow the movement greedily, but aside from that, he's the image of indifference.

"*But I know the truth. He wants this. But he wants me to take the choice from him. I rub myself over my panties, slowly circling my clit again.*"

I follow the directive, nudging my clit beneath the fabric of my panties.

"*Touching myself is nothing new, but with Mr. James watching me, it's never felt better. A moan slips out, and my hips start rocking into my touch. He licks his lips and takes another drink. When he sits back in his seat, I see exactly how much he wants me through his gym shorts. But he doesn't make a move to touch himself.* Challenge accepted."

My eyes drift to Niccolaio's lap, and he gives me a knowing look. A thrilling jolt of lust soars through me at the sight of his massive hard on, straining against the constricting fabric of his suit pants.

"*I take a deep breath and pull my panties to the side, showing him the parts of me no one else has ever seen. I've never been exposed like this... I'm spread out on display for my teacher, and the thought only gets me hotter.*"

Taking a deep, nervous breath, I reach for my white lace panties and pull them aside, giving Niccolaio a clear view of my glistening pussy.

"*Fuck*," Niccolaio groans.

They're Mr. James' words, but looking at the desire on Niccolaio's face, and the way his knuckles are almost white from clenching the beer bottle so tightly, I know they're his words, too.

"*I slip two fingers inside, and they slide in easily with how wet I am. My head drops back, and I fuck my fingers harder, rubbing at the tight bundle of nerves with the heel of my palm.*"

I dip two fingers inside of me to steal my wetness and drag them to my throbbing clit before returning my fingers inside of me. I thrust the fingers in and out of me, fucking them as I use the base of my palms to rub roughly at my clit.

I've read the novel enough to know what Remington says, "*I picture you touching me like this almost every night. And in class. It's all I ever think about.*" The stolen words slip past my lips, barely distinguishable between breathy moans.

"*I stand and walk toward him*," Niccolaio reads, betraying his eagerness by skipping to the part where I bare myself to him completely. "*When I'm standing next to the table in front of him, I slide my underwear down my legs, letting them fall to the floor.*"

I stand on shaky legs, approaching him slowly, and when I'm a foot away from him, I turn around and slide my panties down my legs, giving him a view of my bare ass before I straighten and step out of my panties.

I wish it was my name on his tongue, but instead, Niccolaio reads, "'*Remington,' he warns, his voice still hard and gruff. It's the same stern voice that tells me to stop touching myself. To go to the headmaster's office.* To behave. *Only tonight, I will misbehave until I break him.*

"*Before he has the chance to object, I sit on the corner of the table, swinging one leg around him so he's in between my thighs.*"

When Niccolaio grabs my waist, helping me onto the kitchen counter, I falter, taken aback by the burning sensation his touch leaves on my body. I want him to touch me lower. To trail his hands down my waist and see how wet I am for himself.

My lips part, ready to beg him for his touch, but I don't say a thing. I don't want to break this seductive trance we're in, where he isn't the guy I'm supposed to hate, to stay away from, and I'm not the girl that conned my way into his life. So instead, I put my legs on either side of him, opening myself up in front of him like I'm serving myself up to him for dinner.

"*I prop myself up on one elbow, while my other hand snakes its way back down. His eyes are glued to where my fingers slowly work their way in and out. In and out.*"

I follow his directive before slipping a third finger into my pussy with ease, allowing the foreign sensation to build in me. I say the words before he does, meaning every single one of them, "*I wonder what you taste like... Your lips. Your cock. Do you ever wonder what I taste like?*"

"*What do you think?*" he says, and I wish to know if he means those words.

If he's just saying them because they're in the book or because he wants me as much as I want him—a lot. With shaky hands, I take the tablet away from him and set it behind me on the island, not wanting him to read the next scene. Because when he tastes me, I want to know if it's because he wants to and not because it's in a book.

I lean back onto my elbows, allowing my right hand to return to my pussy. Staring him right in the eye, I let out a long, soft moan, picturing his cock as I begin to finger fuck myself with renewed vigor.

"Niccolaio," I moan out his name, so he knows it's him and not Mr. James I'm thinking about when I bring myself even closer to an edge I've never before leaped off of.

I startle when he uses his knee to nudge my calf, spreading my legs wider for him. I press my leg harder against his, savoring the contact. I'm chanting his name, riding my fingers and rubbing my clit against the heel of my palm. Desperate for him, I lower my body, so my ass is only halfway on the island and my pussy is closer to his face.

And when I feel his breath travel across my pussy, caressing my clit with its warmth, I come hard, screaming his name out like a prayer and jerking so hard off the ledge that his hands reflexively reach out for my upper thighs to steady me. The contact only causes me to come harder, until my wetness is dripping past my lips and making a mess on the cold marble below me.

When I'm finally able to open my eyes again, I see him leaning forward. I tense, thinking he's going to lick me down there, but instead I feel the coldness of the glass rim of his beer bottle swiping upward along the length of my pussy, collecting my wetness.

Sitting up, I watch with bated breath as he raises the bottle to his lips, my walls clenching in renewed arousal as his full lips make contact with the wet rim of the bottle. He looks me in the eyes, his gaze unwavering as he downs the rest of the beer, swiping his tongue around the rim when he's done.

There's a painful second when I wonder if he did that because of the book or because he wanted to taste me. But then, he leans forward against me—his clothed chest brushing against the hardened peaks of my nipples and the hardness of his massive cock pressed against my clit through the expensive fabric of his pants—and says into my ear, "The next time you serve yourself up to me like that, you won't be thinking about a damn book. It'll be *my* fucking orders you take. It'll be *my* words that have you gushing onto my waiting fingers. It'll be *my* cock pounding inside of your tight, wet pussy, not these pretty little fingers."

Leaning back a little, he reaches for my hands, bunching them together and pressing a light kiss on the tips of each finger until he reaches the three that were inside of me. He inhales, groaning at the scent before brushing the residual wetness across his lips and briefly pressing them lightly against mine.

And then, not for the first time since I met him, the jerk steps away from me and leaves.

8
Punctuality
A gentleman does his best to never keep people waiting. He makes sure to plan adequate time for travel and realizes he's not the only one with a schedule. It is in his nature to commit to being early for meetings.
5
Vulgarisms
A gentleman knows that cussing generally signals a limited vocabulary. Try to find words that express your thoughts with more civility.
A
Loyalty
K

CHAPTER TWENTY-NINE

Dumbledore says people find it far easier to forgive others for being wrong than being right.
J.K. Rowling

Minka Reynolds

"Hit me," Jax says, his voice raspy from all of his muffled moaning and groaning.

About an hour ago, he agreed to shut up if I took the nectarine out of his mouth. He's kept his word, and we've been playing blackjack ever since. Of course, his hands and legs are still bound by Niccolaio's heavy duty rope, which makes playing... interesting.

It means that I've been able to see all of his cards as I handle them on his behalf and deal the cards to the both of us. To even out the advantage, I should be playing with both of my cards up instead of just one, but I've never been one to fight fairly.

My lips curve upwards as I deal another card to Jax. It's a bust, causing him to groan. I lean back a little in my seat, disgusted by the radius of his odious breath. I make a mental reminder to ask Niccolaio to bring Jax a toothbrush.

Behind me, the tablet rings, indicating a call from Mina.

Jax's eyes widen, and he pleads, "No, no, no, n—," as I shove the nectarine back into his mouth.

I help him out of the chair and onto the floor in his designated corner. Sometime within the last week since Niccolaio invited me to

Lucy's wedding as his date, I insisted that he lay sheets down for Jax, and for some reason, he actually agreed with me.

Now, there's a makeshift bed down there for Jax. I push him onto it, face him toward the wall for some extra privacy and hurry back to the tablet. Pressing the bright green button, I accept the call, smiling brightly as soon as I see Mina's beautiful face.

"Hi, Minka!"

"Hey, pretty girl." I look at the clock. "Shouldn't you be in class?"

"It was a half day," she says dismissively. "Guess what!" She's visibly jumping in her seat, unable to contain her excitement.

I think about the last time she was this excited and guess, "It was lasagna day in the cafeteria?"

"No."

"Fried chicken?"

"No, they don't have fried food at school anymore."

"Right. I forgot… There was a food fight?"

She frowns and sighs. "*No*… Why are all your guesses about food?"

"I'm hungry."

"Then, eat!"

I flush, remembering what happened in the kitchen yesterday. Niccolaio still hasn't returned since then, and I'm not sure if I should be worried or angry. Either way, I haven't been able to bring myself to step into the kitchen, the memory too fresh in my mind. But I *am* starving, and I need to eat sooner or later.

When I get up to eat, Mina shouts, "But not yet! Guess what!"

I sit back down. "Barbecue chicken pizz—"

"I get to play Juliet in the school play!"

I mash my teeth together, so my jaw doesn't drop in shock. I'm not disillusioned. I realize that people can be cruel when it comes to kids in wheelchairs. Even theater teachers. And that's why I know this may be a once in a lifetime opportunity given Mina's condition.

"That's… that's *amazing*, Mina," I say, and I mean it.

But inside, my heart is pounding, and my mind is running through a million possible scenarios that would allow me to attend her play without putting her in danger, all less likely than the last. Ten minutes ago, I didn't mind hiding out in a safe house. In fact, I was *thankful* to be in this situation.

Growing up broke meant that, every second of every day, I wondered if I'd have a place to sleep, food to eat, and water to drink and clean myself with. It meant rationing a single scoop of peanut butter from the Dollar Store for breakfast and dinner so that Mina could have a decent, balanced meal.

Instant ramen was a luxury I was rarely able to afford, and the best meal I had each day was the free school lunches I more than qualified for. If there was food in the kitchen cupboards, I ate it all—even if it was expired, though that rarely happened, because I seldom had enough food to reach an expiration date.

But now?

If the pantry in the safe house isn't fully stocked, one of the guards stops by to grocery shop for me and Niccolaio or drop off some takeout from restaurants that I would never be able to afford on my own. Heck, I haven't even thought about a bill in weeks.

And the showers? I have to force myself to cut them short—not because I'm too broke to pay the water bill, but because I care about the environment.

But I would give all of that up to go to Mina's play.

There's no way I'm missing out on this.

No matter what I have to do to get there.

"Can you go?" Mina asks me. "It's three Saturdays from now! Please, please, please, please, please!"

I quickly do the math. By that time, I'll have lived with Niccolaio for almost two months now. There has to be some progress by then.

"Of course, I will," I promise.

Mina squeals in delight and quickly shouts her goodbye to me when one of her friends from the group home calls out her name in the background. After I hang up, there's a large pit weighing heavily in my stomach. There's no way I'm missing Mina's play, but I have to consider the safety risks of attending.

"You're not going out," Niccolaio says from behind me.

I jump, startled. I didn't even hear him come in, though that doesn't surprise me, since he moves like a darn ghost. I didn't hear him come in yesterday either, which led to things that must not be named. What does surprise me is that I haven't seen him since he watched me come yesterday and left shortly after, and now that he's here, he's not even addressing what happened. I eye him up and down. He's wearing another outfit, though, which tells me he went somewhere he could change.

Despite my curiosity, I don't ask him where he went. I'm too focused on stifling the burn of my cheeks at the memory of what happened and the anger simmering inside me at being left without a word.

I'm usually never so bashful after a hookup. Then again, it doesn't help that he left me sitting on the island, naked and wet, without even a goodbye. Plus, I've been with my fair share of men, but none of them have been like Niccolaio.

There's always been an agenda for me, but yesterday was purely about pleasure.

My pleasure.

So, I suppose that makes this my first real morning after, as unconventional as it is. And that, along with my anger at being left, is why it takes some time for me to register his words, but when I finally do, my discomfiture and anger quickly turns into an all-encompassing fury. *Who the heck does he think he is, bossing me around like that?*

I scowl at him, and my voice is mocking when I say, "Oh, sorry, *Dad*. I must have missed it when you became my caretaker. Did you sign some adoption papers and everything? Am I grounded? Shall I call you Daddy, too?"

"Is that another fantasy of yours?" he asks, obviously referring to the student-teacher roleplay from yesterday. The edges of his lips tilt upward and his voice dips lower into a seductive lull. "You can call me Daddy whenever you want."

I ignore his words and change the subject, because I pretty much asked for that. "You can't tell me what to do. Don't bother trying."

He studies me, his intense eyes on my face, looking for I'm not sure what. "You're free to do whatever you'd like. I'm not telling you what to do, Minka. I'm reminding you that your actions have risks and consequences." When I open my mouth to speak, he cuts me off, "You know I'm right. What happens when you go to Mina, and you're followed? Is it really worth it?"

He's right, of course.

But that doesn't mean I like what he's saying.

Or that he's the voice of reason right now.

I shouldn't have made any promises to Mina, but this is huge. She's auditioned for school plays several times before, but other than a few roles as an extra, she's never had an opportunity like this.

If I'm not there for her when she needs me, then what's the point of working so hard to be in her life?

But deep down, I know I can't go.

Not unless something about our situation changes.

I run my fingers through my hair, trying to reign in my anger. It doesn't work. "Gosh. How socially inept are you? It's not okay for you to give me unsolicited advice on my personal life without an invitation. Do you see me sifting through your life, demanding to know why there's a hit out on you?"

He's quiet for a moment, his brown eyes glaring at me before they're overcome with a look of resignation. "I killed someone I loved."

"What?" I say, taken by surprise. "I-I... How does this end?" I ask him, finally settling on an appropriate reaction to such a revelation—one where I ignore what he just said because I'm not quite ready for him to confide in me. "How do we end the hit on you?"

For the first time since I met him, he looks uncomfortable. "We can't."

I shake my head adamantly. "No. There has to be a way."

He sighs heavily, and I can almost picture the weight of the world on his shoulders. "There are two ways. One is impossible, and the other involves bloodshed."

I think about it, a sick part of me entertaining the idea if it means I'd get to see Mina play Juliet. "Tell me about them."

"The first way—the impossible way—is for the person who called the hit or someone higher than the person who called the hit to call it off."

"Why is that impossible?"

"Because there's no way the person who called the hit is going to call it off. And there's no Andretti higher than the one who called the hit."

My jaw drops. "How in the world did you piss off the head of the Andretti family? How do you even *know* the head of the Andretti family?"

From what I know about the Romano family, they're a massive organization, and with massive organizations, the big fish don't know the little fish. Just like I doubt the CEO of Starbucks knows all of his employees, I doubt the head of the Romano family knows all of his.

I don't know much about the Andretti family, but I assume the same logic applies. And for some reason, I thought Niccolaio was small game. Yeah, he's intimidating as heck and obviously wealthy enough to be at the top.

But at the same time... it just didn't make sense in my head for him to be a big dog from the Andretti family. After all, he's an Andretti in Romano territory. If he's truly important, wouldn't he be living in Andretti territory rather than on enemy turf?

"He's my little brother."

My jaw drops, and I reel at the information, which is a lot to take in. If the head of the Andretti family is Niccolaio's little brother, then Niccolaio isn't just affiliated with the mafia. He's mafia royalty. And something tells me that if whatever went down didn't happen, I would be living with the head of the Andretti family. Not a disgraced heir in hiding. I can't even begin to wrap my head around that, so I push the thought aside and focus on the other ridiculous implication of his statement.

"Your little brother called a hit on you?!" I nearly shout. "Wait... If he's your younger brother, shouldn't you outrank him? Can't you call off the hit yourself?"

He sighs and takes a seat beside me on the couch. "He called a hit on me, because he hasn't forgiven me for killing my uncle."

At his words, I'm speechless. I can't even imagine hurting a hair on Mina's head, but if push came to shove and I was threatened, I suppose I wouldn't think twice about hurting either one of my "parents."

He continues, "And because I killed my uncle, I was excommunicated, which means I forfeited my spot as the future *capo bastone*—the underboss—and, eventually, when my dad died, the *capo famiglia* —the boss."

"And your brother took your place," I finish and hesitate before adding, "Why did you kill your uncle?"

"Because Asher was going to do it, and it wouldn't have been a merciful death."

My heart weeps for Niccolaio. I couldn't even imagine being put in a situation where I have to kill Mina to protect her from a horrible death. A part of me feels like I'd be too weak to do it.

"Why would Asher want to kill your uncle?" I ask.

"Retaliation. Four days before Asher came to Florida, my dad ordered a hit on Vincent Romano. It failed, and the Romano family sent Asher to retaliate."

"Why did he order a hit on Vincent Romano?"

"Because the Romanos and Andrettis were—are—at war."

"Why?"

He laughs loudly, startling me. "Honestly, I don't know why we're at war, but it's always been that way. Been that way since before I was born, too. Sometimes anger is learned, and that's all you know because it's all you've been taught. That's where Ranie, my brother, is at right now, and there's no getting through to him in that state. That's why I said that Ranie calling this off is impossible. There's no way it'll happen."

"But you said there's another way." I hesitate when I see the somber expression on his face. "W-what is it?"

"The blood debt must be repaid."

"What's a blood debt?"

"Blood is currency in this world. If you take a certain amount of blood, you've gotta give it back. It was the only way that kept us from killing back then, when it was easy to get away with it with the law enforcement."

"And how much blood did you take?"

"I killed some guy named Angelo. He wasn't even an associate yet. They're lowly ranked, ranked lower even than soldiers. And now, I guess, Naz."

"That doesn't sound too bad. You just have to give two lives worth of blood back? I've already seen you shoot two people."

"It's not so simple. Angelo was a recruit. Nobody big. Not even fully an Andretti yet. His life doesn't matter to anyone high up. The situation with Naz is complicated, because he's a nobody, but his father was a somebody to my Dad." He sighs. "But my dad is dead, and unless Ranieri is suddenly getting close to old ass men, it won't matter. Plus, Naz was in Romano territory when that happened. That's enough to escalate into an all-out mob war if a blood debt is called for that. Nobody will win if that happens, so that will go unretaliated."

"So that leaves your Uncle Luca."

"Yeah."

"But the Romanos were in Andretti territory when he was killed."

"But a Romano didn't kill him. I did."

"So, how do you pay that blood debt?"

"He was a *caporegime* for the Andretti family. For the blood debt to be repaid, another *caporegime* has to sacrifice his life."

I gasp. "Like Vincent Romano."

Niccolaio reluctantly nods. "Yes, but I would never let that happen. Neither would Asher for that matter." His eyes meet mine. "There's another way to pay the blood debt."

"How?" I ask, though judging by his expression, I know I won't like the answer.

"When a mafia heir is born, he is automatically and permanently given the title of *caporegime*. Regardless of excommunication."

"What are you saying, Niccolaio?"

But I suspect I know what he's implying. That he can pay the blood debt.

And as mad as I am at him right now, the blood drains from my face when he confirms it.

"If I die, the blood debt is repaid... If I die, all of this ends."

CHAPTER THIRTY

To err is human, to forgive, divine.
Alexander Pope

Niccolaio Andretti

Twenty-Four Years Old

I **don't mind the hard punch** to the stomach.

In fact, I welcome the physical pain. I relish it. I just wish my brother's smug fucking face could be anywhere else but here, gleefully witnessing my brutal beating, as one of his soldiers rains punch after punch on my already sore and bruised body.

Ranie's eyes are full of triumph, as if he caught me, when in reality, I didn't bother hiding. Perhaps it was a mistake to attend my father's funeral, but the old man had been a good father to me before everything went to shit. Four years of banishment didn't erase twenty years of decent parenting, so I figured I'd pay my respects.

And I wasn't going to do it hiding from afar like a fucking coward.

Instead, I arrived at the funeral in the car my father had bought me on my sixteenth birthday, a black 1970 Chevrolet Chevelle SS 396. A car I stole back from the Andretti compound an hour before the funeral.

It wasn't exactly hard.

Almost everyone was either preparing to leave for the funeral or was already on their way to it. And when I stepped out of the car at the cemetery, slipping on black aviators that matched my fitted black suit, I saw several slack-jawed faces turn my way.

Not much had changed since I left, and I could immediately tell everyone's rank by their reaction to my presence. The soldiers tensed, their hands automatically reaching for the weapons they undoubtedly had holstered underneath their suits.

The *caporegimes*, while tense, put a considerable amount of effort into not reacting, which was a telltale reaction itself. They're ambitious little fucks, and any display of fear regarding my appearance would be tantamount to cowardice.

And finally, standing beside my father's closed casket was Ranieri; my dad's old *consiglieri*, or chief advisor; and the new *capo bastone*, the underboss or second-in-command of the Romano family.

The latter two had stoic but resigned expressions on their somber faces, but Ranie graced me with a slight, devilish smirk, which was entirely inappropriate for the occasion and therefore a very Ranieri thing to do.

A murder, an excommunication, and four years later, and all I got from Ranie was a damn smirk.

He made a sweeping gesture with his arm, welcoming me to join him beside our father's grandiose gold- and marble-embedded, jet black-stained casket, a lavish and colossal thing, which was the pretentious variety of shit my father had been known to prefer while he was still alive. I wouldn't have been surprised to learn that my father had chosen it long before he croaked, unwilling to let us mere mortals fuck up choosing one for him.

If my brother and I were on better terms, I would have whispered some witty joke about it in his ear, and we'd make a competition out of hiding our laughter in front of the thousand-strong crowd that came out for my father's funeral today.

Instead, I was greeted with a mocking smile and the immense pleasure of a murderous glint in Ranie's eyes. I suspected that he was letting me attend Dad's funeral out of respect for our father, but I had no doubt that, after the funeral was finished, he had plans for me that involved a cathartic spilling of my blood.

Which brings me to now.

Not even a quarter of an hour has passed since the funeral ended, and I'm already in the basement of my childhood home, kneeling in a pool of my own blood, the blood loss causing my vision to go blurry and my head to pound.

"Release him," Ranie demands, a surprising level of self-confidence in his voice that hadn't existed when I last saw him.

"Why?" I ask crossly, looking a gift horse in the mouth and not giving a damn that I'm spitting on it.

I study Ranieri, taking in the tense set of his shoulders and the grim line of his mouth. Behind him stands Luigi, my father's *consiglieri,* and Mattia, my older cousin and the new *capo bastone*, thanks to Ranie's promotion to *capo famiglia*.

Mattia's discomfort at the proximity between him and my blood is clear on his face, but he's always had a queasy stomach. My father always said that he wasn't cut out for this life, but Dad, Uncle Luca, and Uncle Gabriele, who passed shortly after Mattia was born, are all gone. And aside from Mattia, we don't have any other cousins. That means that Ranie doesn't have very many choices for *capo bastone* if he wants to stay within the dwindling gene pool.

In his place beside Mattia, Luigi has a stern look on his face, one that's fixated directly onto Ranie. Interesting. Luigi's presence means that there's still business my dad wanted complete before he died. Otherwise, Luigi would already have been replaced, given a ridiculous sum of money, and peacefully retired in a lavish Floridian mansion by now—per Andretti tradition for a *consiglieri* that has served his boss and family well, which I have no doubt Luigi has.

I study the body language between Ranie and Luigi, quickly surmising that there's a secret they're keeping from me. A big one. One that, given the situation and date, likely involves my father and most definitely involves me.

Unable to help myself, the corners of my lips turn up into a smirk. "What did Dad say that's got you so pissed off, Ranie?" The glower Ranie sends my way is confirmation enough, so I continue to goad, "Did he tell you I'm his favorite son? Admit it to you on his deathbed?" I feign disbelief. "Are you *jealous*, Ranie?"

Of course, I know it's nothing of that sort. Dad would never make a declaration like that. Ranie was always Dad's favorite and I was Mom's, but Ranie never knew that, and I doubt that Dad ever told him. But I suspect that if I piss Ranie off enough, he'll let what my father said to him slip. At least the young Ranie from four years ago would have. I am curious to see how Ranie has grown up since I've been gone.

Ranie impresses me by brushing off my remarks and saying, "You never know when to shut up, do you, Niccolaio?"

Mattia chimes in, a nostalgic smile on his face, "We all know you're the talker, Ranie."

I snort, the sound coming out like a pig's oink, given the present condition of my face. But pain aside, for a brief moment, everything feels normal. I'm not getting beat up in front of my family in my childhood home by men that used to serve me. I'm not on the run from the people I love, and my dad hasn't died. I'm just a guy, laughing at a joke his cousin told, one that speaks of a familiarity, a kinship between the three of us.

And damn if that doesn't blow up my walls into a million sharp pieces.

I suspect that Ranie feels the past trickling in, too, because his face is a conflicting mixture of pain, humor, and anger. He takes a deep breath before his resolve visibly hardens, and I watch him overcome whatever internal turmoil he was struggling with.

"Clear the room," he commands, and the lone soldier and two *caporegimes* that were carrying out my beating immediately leave.

Luigi and Mattia, however, remain in the room.

Ranie doesn't bother turning his body when he repeats, "Clear the room."

Mattia leaves, but Luigi remains. I narrow my eyes at the unspoken implication. Whatever Dad told Luigi to make happen involves what's happening right now. Ranie's treatment of me. I'm sure of it. The curiosity is eating at me, and I wonder yet again what my dad told Ranie. The man sent a clear message when he excommunicated me, so I doubt it was anything good. But still...

"What did Dad say?" I repeat.

Ranie ignores me and turns to Luigi. "I won't repeat myself," he warns.

It dawns on me that I might not know the Ranie in front of me. The Ranie I knew would never have talked to Luigi like that. While I was never particularly close with Luigi, Ranie was. At least they had been when I left. The revelation that I no longer know my little brother is far more painful than the cuts and bruises on my body.

"*La Volontà del re*," Luigi begins, saying the Italian phrase for "The King's Will," "follows the successor, even in death."

And with that, Luigi leaves, parting one last stern look at Ranie and sparing me a sympathetic glance. But clearly not sympathetic enough to remove my binds, though Ranie did say that I could go earlier.

I study Ranie carefully. The King's Will refers to the last wishes of a mafia boss, a list of things or even a single wish that is forced upon his successor. Not every mafia boss gives his successor a King's Will. Some die before they get the chance to. But my dad died slowly in a hospital bed after a car crash, of all mortal ways to die. There had to have been plenty of time to dictate a King's Will. Given what I've seen, whatever he said has to do with me. And judging by Ranie's reluctance, he doesn't want to do it.

My heart quickens at my sudden, painful realization—Dad's King's Will was to order my death. It has to have been.

"What's eating at you, Ranie?" I soften my voice, because as much as I hate this situation right now, I have to sympathize with my brother.

He lost his father, and now the man who took his uncle from him is in the same room as him. And perhaps he's been given the directive to be his own brother's executioner. I know I wouldn't be able to do it.

"You don't have to do it," I tell him quietly. "You don't have to kill me. No matter what anyone tells you."

I'm urging him to go against the King's Will. I shouldn't be doing this, but I'm not doing it for me. I'm not begging for my life. I'm begging for the boy I knew four years ago. The one whose sleepy eyes flashed with heartbreak at the sight of his older brother's betrayal.

The Ranieri I knew back then could never do this, and I don't want him to have to.

But again, Ranie surprises me when his eyes flash with cold anger and he says, "It may not be today, but you *will* die. It can be tomorrow or ten years from now, but you'll die, Niccolaio, and it'll be from my hands. Make no mistake, you'll answer for your sins."

My eyes widen. "The King's Wi—"

He cuts me off, "He was your uncle."

"And I'm your brother."

"I have no brother."

CHAPTER THIRTY-ONE

I could easily forgive his pride,
if he had not mortified mine.
Jane Austen

Niccolaio Andretti

Present

Minka is angry at me, which doesn't surprise me in the slightest.

Since we relocated to the safe house a few weeks ago, we came to a tentative truce, but that ended last night when I told her that she couldn't go to her sister's play. Hell, that probably ended the night before that when I ditched her after she came.

But I couldn't stay in the same room with her. Not when she was so fucking tempting, her perfect, naked body pressed against me and her face flushed from coming harder than I'd ever seen a woman come.

I shouldn't have even indulged my attraction to her. I should have left as soon as I came into the safe house and saw her touching herself. But I couldn't. She was like the best gift I've ever received, laying on the bed for me to unwrap and play with.

And when I finally saw her come undone, I forcibly reigned myself in as well as I could until I couldn't stay in the same room as her any longer. I dashed out into the alleyway; whipped myself out; and like a fucking scumbag, jerked off in the empty alley to the image of her pretty pussy opened up in from me. The only saving grace was that I was hidden from view of the street by the giant blue trash container.

The real surprise, though, was yesterday, when she didn't suggest that I give myself up to the blood debt. I'm still surprised that she hasn't brought it up, especially since I can feel her anger radiating off of her in waves right now, as I park the car in the full graveled parking lot of an abandoned miniature market.

"What the heck?" she asks, smoothing down the dress I gave her earlier, a smoking hot, formfitting red number that reaches down to the middle of her thigh. Earlier, I had to force myself not to tear it off of her and demand a repeat of last time. "This is where they're getting married?" For the first time since yesterday, she looks me in the eye. "Lucy's not normal. At all."

"None of this is normal," I mutter, referring to us, but obviously I agree with her.

Ever since I met her, I've noticed that Lucy continually flirts with the border between sanity and insanity, but whatever. She's happy. Asher's happy. And I suppose, at the end of the day, that's all that matters.

I give Minka my arm, and she reluctantly takes it, knowing she doesn't have a cat's chance in Hell of walking in her heels on this cobbled road unscathed without my help. I lead her to the front of the rundown, dilapidated building and knock on the door three times—one long knock, followed by two quick ones. The eye level slit on the door slides open, and we're met with silence on the other end.

"*Siamo qui per il matrimonio*," I say in perfect Italian, telling the guy that we're here for the wedding.

"*Nomi*?"

"Niccolaio Andretti *e* Mink—"

The sound of the slit sliding shut cuts me off, and the door immediately opens after. My reputation must precede me, because the guard, probably an associate but no higher than a soldier, averts his eyes as he leads us down the musty hallways into a stairwell that only goes down.

Minka's grip tightens on my arm, and I refrain from patting her hand reassuringly. She'd no doubt find a way to take offense to such a gesture. I slow my pace, so she can keep up on the wobbly stairwell in her spectacularly high heels. Once we reach the bottom, we're greeted by a maze of tunnels.

"Where are we?" Minka whispers, but the resounding echo of the tunnels carries her voice loudly.

"During the prohibition era, the Romano boss had the bright idea of building tunnels that connected his businesses. They're all over New York City. They used them to smuggle alcohol, which made them even more money than drugs did. We'll be going to one of the old smuggling stops right now," I reply, helping Minka into the golf cart.

"And where's that?"

"The church."

Minka mutters something, and knowing her, it was probably a PG-rated curse. We're both silent as the guard drives us to the stairwell that exits into the church. As soon as we're out of the golf cart, the guard, with his eyes still averted from me, murmurs a quiet salutation in Italian and leaves without another word.

"Why all the cloak and dagger?" Minka asks as we make our way up the stairs.

"To avoid paparazzi. We were assigned to that post, but there are several assigned routes for today in order to get all of the guests to the church in a timely manner."

When the guard stationed at the top of the staircase opens the door for us, we're greeted by the sight of John with Red Senior.

He glances past us quickly before doing a double take and approaching us, a resigned and reluctant expression on his face. "Nick. Minka," he says, inclining his head slightly to each of us. "I don't believe I've properly introduced you to Ashley."

"Nice to properly meet you both," Ashley says, hiding her uncertainty behind a shaky smile.

I notice that she has a ring on her ring finger.

"Congratulations!" someone says, approaching our small group and slapping John on the back. Ashley looks grateful for the interruption, and together the three of them leave us alone without another word.

I lead Minka down the aisle towards one of the rows in the middle. Usually, the groom's friends and family sit on one side of the aisle while the wife's friends and family sit on the other, but the seating arrangement is open, since Lucy is a foster child with very few friends, except for some chick named Aimee. Speaking of Aimee, Lucy's maid of honor, I make a mental note to stay clear of her. I've only heard bad things about her.

That she's funny. Hilarious. A riot.

Gross.

"You're grumpy again," Minka remarks as we slide into one of the pews in the front.

"No, I'm not."

She looks pointedly at the thinly set line of my mouth.

"Fine," I admit, "maybe I'm a little grumpy. I don't like weddings."

"Why not?"

"Actually, I don't like *Romano* weddings. Too many trigger-happy people that have been taught all of their lives to hate someone with my last name."

"And do they?"

"What?"

"Do they hate you because of your last name?"

"Y—" I cut myself off and really consider it. "Huh. They don't."

If I really think about it, they do avoid me and avert their eyes, but it's not because I'm an Andretti. It's because I'm the fixer. It's the same reaction I've seen Asher garner, and I suspect that, like Asher, I'll get these looks long after I retire from this position.

I'm startled by the realization, but now that I'm aware of it, it doesn't take me long to figure out why it's been years since I've been treated like a pariah thanks to my last name—Vincent Romano.

As the fixer, I've worked under his tutelage as the head of enforcement from the start, and he's always been quick to punish people who have mistreated me. To set them straight with the words of a well-respected man. And in the rare chance that didn't work, to force them into submission.

I look diagonally across the aisle at Vincent Romano, wanting to study him after this revelation. But I frown when I see him. Something's off about him tonight. He looks a little ragged, a little less put together.

In normal circumstances, this would be concerning... but this isn't a normal circumstance. This is Asher's wedding, which makes it even more alarming, because we all know Vincent would give up his life to make this day perfect for the man he considers to be his son.

One glance at Asher standing before the Romano boss, who was ordained to complete the ceremony, and I can tell that Asher sees it, too, because he keeps glancing at Vincent when he should be clearing his mind and focusing on Lucy and this wedding.

I make eye contact with Asher, and he quirks a questioning eyebrow in Vincent's direction. I shrug, hoping it conveys my confusion. Asher nods, his frown deepening, but it immediately clears when the wedding music begins to play and the flower girl, one of Vincent's nieces, Bastian's youngest sister, starts walking slowly down the aisle and tossing flower petals or some shit.

I ignore the procession of women and men walking down the aisle, glad that Asher didn't bother asking me to be one of his groomsmen, because we both know that I'd hate it and do a shit job of planning everything except the bachelor party.

Next to Minka, one of the notoriously handsy *caporegimes* tries to subtly scoot closer to her. I cut him a glare so harsh it quickly takes care of that problem.

Minka looks startled by my reaction before amusement and a dash of determination quickly take over her features. "For someone who was so quick to run a couple of nights ago, you sure are possessive." Her tone adopts a teasing lilt, but I suspect she's serious when she says, "You know, it would be great if you could get over this crush you have on me."

I barely refrain from scowling. "I don't have a crush."

"Then, what do you call this?" she asks, gesturing to our proximity and the way I've angled my body to ward off other unwanted assholes.

I sigh in resignation, putting a little distance between us, not even bothering to wonder why she says half of the shit she says. She wasn't complaining when I was watching her come undone in front of me.

"Aren't you supposed to be mad at me?" I ask.

Her eyes widen slightly, like she's just remembering that she doesn't like me, and she returns her attention to the wedding. Aimee, Lucy's maid of honor, and Asher's best man, some friend he knows from his childhood, have finally reached the end of the aisle, and everyone has turned their attention to the entrance, where Lucy is now standing.

Sometime in the past ten minutes, Vincent exited the room from the side and made his way to the entrance, where he's now escorting Lucy down the aisle. When she passes the first row, Lucy sends a beaming smile to one of the older ladies sitting on the pew, who I recognize as Lucy's former social worker from one of the background searches I conducted when I finally learned Lucy's real name.

When I return my eyes to Asher, I see something flash in his eyes. Nerves, maybe? I doubt it. Then again, he *is* about to hitch himself to Lucy, who's weird as fuck, for all of eternity. And that's exactly what's happening.

For. All. Of. Fucking. Eternity.

After all, Asher doesn't do things half-assed.

I know this because when he offered me refuge in Romano territory after I saved his life, he set me up with a forty million dollar brownstone, a high-paying job and eventually two security guards from Black Security. And just when I thought that was the end of the surprises, he took me by surprise again by befriending me.

And as Lucy and Asher exchange vows and give each other genuine promises of forever, I find myself pushing aside my derision for marriage and wondering what it would be like to find someone who I'd like to spend forever with. Or, baby steps, the type of woman I'd like to date to begin with.

Whoever she is would have to be able to put up with my asshole tendencies. She'd have to be fierce and capable of one Hell of a mean streak. Nice girls are overrated. Sure, I want a woman who can be kind, but I also want her to have a spine. One hell of a backbone. Preferably one that leads to an ass as fine as Minka's.

Hell, who am I kidding?

It's Minka I want.

CHAPTER THIRTY-TWO

Forgiveness is an act of the will,
and the will can function regardless
of the temperature of the heart.
Corrie ten Boom

Minka Reynolds

I fidget in my seat at my table in the banquet hall, remembering the odd looks Niccolaio sent my way during the wedding, which is just about the worst occasion to be sending a girl looks like that.

Gone was his usual blank mask and in its place was a distinct look of wonder. He tried to hide it, but I saw it, lurking beneath the depths of his eyes as he studied me when he thought I didn't notice.

But the problem is I did notice. I notice everything about him. I've been trying to chalk it up to lust, so I can dismiss it as nothing more than a meaningless crush, but I don't think that's what this is.

At least, I can't reduce it to lust when my heart pounds at the thought of him and I feel my throat swelling in so much feeling when I think of all he's done for me. Like going out of his way to call in favors with Asher, so I can talk to Mina every single day. And making Mina laugh whenever he's there while I'm video chatting with her. And being someone I can talk to about my past—and present—without feeling judged by every wrong (and right) decision I've ever made. And giving me a place to stay when we both know he doesn't need to do this, since I'm not going to go blabbing my mouth about him.

I sigh, swirling my soda in my glass as I watch him talk to the mayor across the banquet hall. Yeah, the *mayor*. And earlier, I think I saw Beyoncé and her daughter running around this place. I shouldn't be surprised that Asher knows all of these people or that Niccolaio is so casually talking to them, but I am.

In his hand is a glass of tea, filled a third of the way. Earlier, he asked a waiter for a glass of whiskey, poured it into one of the nearby plants, and refilled the whiskey glass with some tea from the table's pitcher. Sly Devil.

"Having fun?" a voice asks from beside me, causing me to jump.

The Sprite in my hand splashes outside of the cup from the movement. Asher hands me a napkin, and I hastily wipe the spilled liquid off of my hand.

"I didn't hear you sit," I say the obvious.

I wonder if Asher taught Niccolaio that or Niccolaio taught Asher that. Or maybe these mafia men are just born with the inherent knowledge of how to sneak up on people and scare the living daylights out of them. Seriously... How do you sit down *beside* someone so quietly that they don't hear?

Asher shrugs, smirking a little as he glances at Lucy on the dance floor with Aimee. "Are you having fun?"

"Yes."

"Don't lie. It's unbecoming."

I sigh. "Fine, but it's not like I'm *not* having fun. I'm just... This is weird."

"What is?"

"I mean, thank you for donating the tablets. That means the world to me. But... You hate me. Lucy hates me. Aimee hates me."

He studies me before relenting, "I donated the tablets because I wanted to, not because of Nick or you. I did it for the kids." His words remind me of an article I read on his philanthropy for underprivileged children, and I suppose it makes sense with his background. "And I don't hate you," he continues. "No one does."

"I haven't forgotten what you said to me at Carmen's Cantina."

I know your type. You're not at Wilton for a degree. You're there to find someone to marry. Some rich sucker you can leech off of for the rest of your parasitic life. Come near Lucy again, and I'll blackball you so fast, no man in the city will dare touch you with a ten foot pole. You clearly know who I am. You know I'll do it.

Yet, here I am, sitting in the same room as Lucy, at her wedding no less, and I haven't been blackballed. But that doesn't lessen the lacerating sting of the words as I remember them. Mostly because he was right about everything except for the Wilton part. I *am* parasitic. I *am* looking for a rich sucker I can leech off of for the rest of my life. Well, for as long as I think Mina needs me to.

"It's pretty cowardly to hold a grudge."

"Are you calling me a coward?"

"Well, you're not exactly acting brave."

When he smiles, I realize he's joking, and that surprises me more than it would if I learned he wasn't joking.

After a minute of silence, Asher shrugs carelessly and mocks my earlier words, "I haven't forgotten what you've done to Lucy."

I frown, remembering how awful I was to her. "Are we enemies, Asher?"

"No."

It's stupid, but I ask, "Why not?"

"You've been horrendous to deal with, yeah. But part of what you've done was give her a safe place to stay when she was in danger. When it counted the most. I haven't forgotten that, and I won't ever forget that."

I lean back. "But I've been so mean to her."

"You haven't since, and I don't think you will again." He looks me in the eye. "It seems like the only person who's finding it difficult to forgive you is you."

And with that, he's gone.

He's just as irritating as Lucy.

Shortly after Asher leaves, Aimee and Lucy join me, but this time I'm not surprised—I could hear their raucous laughter from across the room.

Aimee gives Lucy a dubious glance. "We like her now?"

Lucy elbows her in the stomach and turns to me. "Thank you for coming."

"No problem," I say, and I mean it. "I'm glad I came."

And I am. I needed to hear from Asher, from anyone, that I'm forgiven for my past. Lately, as I've started to question whether or not my choices have been good ones, I've also abhorred my inability to reign in the ugliness of my emotions and how I've treated others.

I needed to hear that I'm not beyond redemption.

Aimee breaks the surprisingly comfortable silence that stretches out, "Hey, Loosey Goosey?"

"Yeah?"

"No one shot you down today."

Lucy smiles. "I haven't been poisoned either."

Aimee snorts, and I give them polite smiles that hide the *What in the firetruck?* I'm thinking in my head. I have to remind myself that I reevaluated my opinions on Lucy after our last talk in Vaserley Hall.

I mean, I still think she's crazy... but now I understand why. She's a fifty year old woman trapped in a twenty year old's body, and all that age-old wisdom crammed into that youth has turned her insane.

I'm not sure what Aimee's excuse is.

"So, Nick, huh?" Lucy asks me.

I look at him, talking at the edge of the dance floor with Asher. He has a smile on his face that I haven't seen on him with anyone other than me. And while I'd love for it to be reserved for me, I'm glad he has Asher. They seem good for each other.

Around the dance floor, men avert their eyes from Asher and Niccolaio. I saw it in the tunnels, too. The guy who led us through them couldn't even meet Niccolaio's eyes. And when we made our way through the pews in the church, people backed far away from us, some of them even noticeably cowering.

And I realized that Niccolaio is an intimidating man.

So why have I never felt that about him?

As if he knows I'm thinking about him, Niccolaio's eyes meet mine, and I'm ensnared by them.

On the other side of Lucy, Aimee loudly whisper-shouts into Lucy's ear for all of us to hear, "Fuck, they should just sleep together and get it over with."

Abruptly, I feel several pairs of eyes from the surrounding tables turn to me. Lucy is quick to jab Aimee roughly with her elbow (again).

"What the fuck?" Aimee asks defensively, rubbing her rib cage with a look of surprise on her face.

"We're in a church."

Well, we're in a banquet hall built into the back of the church, but still…

Aimee's eyes widen. "Shit, I forgot." Her face half somber and half apologetic, she corrects herself, "*Holy* fuck, they should just sleep together and get it over with."

Lucy groans and rubs at her forehead, giving up on Aimee. Instead, she sends me an apologetic look, which I shrug to. As long as Niccolaio didn't hear that, I'm not too mortified. I steal another glance at the man in question and am surprised to see him making his way towards me.

Around me, I hear the girls quickly reacting, and I wonder if they'd be reacting the same way if he was uglier or if they'd cower away from Niccolaio like all of their male counterparts seem to do.

"Care to dance?" he asks me when he reaches me.

I nod, saying my goodbyes to Lucy and Aimee. He leads me to the dance floor, holding my hand tightly in his. People naturally part for him, for some reason repelled by him when all I seem to be able to do is get closer.

When he pulls me closer, I inhale his seductive scent. I can feel his laughter against my chest, but I don't care. I'm not even embarrassed by my reaction. I'm resigned to the fact that I'll always react this way to this man.

"Did you just sniff me?"

"Yes," I mumble into his suit jacket.

"I think it's only fair if I do the same."

He leans into my neck before I can prepare myself for it, and I tense, my skin erupting into a million goosebumps as he trails his lips against the curve of my neck. I can feel my nipples pebbling against my dress, unhindered by a bra, and I push myself closer to hide them from the crowd. Or at least that's what I tell myself.

When his mouth reaches the space below my ear, he takes me by surprise by lowering my body into a dip, twirling us into a half circle at the same time he raises me back up. A genuine smile spreads across my lips

"You should smile like that more often."

"You should dance with me more often."

"Okay."

"Wait. What?"

"Let's go."

"Where are we going?" I ask, as he leads us to the tunnels, barely pausing to send a boyish head nod Asher's way.

"I'm taking you on a date, Minka Reynolds."

I've never been on a date.

CHAPTER THIRTY-THREE

True forgiveness is when you can say,
"Thank you for that experience."
Oprah Winfrey

Minka Reynolds

Of course, my first date happens at a movie theater.

Original.

But honestly, with Niccolaio as my date, I can't even bring myself to care, and when we walk into the completely empty theater lobby, I know why we're here and not somewhere more crowded. Not for the first time, it occurs to me that Niccolaio is always thinking a dozen steps ahead.

"This is a dollar theater that plays movies that have been out in theaters for a few months, and honestly, it should be out of business already. None of the theaters are in decent viewing condition, so no one goes."

I see what he means when we enter the theater, and there's a gaping hole in the top left corner of the screen. In the center right, there's a giant stain on the screen, also. How that happened, I have no clue, but I'm not impressed. Again, I also don't particularly care, though I am amused and confused as to why Niccolaio took me here. Surely, he'd be able to find another place that isn't frequented by people.

We sit down at the center of the handicap row. Normally, I'd be more sensitive about using up a seat reserved for handicap people, but this place is a ghost town. There's even only one employee running the whole place.

"Are we in the right theater?" I ask as I stare up at the screen, where Emma Watson is looking into a handheld mirror at the Beast.

Given what I know about the fairy tale, it looks like the movie is at least two-thirds of the way done.

"Yep. This is the one."

"Do you want to catch a later showing?"

"No. Do you?"

I frown at the amusement in his voice, but I shake my head and stay silent as we watch the last twenty or so minutes of the movie in silence. Five minutes in, he does the stereotypical yawn, stretch, and hand around the back move, which makes me roll my eyes.

"I shouldn't have told you that this is my first date. Now you're pulling out all the big moves," I say, leaning my head against his firm bicep and gesturing to the giant hole in the movie theater carpet, which has to be some sort of hazard. Definitely a lawsuit waiting to happen.

He gives me a boyish grin, and his face instantly transforms from the face of Niccolaio Andretti, the killer the darkest people in this world know, to Niccolaio Andretti, the guy who doesn't judge me and says silly, ridiculous things to make my little sister laugh.

"Damn, I should have splurged for the popcorn," he says, looking at our stash of boxed candy in mock disappointment.

I try and fail to stifle my stupid smile, because I was the one who pointed out the greenish hue of the popcorn in question. Good God, this place needs to be shut down, but man, if it isn't quickly becoming one of my favorite places.

"I think I'll have to dock two or three points off for that."

"I think I can live with a 98%."

"On a scale of one to five."

"Ouch."

"Do you want me to kiss it and make it better?" I say, grinning at the foreign feel of flirting for fun.

Without an agenda that involves men that I have no desire to be with.

"Depends on what *it* is."

"Have you always been such a perv?"

"Since I reached the double digits."

"You know, I can picture ten year old Niccolaio trying to peak up ladies' skirts."

He rolls his eyes, but the smile is still on his face. "Shut up and kiss and make it better already."

With pleasure.

I lean forward, my breath hitching, as I shift my body his way. He surprises me by reaching across me and grabbing my waist, lifting and swiveling my body so I'm straddling him. Grinding myself harder against him until he groans, I lean forward to kiss him, my lips almost touching his.

And then the movie theater attendant enters the theater, making his rounds up and down the rows in the theater, even though Niccolaio and I are clearly the only ones in here. I stifle a laugh as the embarrassed teenager power walks past us, unable to avoid it given our placement in the handicap row.

Burying my face in Niccolaio's neck, I wait until the poor kid leaves before I let the laughter burst past my lips.

Niccolaio looks at me in amusement. "You're smiling, and I didn't even have to dance with you."

It's then that I realize that I haven't smiled or laughed this much in... well, ever. I've never had the chance to be a kid. I was abandoned, and when my parents came back, I was forced into drug dealing. And then Mina came, and I learned how to be both sister and mother at once, and I haven't stopped since.

But now, I feel my age. I feel young and free, like the possibilities in life are endless, even though I'm just sitting in a seat in a rundown dollar movie theater, hardly watching the movie that's playing on the screen.

Heck, I even almost forget what's playing until, a few minutes later, the end credits come on, and the song "Beauty and the Beast" begins to play. I stand up to leave, disappointed that my time in the dark with Niccolaio is over.

But when I head towards the exit, Niccolaio grabs my hand and pulls me back to him.

"What are you doing?" I ask as he begins to guide my body into a sway.

"We're dancing, Minka. Go with it."

And I do, the happiest I've been in so long, swaying to the sound of John Legend and Ariana Grande as Niccolaio pulls me tighter into his arms and dips me like a seasoned pro.

I'm grateful when Niccolaio doesn't turn in the direction of the safe house. I was worried that this date would be over so soon, but I should have known better. I suspect that Niccolaio will always exceed my expectations.

My cheeks flush as my mind automatically drifts to sex. I want a kiss from him, and not a light pressing of our lips together before he ditches me without a word, though, heck, I'd take that, too, at this point.

"What are you thinking about?" he asks.

"Your lips on mine. My hands sliding down the front of your pants, gripping your bare cock. Your fingers on my chest, pinching, teasing, tugging on my hardened nipples," I answer honestly.

Perhaps too honestly, but oh, well.

"Fuck," he groans, pulling the car over, and for a brief moment, I perk up in excitement, thinking that he's going to give me exactly what I want, but he doesn't.

Instead, he unbuckles my seatbelt, exits the car, and opens my door for me. I grab his hand and accept his help when he lifts me onto the hood of the car. Before me is the Hudson River in all of its smelly glory.

He smirks at my scrunched up nose and says, "Almost nine million people live in this city, and all of their trash gets taken across the river to be incinerated. The wind still picks up the scent and drifts it back across the river, hence the stench."

"Lovely." I joke, "So, you've taken me to the last twenty minutes of a movie at a place that's more safety hazard than it is a theater and now a stinky river across from nine million people's worth of trash. Is this the part of the night when you chop my body up and throw the pieces into the water?" I lean into him as he takes a seat beside me on the hood of his car. "Niccolaio Andretti, you're absolutely charming. Do what you want with my limbs, but do you promise to keep my ass intact? I'm rather fond of it."

"Laugh it up, but this is my favorite place in the entire city."

"Why is that?"

"We live in a city with nine million other people. Nine million. And that isn't including the shit ton of tourists New York City garners, too. Sometimes, I just need a break. To remind myself that I'm free. That I'm not tied to this town in the ways I sometimes feel like I am. And here, I'm alone. I'm my own man. I can think my own thoughts without them being clouded by so many other people."

"Don't you ever get tired of being alone? You lived by yourself in that brownstone."

"Well, yeah, but that's different."

"How so?"

"I'm trapped there, and I'm not here. I'm not sure there's another way to explain it."

"I like it here," I decide.

"Even if it's smelly?"

"Especially because it's smelly."

"No shit?"

"If it wasn't, I think more people would be here, and then, I'd really hate it."

He barks out a laugh. "You're something else, you know that?"

"So says the man that goes to a putrid river to get away from nine million people that don't even know him." My expression sobers as I look at the city from our viewpoint. "I know what you mean," I say softly. "It feels like freedom here. It's far enough away from the city that I don't feel trapped by all of my responsibilities and close enough that I still feel like I can be there for Mina if she needs me." I turn to him. "Thank you for taking me here."

We sink into silence together, enjoying the sound of the water and the breeze before he asks, "Why don't you curse?"

I do curse when it comes to filthy words, because there's just no substitution for that, but I suspect he's not referring to that, so I say, "I promised myself I'd stop around the same time I promised myself that I'd become the person I need to be in order to get Mina back."

The reference to my gold digging is sobering, laying between us like the elephant in the room. I'm grateful when he doesn't bring it up, because I don't want to face that reality yet. I don't want to gold dig, but I still need to. Mina has six more years in the foster care system if I don't do anything about it.

But for now, I just want to enjoy this moment of normalcy, with a boy that I really, really like. And I do like him. He's maddening, absolutely infuriating, but he's also everything I never knew I wanted. Is it so wrong to lead him on like this? He's a big boy. I'm sure he can handle it.

"Why don't you try cursing right now?" he asks.

"It's a slippery slope."

"Not even a little?"

"Are you trying to corrupt me, Niccolaio?"

"You're already corrupt, Minka. Or shall I say Remington?"

I shove my shoulders lightly against his, forcing the memories of that night away but also wishing he'd just kiss me already. I want to know what it feels like to be kissed—really kissed—and like it.

But I don't want to be the initiator. Not when I'm already leading him on.

So, instead, I say, "Tell me a secret."

"What do you want to know?"

"What happened that night?"

"It was four days after a botched hit on Vincent. We all thought the Romanos were going to retaliate on my dad, so he had me and Ranie stay at our Uncle Luca's place. I couldn't sleep and was walking around the place when I noticed that all the guards were missing. I didn't have my phone on me, and Ranie's room was on the other side of the mansion, so I drew my gun and cleared the rooms until I reached that hall. Where I met Asher for the first time. He gave me an ultimatum—Ranie's life or Uncle Luca's."

"And you chose Ranie."

"I don't regret it either."

"How can he be mad at you for what happened if you did it for him?"

"I don't think he knows I did it for him. I don't think anyone knows what happened. Or if they do, they just don't care. I did kill a *capo*."

"Did you try to explain what happened?"

"I fled as soon as it happened, but I tried to call and email for a little. But then I realized they could track that, so I reverted to mailing letters to my dad and Ranie without a return address. I don't know if they ever got them. Either way, it doesn't matter. My dad's dead, and Ranie put a hit out on me. *La volontà de re*. The King's Will."

"What does that mean?"

"It's like a deathbed wish from a mafia boss to his successor. And traditionally, it has to be carried out."

"And your dad made a King's Will? What was it?"

"My death."

I shake my head, unable to believe it but no longer wanting to talk about something so dark, so serious on my first date. "Tell me something else. Something positive."

He leans back, so he's laying entirely on the car now, and I join him, resting my head on his chest. “I want you, Minka Reynolds. You’re going to be mine. It’s just a matter of time.”

“I don’t have a say in this?” I ask, amused.

He decided that he wants me, and it’s just a matter of time. That should piss me off, but it doesn’t. Because if I’m being honest, I want him, too.

Even if I know I can’t have him.

CHAPTER THIRTY-FOUR

I wondered if that was how forgiveness budded; not with the fanfare of epiphany, but with pain gathering its things, packing up, and slipping away unannounced in the middle of the night.
Khaled Hosseini

Niccolaio Andretti

M**inka's quiet as we** drive back to the safe house. It's on my mind to say something, but I notice a car following us once we reach a one block perimeter to the safe house, and I have to push the thought aside.

"Take the wheel for a sec," I tell Minka.

"What?!" she asks, the alarm clear in her voice. "I've never driven a car!"

"How old are you?"

"Twenty-two, you jerk! I'm a New Yorker! We don't drive."

I smile at the sass in her voice. Aside from earlier in the day, she's been tamer than usual today, and I was worried that taking her on a date might pacify her defiance.

I look her in the eye, so she knows I'm serious. "I'm going to let go of the wheel. If you don't take it, I can't guarantee we won't crash."

I let go of the wheel, and her eyes widen.

She grabs it, shouting, "You asinine jerk!"

I laugh, my head turned away from her as I dig through my go bag and say, "Careful. Your Wilton is showing."

Surveying my options, I grab a knife, my colt and an EMP gun from the bag before swiveling back to the front seat with my goods.

Minka's eyes widen as she takes in my selection. "Oh, my God. You're crazy. You almost killed us for *that*?! What are those for?"

"I didn't *almost kill us*. You're a natural driver."

"You weren't even watching me drive!"

"We're alive, right?"

"Unbelievable. And this date was going so well."

It was. It still is. I was going to drop her off at the door to the safe house, like I'm pretending to drop her off at her parents' house; give her a kiss that would blow her mind; and then, jokingly sneak in a minute later.

But now she's about to watch me kick some ass, and isn't that better?

I take the wheel from her and drive past the alleyway to our safe house.

"Are we going somewhere?" Her eyes light up when she notices that we passed our place, and I'm tempted to take her someplace else, to make this night last as long as it can. "Gun range?"

"Someone's following us."

Her eyes widen, and she stares at my weapons again before relaxing in her seat, a resigned sigh escaping into the air.

I hand her the EMP gun, even though I'd love the opportunity to use it for the first time. "Want to shoot it?"

"I've never shot a gun before. My aim probably sucks."

"It doesn't shoot bullets. It shoots an electromagnetic pulse, so your aim doesn't have to be too good. Just shoot in the direction of the car when I tell you to."

A sly grin spreads across her face, and holy shit, I think I'm in love with this woman. Okay, maybe not, but I could be. I can see this going there, and I'm eager for every little moment that she surprises me. Like right now, when there's excitement in her eyes when there probably should be alarm.

"Hold onto the *Oh Shit!* handle," I warn, before slamming on the breaks and using the momentum to swivel the car one hundred and eighty degrees, so I'm now facing the car that was following us.

I take in the widened eyes of the driver, his mouth slightly agape as he quickly presses on the breaks of his car, and it halts with a sudden jerk. His face says it all—he's in way over his head. But I've never been one to have mercy. This guy decided to come after me while I'm with Minka. With that thought in mind, I rev my engine, and the other car begins to reverse. I follow it at an increasing speed. Beside me, Minka's face is flush with adrenaline, and she's never looked more beautiful to me.

"Can I shoot it?" she asks.

Her burgundy hair is blowing wildly in the wind, her flushed face is a rosy pink, and the EMP is delicately nestled between both hands, and she's the hottest thing I've ever seen in my life.

I bite back a grin and say, "Almost."

I turn my wheel a little to the right and pick up speed, so my front left bumper is next to his front left bumper, and then I start to turn the car in his direction. He adjusts his wheels, shifting the direction of his car, so I don't bump into it. When he realizes where I'm leading him, he tries to turn another way, but it's too late.

I've backed him into the dead end alleyway adjacent to our safe house. He revs his engine, a threat that he'll ram us down, but I call bullshit.

Just in case, I tell Minka, "You can shoot it now."

She sticks the EMP gun out of the window, the size of it a little too big for her, and I watch her struggle to balance it with a slight grin on my face. A few seconds after she pulls the trigger, the other car's engine starts to die.

"How are you not upset about this?" she asks, her eyes eagerly devouring the scene before us.

But I am upset. I just hide it well. Instead of telling her this, I say, "I was prepared for something like this to happen."

I just didn't think she'd be there when it did, and fuck, that makes me mad. And as the adrenaline fades, I realize how fucked up this is.

I put this woman in danger. If she gets hurt, that'd be on me, and I know without a doubt that I would never recover from that.

My expression sobers as I stare at the opposing car, allowing my anger to simmer beneath my skin, hidden to everyone but me. Unfortunately for the guy in front of us, he's the source of my anger, and I've never been one to forgive and forget. *It must run in the family*, I can't help but think in the back of my mind.

The driver rolls down his window and sticks both of his hands out for me to see. He places one hand on the roof of his car and uses the other to unlock the car door from the outside handle. I wait impatiently as he steps out, my gun at the ready just in case.

When he's completely out of the car and pressed against it, I get out and approach him, Minka following closely behind me. I cuff his hands together with a zip tie I grabbed from my go bag and lead him into the safe house, using him as a human shield in case any intruders got in while we were gone, though I suspect not, because I haven't gotten an alarm alert on my phone.

After I clear the room and am certain that only Jax is in here, I grab a bag for Minka and toss it to her. "We have to switch safe houses."

She doesn't protest, and while she packs up her things, I grab my bag and place it by the door. I didn't bother unpacking when we came here in case of a scenario like this. I grab Jax, whisper a plan in his ear, grab a seat from the kitchen, pull it in front of the couch, and sit him on it before pushing the driver onto the small couch.

As soon as his sorry ass lands on the cushion, I ask, "What's your name?"

He stays silent, so I grab his wallet from his front pocket and pull out his driver's license.

"Hi, David." I toss his wallet and license on the floor at his feet and gesture in Jax's direction. "This is Jax. He tried his hand at the bounty, too, and has been living with us since. How long ago was that, Jax?"

"I d-don't know."

"Guess."

"A year?"

I hold back a snort at his theatrics. "And why haven't I killed you yet?"

"Because your girl likes me."

"Right. My girl likes you." I call out, "Minka?"

She peaks her head out of the closet, and I raise my gun and fire three bullets in Jax's chest in quick succession. He falls back, the movement causing his chair to fall with him, landing on the ground with a thud.

I wait with bated breath for Minka's reaction. I probably shouldn't have done that in front of her, and it's certainly an indicator that I haven't—and probably never will—abandoned my asshole ways.

But something about this situation and today has me feeling on edge. This is the life I lead. I will always be in danger, and I'll always be putting others in danger. If Minka can't accept that, then we should end this—whatever this is—now. And… maybe I want to give her a reason to do so, because I know I sure as Hell won't.

I'm already too far gone, trapped in the way she makes me feel. Her eyes, her hair, the flush of her soft skin. The way her face lights up at the sight of her sister. And her selflessness, completely misguided but there nonetheless.

Minka lets out an alarmed gasp and eyes Jax's body with shocked eyes. I try to stand there expressionless, to let her see me for the monster that I am, but at the last minute, I unravel. I fucking *wink* at her, my face angled away from David, and she relaxes and returns to her packing. And goddamn, the way she trusts me just like that is alarming.

But also exhilarating.

On the couch, I see David jerk back in shock from my peripherals, still staring at Jax, though the chair is covering him from view.

"Are you going to answer my questions?" I continue when he nods, "How did you find me?"

"Someone texted me the location."

"Who?"

"I-I d-don't know."

"So, some stranger just texts you my location out of the blue?"

He nods. "Check m-my phone."

I grab his phone from his front pocket and open up his text messages. There's a picture of my face in the first text.

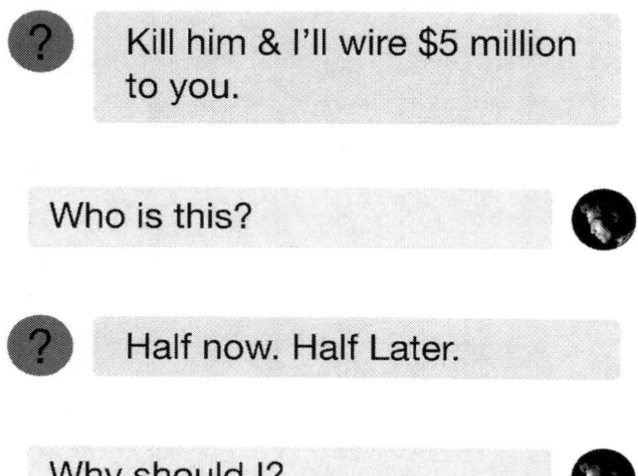

The next text has an image of David playing cards at a casino somewhere.

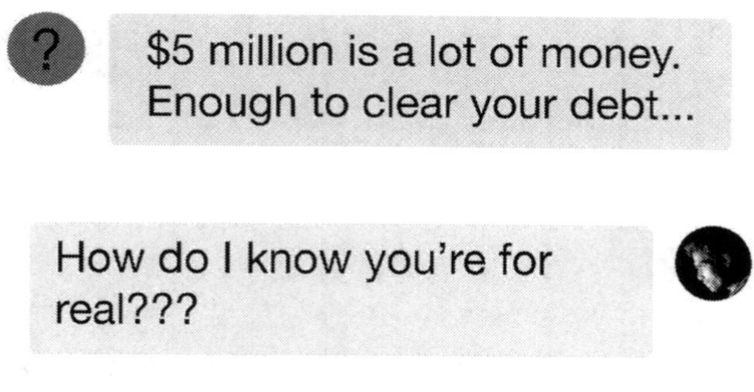

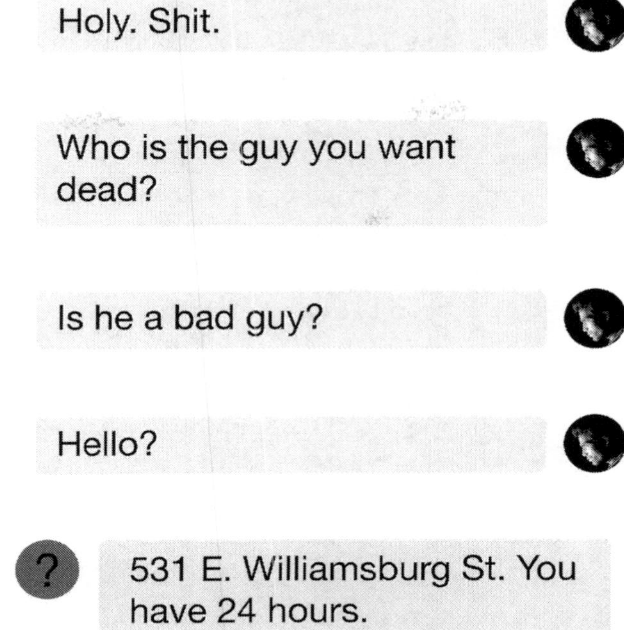

I take in the text, my jaw clenching at two realizations. One, whoever this is has money, which may mean power. And two, the unknown number knows where the safe house is, which can only mean one thing.

"Can I get up now?" Jax asks from the floor, startling David.

"W-what? B-but you were... What?" David's face is the image of confusion.

I spare him a pitying glance. "Blanks don't come even remotely close to sounding like the real thing. Next time you consider taking out a hit, don't. You're out of your league."

"They were blanks?" Minka asks, approaching me with the few things she owns. At my nod, she says, "I figured it was something like that."

Translation: she trusts me enough not to go against my word after I promised not to kill Jax when she asked me not to a week ago.

Fuck.

Someone in this world *trusts me* again.

I think my heart stutters for a staggering moment, but I don't want to admit it, because admitting that means admitting a whole lot more than I'm ready for. But if I'm being honest, I don't think I'll ever be ready for her.

I have a hit on me; she's trying to get her sister back; I'm not a good person, and my reputation is worse. The danger that precedes me will forever get in the way of us, so what the Hell am I doing?

I don't voice these doubts. Instead, I send a text to one of my guards to deal with Jax and David, take Minka's stuff from her hands and lead her to the car. We drive in silence, the adrenaline no doubt having left her a while ago. I can see it in the heavy hooding of her eyes as she struggles to remain awake as I drive to the new safe house. A safe house that I set up a while ago, one that only I know of.

And now Minka.

It's a warehouse near the spot along the Hudson I took her to earlier. The warehouse is rusty on the outside and full of blackened windows, but on the inside, it's like a home. In fact, it's modeled after the west wing of Uncle Luca's estate.

I couldn't help myself. It started out with laying down the same Carrera marble that laid on Uncle Luca's floor, and next thing I knew, I was painting the walls the same color, adding rooms to match the layout and even scouring the internet for similar furniture.

For the past seven years, I've put my heart and soul into renovating this place by myself. It was a way to pass time when I had no one but Asher and Vincent in my life, and as Minka looks around the place in wonder, I'm grateful for it.

"What is this place?"

My safe haven.

"My safe house."

"I thought we were just at your safe house."

"That was Vincent's. This is mine."

And it was always meant to be a last resort, but I suppose my life has reached that point. In fact, I'm surprised it hasn't come sooner.

Minka takes her stuff from my arms and sets it down on the floor by the entrance. She turns to face me. "What are you going to do now?"

"I'm going to find the person who sent David after us, and I'm going to take care of him."

"It wasn't your brother?"

"No. Only one person knew about that safe house."

"Who?"

I release an unsteady breath. "Vincent Romano."

CHAPTER THIRTY-FIVE

Forgiveness is not an occasional act.
It is a constant attitude.
Martin Luther King Jr.

Niccolaio Andretti

The street is ominously silent as I park my car in front of Vincent's brownstone. I reach behind me and grab my go bag, sifting through it for the plastic canister I'm looking for. When I find it, I slide it between my sleeve and the inside of my forearm, hiding the extra bulk with another coat, thankful that it's appropriate for the weather.

It's one of those odd summer days, where it's hot as balls, but it still looks like it's going to storm. I suspect that it's going to happen sometime tonight or early tomorrow, and the thought excites me. I've always been a dramatic fuck, and I can't think of better weather than one that matches the storm brewing inside of me.

I knock on the door, and after a brief moment, it opens. "Sergio," I greet, slapping the guard on the back, schooling my features so everything appears normal.

"Everything good, bro?" he asks, making a gesture for me to spread my arms and legs.

I hand him my guns first before spreading my arms and legs, grateful I paid a little extra for a plastic canister of the sleeping gas. As he runs the metal detector across my body, I say, "Not really, man. Safe house was just breached."

"Asking Vince for another?" he asks.

"Yeah. Is he here?"

Serg nods and leads me to Vincent's office, where he leaves me with a "he'll be down in a moment."

I nod my head, and as soon as he's gone, I grab the canister and unlock it, placing it into the air vent at the top. I inject myself with the counteragent as the sleeping gas makes its way through the house, and I hear the thud of Serg's body dropping from his guarding post outside of the door.

I wait another minute before I leave. I grab a few zip ties from Sergio's back pocket, where I know every Romano guard keeps a few, and tie him and the nearby guards up in case they come to before I'm done with everyone else.

I do the same with the men around the house before I reach Vincent. I carry him over my shoulder, fireman style, and haul him into the dining room, where I've gathered the rest of his men and lined the twelve of them up in a row against the wall.

Vincent's guards wake up before he does, and I can feel Serg's betrayed glare on the side of my face. I shut it out, letting my anger fester. I barely even know the guy. I've only talked to him when I needed to see Vincent, and that's it.

But still... the betrayal bothers me, and I can't help but remind myself that at least Minka trusts me, and I care a hell of a lot more about her opinion than Serg's.

Still, I say, "He gave out the location of the safe house."

A glare still in his eyes, Serg says, "You know he didn't."

But I don't.

I don't know that.

Am I supposed to abandon my gut and trust everyone? All evidence points toward Vincent. He's the only person that knows both the location of my brownstone and the safe house. I chalked it up as a coincidence that I was found by both Jax and Naz in the first place, but after today's attack, I'm no longer so generous.

And I'll be damned if it happens again.

I wait for ten minutes until Vincent rouses with a violent, hacking cough that causes my lips to tug downwards. When he opens his eyes, he blinks them slowly, the confusion evident in his face, and I wonder for the first time if he had always been like this—slow, weak —and, too distracted by the feel of a fatherly figured, I never noticed.

"Good," I say, straightening up and double checking the ropes binding Vincent's arms and legs to the dining room chair with my eyes. "You're up."

"What is this?" he asks, his voice calm and strong despite the situation.

And *that's* the Vincent Romano I, and the world, knows.

"What have you been up to, Vincent?"

"Vince," he says, a smile on his face, and I gotta hand it to him.

He's got balls bigger than I've ever seen.

I straighten up, inching closer and drawing the knife I nabbed from the kitchen out of my sleeve. Against the wall, Sergio jerks forward, a growl more feral than a wolf could manage escaping his mouth.

"Now, now," Vincent says, his eyes on Sergio. "We're all friends here. Right, Niccolaio?"

"No, actually. I don't think we are."

And with that, I wind up my fist and punch Vincent straight in the face. Sergio reacts, thrusting himself off the ground but falling straight on his face, thanks to the way I've hogtied him. I was never a boy scout, but I've got some mad skills when it comes to rope and, apparently, zip ties.

"Now that's just cruel," Vincent says, but his voice doesn't have as much strength now.

Instead, he wheezes a little, and I frown. I thought he could take a punch better than that. He's not that old. Come to think of it, that ill-omened feeling I got at Asher's wedding is still there, and I study him again.

He's lost a lot of weight in the past few months. His face, which used to draw women in like catnip, is now slightly sunken in. His eyes are bloodshot, and his hair is a little less full. Not a lot less, but still... It's noticeable when you really focus on him.

I noticed these things at the wedding, but it was more like a passing observation. After all, one doesn't just stare at Vincent Romano unless they're looking to fuck him or looking to get their teeth kicked in by an eager Romano soldier.

And it isn't like Vincent is some sort of attention shy dictator. It's just that everyone—and I mean *everyone*—he's ever met has an immense amount of respect for him. I don't think he's ever met someone he couldn't charm.

Yet, here we are—my fist dripping with his blood and accusations on my tongue that I can't turn back from. What would Asher think? He went into the heart of Andretti territory, which should have been a suicide mission, after a botched hit on Vincent. No one even touched a hair on Vincent's head that time. I, on the other hand, drew blood.

And I'd be lying if I said my reaction isn't stronger, more violent, because Minka was involved. Because I'd put her in danger, and I'd rather lash out than accept it. Nevertheless, Vincent leaked my location, and there's hell that needs to pay.

"Why did you do it?" I ask him.

"Do what?" he has the guts to ask, a look of pity in his eyes that I don't understand.

Why would he pity me?

Perhaps this is how Vincent became the head of enforcement. Playing fucked up mind games like this.

"Leak the location of the safe house."

"Where you attacked?" he asks, a convincing amount of concern in his voice. "Are you alright? Minka?"

Somebody hand this man a fucking Oscar.

"We're alright." My voice is dripping with venom. "No thanks to you."

Vincent sighs, a resigned look on his face. "You know what your problem is, son?"

"I wasn't aware that I have any."

He ignores my attitude. "You're too guarded."

"And I have reason to be." I look pointedly at the tied up men surrounding Vincent, all willing to and happy to lay down their lives for him.

The hypocrisy, to me, is obvious.

Again, he ignores me. "Yet, in the oddest of moments, you're willing to sacrifice so much for people."

"Perhaps that's why I'm guarded. I've sacrificed too much for others. Maybe I'm sick of being burned?" I say, referring to the sacrifices I made for my brother and even Naz.

"Perhaps," he agrees. "But that's a sad way to live life, no?"

I grunt in agreement, because how can I argue with that?

"Look, Vincent. Cut the bull shit. We can stand around all day or we can end this now. You gotta know I won't let up. Why did you leak our location?"

"I didn't, son," he says, and his voice is so damn earnest that I believe him for a second.

But who else could? Aside from my guards, who I monitor without their knowledge, no one else, not a single other person, has the location of the safe house. No one. Only Vincent fucking Romano, and here he is telling me he didn't do it?

Fucking bull.

"Doesn't the lying get old?" I ask.

"I don't know. Does it?"

"What do you mean?"

"You lie to yourself every day, Niccolaio Cristiano Andretti. You miss your brother, but you hide behind your anger for him." I suck in a sharp breath, but he doesn't relent. "You're lonely, but you refuse to spend time with me or Asher when we offer. And we do. Often. You look at me like a father figure, but you push me away every time we talk. Hell, I bet you do the same with that girl of yours. Minka. You love her, don't you? What do you do there? Weave a grand tale of woes and danger? Tell yourself you can't be with her, that one of you isn't good for the other?"

Jesus. Vincent Romano is tearing me apart. He's taking the man I think I am, and he's dismantling it. I want him to stop, but I don't have any words in me to speak out. Why is he saying this? Why does he even care to say this? Is this some sort of reverse interrogation tactic that I've never in a million years thought of employing?

And that stuff about Minka. *Christ.* I don't love her. I can't. And I *am* bad for her.

At my silence, he pauses and looks me in the eye. "When will you let yourself be happy, son?"

"How can I be happy with there's a goddamn hit on my head? A hit my own brother put out on me."

"Stop feeling sorry for yourself, Niccolaio. You're angry. I get that. But at some point in your life, you've gotta learn how to forgive. Otherwise, your anger will eat away at you until the only thing left is that pride of yours that's done you no good anyway."

"Stop," I demand. "Stop it and just answer my fucking question. Why did you release the address?"

"I didn't. And if *you'd* stop, you'd realize that I care about you too much to do that. Just look at me."

"What?"

"Really look at me, and what do you see?"

I see... a man who's strong of mind but not of body. How the hell did that happen?

"What... what are you trying to tell me, Vince?"

Vince.

Not Vincent.

What's wrong with me?

"Look at me and then look at that picture on the wall," he says, referring to the large canvas framed of him with his family.

And I look at it, but I don't really look at it. Instead, my mind is reeling, because I'm an idiot. I'm a hotheaded idiot that got angry and didn't think. Didn't stop to realize that there are other ways to track me without following me. Cameras. Like the ones Dex, John and I share.

And this sure as hell isn't Dex.

How did I get this so wrong?

Regret churns violently in my stomach, and I force myself to look at the picture, because it's the least I can do. In it, Vince is vibrant.

He's full of life. Healthy. The man before me isn't frail—I don't think Vince could ever be frail—but he certainly doesn't look like the man in the picture.

I don't know how I didn't notice it before. The changes were so gradual, happening in such little, tiny baby steps that after a change happened, I'd get used to it, and then the next and the next and the next and so on. And now, here I am. Feeling like the biggest idiot in the world.

The biggest asshole.

"Are you sick?" I ask Vince as I lean forward to cut his binds.

I hand him an extra knife, and together we make our way to the guards, but as soon as I cut Sergio's binds, he tries to restrain me. Since I deserve it and worse, I don't even put up a fight, though we both know I can easily best him in one.

"Let him go," Vince orders, and after a moment's hesitation, Sergio does.

"Are you sick?" I ask again. "What's wrong with you? Why haven't you told anyone?"

He sighs. "I have cancer. It's late stage, and it isn't going away. I have time left, but it's not much. I don't want to put myself through chemotherapy, and I wanted to give Asher and Lucy time to enjoy their honeymoon before I tell anyone." He looks at me expectantly.

"I won't tell Asher until you're ready to," I promise, though the promise makes me uneasy.

Asher would want to know. Right away.

"And you won't tell anyone about what you did tonight," he orders.

"But—"

"Asher is going to need you when he finds out. He won't say anything to you, but he will need you. If you must, you can tell him later. Much later."

"I'm so—" I start to apologize, but the words get stuck in my throat, strangled by the emotion there.

"It's okay," Vince insists. "You didn't know."

But it's not okay.

Because Vincent Romano has always been kind to me. He's always treated me like a son, and ever since I met him, he's had my best interests at heart.

And this is how I repaid him.

Fuck, I'm a monster.

CHAPTER THIRTY-SIX

Resentment is like drinking poison and then hoping it will kill your enemies.
Nelson Mandela

Minka Reynolds

Niccolaio doesn't come home by the time I've fallen asleep. But sometime in the night, I wake up to the sound of pounding. There's rain pouring down on the roof of the warehouse, but in addition to that sound, I think I hear another.

I jump out of bed, wary to investigate. When I exit the bedroom, I follow the sound to an open door at the end of the hall. There's exercise equipment set up everywhere in it, but when my gaze lands in the center of the room, I stop, startled by the mess in here.

There's some sort of sand pouring out of a disfigured black leather thing in the center of the room. Beside it stands a shirtless Niccolaio, a knife in one hand and in the other a clenched fist.

I eye him warily. "What's this?"

"A punching bag."

"Doesn't look like one."

"I was mad."

I hesitate. "At who?"

"Myself."

Again, I hesitate. I'm not used to comforting anyone but Mina, but lately, she hasn't needed much comfort. In fact, I think she's been pretty happy for a while now. So, I'm wary when I take a few steps forward, towards Niccolaio, trudging on only because I hate seeing him like this. So angry. Raw. Defeated.

"What happened?" I ask.

He stops slicing the bag and drops the knife on the floor, but his back is still facing me, the tan muscles rigid. "Vincent Romano has cancer," he says, his voice defeated.

"What?"

"Vincent Romano has cancer, and I just tortured him. I punched him. I accused him of leaking our safe house, but it wasn't Vincent. It was John. *FUCK!*" he shouts before his voice dips into a broken whisper, "I'm a monster, Minka. You're better off without me."

"I— Joh—" I struggle with what to say, overloaded by the information he sent my way.

With the lives we've lived, we both always assume the worst. It's been programmed into us. It sucks, but it's the way life made us. I refuse to believe Niccolaio is a bad person. Not given what I've seen of him.

For a while, words evade me, but finally, I settle on what I mean the most. "You're not a monster, Niccolaio. You're a good person. You've defended me. You jumped in front of a bullet for me. Twic—"

"If you think I'm a good person when I'm defending you, then I'm doing it wrong."

"You know what? Exactly. Defending me tonight... You're doing it *right.* What happened tonight... You were just reacting to me being in danger. You can't hate yourself for that. You're not a monster, Niccolaio."

I approach him and hesitantly put a hand on his bare back, shivering at the contact, until he shrugs me off. Instinctively, I take a few steps back, as if the distance will protect my heart from the sudden stab of pain at his dismissal.

Finally—*finally*—he looks me in the eyes... and says, "You're better off without me."

And then he takes off, not once looking back. He doesn't even slow. I reach out to touch him, but he slips past me, angling his body away from me, so it doesn't brush mine as he passes.

And I don't know why he's fighting me. Fighting this. Us. But it hurts.

It hurts so darn much.

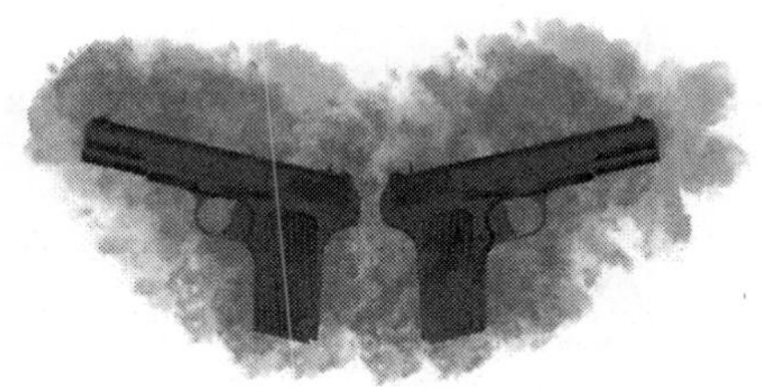

I'm grateful when Mina calls me, happy for any distraction from Niccolaio. After our discussion earlier, he entered one of the bedrooms in the warehouse and hasn't left since. I couldn't go back to sleep, and the whole day passed by with an agonizing slowness. Now, it's nighttime, and I still haven't seen him leave the room.

And I may or may not have been lurking in the halls every few minutes.

Mina happens to be catching me during one of those times. I press answer for the video call and head down the hall towards the office, where the Wi-Fi connection is strongest. I stay in the hall, though, uncomfortable with the idea of entering Niccolaio's office uninvited.

"Hey, Minka!"

"What's up, kiddo?"

"I'm twelve," she reminds me.

"Still a kiddo even when you're thirteen times that age," I remind her, though it's half-hearted.

I'm distracted by my thoughts of Niccolaio.

"What's wrong?" Mina asks, perceptive as ever, and I'm reminded that she's about to turn thirteen and will be in high school in the blink of an eye.

I open my mouth to tell her, but the words die in my throat. Sometimes I wish I could tell her about these things, like I would if we had a normal sibling relationship, but we don't. I'm both her sister and her mother, and this means there are lines of propriety that need to be drawn between us. And that includes not talking to her about my stupid boy troubles.

And apparently, Mina has picked up on this, because it's her turn to frown. "Why do you always do this?"

"Do what?"

"Keep things from me. Things that I know you want to say."

"I—I don't do it on purpose."

Her face falls. "Yes, you do."

"I just... You're my sister, Mina, and I love you. I don't want to burden you with my problems."

There's a shocking flash of anger on her face. "Like I do to you?"

"What?! Where is this coming from? You're not a burden, Mina. *Never*," I say emphatically, meaning it.

But Mina's head is already turned, her attention on someone else. My face sours when I hear Erica's voice in the background. It sours even more when I see Mina's face light up at whatever Erica is saying.

It hurts. More than I'd like to admit. Deep down, I know it's petty to resent the fact that Erica can make Mina happy. I should be happy that Mina is happy, but I can't help it. As Mina's social worker, Erica played a huge role in taking Mina from me, and I can't ever forgive that.

I don't *want* to ever forgive that.

I close my eyes, not wanting to witness Erica making Mina happy while I'm pretty much useless—unable to visit Mina and unable to do anything to cheer Niccolaio up. I sink into self-pity, hating myself for being this type of person but unwilling to change. Not when it means the alternative—taking responsibility for my role in how messed up my life is.

"You hate Erica. Don't you?" Mina says, her words startling me.

I'm glad my eyes were closed.

After I reign in my shock, I open my eyes, sigh, and say, "I… yeah."

I don't want to lie to Mina anymore.

She deserves the truth.

"She's not a bad person. I like her."

"You told me you hate her."

"I was eight, and they had just taken me from you."

"And now?" I soften my voice. "You're not a burden to me. Never."

"I know what you do."

"W-what?"

"You're with yucky men, because you think you need money to get me out of here, but you don't need to get me out of here."

My jaw drops, and I'm taken aback. "W-what? How? Who told you this? I don't d—"

"Minka," she says, stopping me with her tone. On her face is a somber expression a twelve year old girl has no business having. "You don't have to do this."

"What? Of course, I do."

"*No*, you don't," she insists, her tone adamant.

"What are you talking about?"

"I…" she hesitates. "I'm happy here, Minka. I love you so, so much, but I don't want to leave. I don't feel the same way I used to. It took time, but I like it here now. The school I go to is so much better than my old one; people are friends with me; the teachers are nice to me here; I don't have to watch you eat half a packet of cup noodles while you spend all of your money on my food; and honestly, I know it's better for the both of us if I stay here."

I think I whimper, but I don't know for sure. I'm too startled by her words to pay attention to anything but her. "But—"

"I like it here, Minka. That doesn't mean I don't love you," she says, always sounding far wiser than her years.

I guess that's what happens when life forces you to grow up too fast. Did I sound as wise as her when I was her age? Because I certainly don't feel wise now.

She continues, "It just means that staying here is right for me."

And for the first time since I started this soul-sucking gold digging plan of mine, I'm questioning everything. What if Mina's right? What if she's better off there instead of with me?

Oh, God.

Did I just waste all these years—and my sanity—trying to gold dig? I feel a tear stream down my cheek, and I hastily say a goodbye to Mina before ending the call, because I don't want her to see me like this.

Weak.

Broken.

Pathetic.

From behind me, strong arms wrap around me, and I sag into them. Deflated, but thankful for the contact.

"I'm sorry," Niccolaio says.

"For what? You didn't make Mina say those words."

"For being an ass earlier when you were just trying to help. I just... I needed time to process everything, and I'm not used to letting others help me." He hesitates. "And Minka... Your sister is right."

I tense, and it's a warning for him to stop.

Now.

Even nice people have their limits, and no one has ever accused me of being nice.

But Niccolaio doesn't heed my body's warning. Instead, he continues, "Gold digging isn't the solution to your problems. In fact, it *is* your problem. You're smart, beautiful, funny, feisty, and so fucking amazing. Goddamn, Minka, you're perfect. I truly mean that.

"You could be happy. You could be free. But instead, you're angry and frustrated, and you hate what you're doing with your life. I'm not saying Mina was ever a burden, but I *am* saying that maybe you should listen to her when she says she should stay and accept the positive life changes that'll come with that." He takes a deep breath. "Maybe you two are better living apart from each other."

"How can you say that?" I throw my hands up in frustration. "That's my sister you're talking about!"

"And I have a brother, who I've been away from for years."

"But that's different. Don't be delusional, Niccolaio. He put a hit out on you."

"It wasn't always like this."

I snort, unbelieving. I've been around Niccolaio long enough to know he's intolerable most of the time... like now. If I had the money and you asked me a month or so ago, perhaps I would have put a hit out on him, too.

"Look, Minka. This isn't about me. This is about you. Not me. Not Mina. *You.* You have to stop focusing on other people and start focusing on yourself. You think you're this awful person, but you're not. In fact, you're the opposite. You're selfless. *Too* selfless. And you've given your life up for a person who is now telling you that you no longer have to. Maybe you should listen to her." His voice drops. "You deserve more than this. More than gold digging."

I ignore everything else he said and focus on the last part, because part of me fears that he's right about everything. "It's my body. I can do what I want with it."

"You're right, and that's the problem. Is this really what you want?"

It's on my tongue to say *no.* To stop lying to myself and everyone around me. But instead, I say, "Yeah. It is. So, what?"

"There are other options," he says to me, like I haven't already considered that. His voice is raised, though, and I realize how much this conversation is affecting him.

One moment, he's the one fighting whatever this is between us, and the next moment, it's me. Maybe we should just give up. Maybe we should end this before someone gets hurt. But even as I think the words, I know I won't.

I can't.

I want him too much. And I'm too far gone. If this ends, I'll be devastated. And as horrible of a person as it makes me, I hope he feels the same way, because, heck, I don't know why we're always fighting with each other when all we want to do is consume one another.

"Look at you, Minka," he says, and I know whatever words he says next will piss me off. "Anger, bitterness and resentment. Those things only hurt *you*, Minka."

I stare at the ceiling, hoping it'll take away the same feelings he's calling out. But it doesn't. So, I fixate on a hole in the ceiling where an expanse of darkness and a sea of stars peak into the remodeled warehouse.

How can the stars still shine so brightly when there's so much darkness between the two of us? My eyes fixate on the stars, as if the stars will answer all of my questions. The jerks, of course, don't.

And so, I fixate on the darkness of the night sky instead. And the darkness of us. Darkness is tethered to Niccolaio's DNA, and I'm not sure what is the darkness of the night and what is him. It startles me that I can't tell the difference, but more so that I don't care.

I sigh, but my words still come out angry, violent and loud, "How can you say that when you're exactly the same way?!" I take a step towards him, my fingers clenched into a familiar tight fist. "I see you Niccolaio. You're more broken than you care to admit."

And he is.

I don't add that I think the fractures in his soul are beautiful. That I'd take every imperfection of his before I'd take anyone else's perfections.

CHAPTER THIRTY-SEVEN

Grudges are for those who insist that they are owed something; forgiveness, however, is for those substantial enough to move on.
Criss Jami

Niccolaio Andretti

"You know what? I am. I *am* broken," I admit. I don't even bother hiding it, unwilling to do so after Vincent, of all people, pointed it out after I fucking stained my fist with his blood. "But so are you, Minka. And there's nothing wrong with that."

She scoffs. "Get off of your high horse, Niccolaio," she says, and I wonder if we're horrible for each other.

Maybe we are. Maybe we both know this. But even so, our hearts aren't listening. Mine is aching for her in ways I never knew possible, and I know she feels the same way. I'm sure of it. I can see it in her eyes, in the way her eyes flare every time I drift closer, even if it's in anger, frustration and disappointment.

She can't stand me, but she can't stand to be away from me either.

"There are consequences to your actions," she says, referring to Vincent, and it doesn't bother me, because I know she's hurt. That she's just trying to piss me off. To push me away like she does everyone else, except Mina.

No, Mina she tries to pull close.

Too close.

"That's your problem right there."

Her eyes seductively flash with anger, and my cock rears its head. The damn thing wants angry sex, but I can't. Not with her. Not when everything is so damn complicated right now. I can lust after her, sure; I can crave her, yes; I can help her on the right path, absolutely; and I can kiss her, perhaps.

But I certainly can't fuck her.

Not when I know I won't be able to let her go afterward.

"I don't have a problem," she protests.

"You do. It's that you live life worrying about the consequences."

She snarls. "I'm not going to listen to advice from you. You didn't give a damn about consequences, and now you have a hit out on you, taken out by the Andretti family, by your own brother." She scoffs. "If that isn't enough to support the merits of my way of thinking, this discussion with you is pointless."

I shouldn't have told her that. I shouldn't have told her about my past, about my family. I don't know why I did. Sometimes I feel like I hate her. Like I hate her so fucking much. How dare she say these things to me? How dare she speak the truth? And why do I want to be around her if I hate her so much?

But I know, deep down, that it's because I don't hate her.

She's just too real with me, too eager to confront my darkest demons. She always has been. And fuck, it rouses every emotion in me—the good and bad. It wakes up the monster in me. It rises the beast. And it dawns on me that she wants me like this. She wants me to be mad at her so that I can forget about what we're arguing about and focus on the fury.

She knows to do this, because we're both the same.

We're both animals, always succumbing to our rage. Our inability to forgive.

But not tonight.

Tonight, I won't let her push me away.

And when she storms out of the warehouse, practically scorching the place in her wake, I follow after her. I can feel the waves of anger radiating off of her, yet I choose to follow her. I choose to pursue this woman that I want more than I've ever wanted anything else. More than I want my next breath.

When she sees that it's raining and she's only wearing her tiny fucking sleeping shorts and a t-shirt—Christ, *my* t-shirt—she doesn't even stop. She continues down the alley, opening her mouth, pivoting to face me, and yelling, "Just stop, Niccolaio. Not tonight. You won't win this fight."

But she's standing there, opening that too smart for her own good mouth of hers, rain dripping down her hair, her face, her body, and I hate her. I hate what she does to me. I hate that this is a fight that either both of us will win or both of us will lose. And of course, I want both of us to win...

I want to fucking kiss her.

She sees the look in my eyes—feral, animalistic, and deranged. And she doesn't move away from me.

She. Doesn't. Move. Away. From. Me.

I don't know who moves first, but within seconds, her lips are against mine.

Angry. Clashing. Warring.

And so fucking delicious.

Holy fuck.

I'm kissing her.

I'm *kissing* Minka.

I press her against the wall of the warehouse, both thankful and furious that we're so far away from civilization. The animal in me wants to fuck her against the hard metal for everyone to see. To see me claim this beautiful woman as mine. But there's no audience here. Just her, me and this amazing magnetism between us.

Her tongue dives past my lips, brushing against mine once. Twice. Three times, and I'm gone. I'm lost in the magic that is her. Her lips. Her hair. Her skin. It all consumes me until my hands grip the round globes of her ass and lift her into the air, her legs wrapping around my waist.

She grinds herself against my erection, moaning sexy little noises into my mouth. My lips drift from her bottom lip to her neck, where I nibble on the sensitive skin, trying to be gentle but not doing a very good job. Especially when she rubs herself on my cock again, trying to fuck me through my pants.

"I'm on the pill," she whispers into my mouth, the best invitation I've ever heard.

I respect this woman. A lot. I think she's a strong woman, stronger than any other woman I have met, but tonight, I'm not going to treat her like it. I'm going to dominate her, fuck her like I've been wanting to since I met her.

I pull back a little and force her lust-filled eyes to focus on my face when I warn, "I'm going to fuck you now. It'll be hard, it'll be rough, and it'll hurt. But I promise you'll feel good. That your pussy will come so hard on my cock that I won't be able to move it as the walls of your tight, little pussy clamp down on me. Okay?"

Her lips part, her eyes glazing over in arousal, but I need her to nod her head. To give me her permission.

"How do you want me?" I ask, hoping she'll let me dominate her, because fuck, I need this.

"Hard. Rough." Her voice lowers, and she rubs her pussy against my cock, our bodies separated by our damn clothes. "And *bare*."

I growl at the filthiness of her words and the trust in me they reveal. My fingers dip into her tiny shorts, ones that I'm starting to love, and it's a shame that I have to rip them off of her. And I do, tearing the shorts and her sexy lace panties at once, until she's bare for me, her pretty pussy glistening in the moonlight.

I don't even bother taking anything else off, leaving my shirt on her torso because I want her to remember that she's mine.

My hand dips into my pants, wrapping my fingers around my cock. I stroke it once, groaning as she takes my bottom lip into her mouth and sucks on it, grazing it with her teeth before she releases it. I fist my cock and run it along her slit, soaking it with her wetness, which has left a trail down her inner thighs.

She moans into my mouth, and I ram my cock into her waiting pussy without a warning. She screams at the contact, her mouth moving to my shoulder and her teeth biting down hard on the muscle there. Her nails draw blood from my back, but I don't fucking care.

Dominant and in control, I command her body, using her pussy like it's a vehicle for my pleasure. I pound into her, unrelenting as she chants my name like it's a prayer. Each thrust of my hips pushes her harder into the wall, but she doesn't complain as she takes everything I give her and gives it back as she meets each of my thrusts. My lips drift down to her nipples, and I suck on one of them roughly through my shirt that she's wearing, biting down on the hardened bud and enjoying the tantalizing smell of both of our scents mixed together.

I feel like I'm marking her. Claiming her. Making her mine. But I need more of her, more of this. I knead her ass roughly with my hands before moving them to her narrow waist and gripping the skin there. I grab her waist and slam her down onto my cock to meet each of my hard thrusts, the need to come overwhelming now, but I refuse to let go until she falls apart on my cock.

And when my fingers brush against her clit, it's all it takes for her to start spasming around me, and only then do I empty myself inside her, the tight clenching of her walls milking every single drop out of me. When we're done, I don't pull out of her. I don't think I can.

"That was..." she trails off, struggling to find the right words.

But there aren't any, so I just say, "Yeah," agreeing with her.

I keep her in my arms as I carry her inside of the warehouse, taking her into my room. I reluctantly pull out of her pussy and place her on top of my bed. I get in behind her, curving my body around hers and pulling the sheets over us.

I should probably clean her, but I don't want to. I want part of me in her even as I pull myself out of her, and that should scare me, but it doesn't.

Good God, I think I'm finally ready for this.

For our relationship.

There are a million things I need to do the next morning, but I can't help but wake Minka up with my mouth on that sweet pussy of hers, my teeth grazing her clit. And my God, when she rides my tongue, coming hard around it, I nearly spill my load on the sheets like a fucking teenage boy.

"I don't think I'll ever get used to that," she says, a post-coital glow on her beautiful features.

I smirk but don't respond, because I plan on waking her up like that as often as I can. We still haven't resolved the argument from last night, but I know she'll accept Mina's words when she's ready to. And I'll be there for her when that happens.

Until then, I plan on showing her that there's a silver lining to this. While she's showering and getting ready for the morning, I make breakfast and pack it in a picnic basket along with a blanket. When she's done, we go outside, and I set up the picnic in front of the river, ignoring her smirk as she watches the domestication of the panther that used to be me.

When we're done eating, I stare at her and say, "Curse."

Her eyes widen, taken off guard by the unusual demand. "What?"

"That's something you gave up years ago for this quest of yours. But you no longer have to."

She glances uneasily at me. "Not filing for custody of Mina doesn't mean I should stop trying to be a good role model for her."

"True, but the way you choose to be a good role model will be on your terms. Not because you think Social Services will hear you cursing and snatch her away from you."

She opens her pretty mouth, no doubt to argue my statement, but she closes it immediately when she realizes that I'm right. I can see it in her eyes that she *has* had that fear before. In fact, she's probably spent the past four years fearing that anything she did at any second may have resulted in the fury of Social Services.

And now that she no longer has those worries, I hope that she feels free, untethered to the responsibilities that were weighing her beautiful soul down.

She throws her head back and yells to the water, "Fuck, fuck, fuckity fuck!"

My eyes widen for a moment. For a second there, I didn't think she'd actually do it. My mouth spreads into a grin, and even though it sounds ridiculous, I shout with her, "Fuck, fuck, fuckity fuck!"

"Damn it!"

"Jackass!"

"Shit!"

And because I want to make her laugh, I yell, "Asshat!"

I'm rewarded by her laughter, and Minka and I curse all morning long at the Hudson, until our throats are sore, our faces hurt from smiling, and she whispers, "I'm falling in *fucking* love with you."

CHAPTER THIRTY-EIGHT

Forgiveness has nothing to do with absolving a criminal of his crime. It has everything to do with relieving oneself of the burden of being a victim— letting go of the pain and transforming oneself from victim to survivor.
C. R. Strahan

Minka Reynolds

It dawns on me that I can leave at any time I want. I no longer need to gold dig, I don't need to find a Social Services approved place to live, I don't have to study for my LSATs, and I'm not in danger if Niccolaio takes care of the only threatening person who knows about my involvement with him.

But as we head towards John's brownstone to deal with him, I'm certain that, more than anything, I want to be by Niccolaio's side. And earlier, when I told him that I'm falling for him, I meant it.

This thing we have is more real than I ever thought possible, and I can't picture my life without Niccolaio. I don't care if danger follows him wherever he goes. I don't care if I'm put in danger by the hit his brother called on him.

I want to be with him in any way I can.

And that thought has me pulling him in for a kiss after he parks the car in front of his brownstone.

"What was that for?" There's a cocky glint to his eyes, and I realize that I quite like it there.

"Felt like it."

He smirks, "Because you're *falling in* fucking *love with me*?"

I scowl, shoving his shoulder with my hand as hard as I can. His massive body doesn't even budge an inch.

His smirk dies down, and he says, his voice genuine, "You know I feel the same way, right?"

I preen at his words, and I'm smiling even as John opens the door with Ashley—or Red Senior, as Niccolaio calls her—at his side after Niccolaio's incessant knocking.

John scowls. "What do you want? You could have called."

"Hey, asshole," Niccolaio says, before greeting John with his fist.

John's face snaps back, and I leap forward, covering Ashley's mouth with my hand to mask her scream. Only after she stops screaming do I release my hand, and by that time, Niccolaio already has John's hands and legs zip tied.

I zip tie Ashley, my face apologetic as I sit her on the couch beside John. At least the couch is comfy.

I hold up the ball and gag that Niccolaio picked up from Dex before we walked to John's. Apparently, Dex is into some kinky stuff, and honestly, the thought reminds me that I'm down to try anything with Niccolaio at least once.

Except maybe the ball and gag.

With it still in my hands, I say to Ashley, "Scream, and this will go into your mouth." I grimace. "We got it from Dex, so who knows where it's been?"

Even now, I'm holding it by the end of the leather strap, unwilling to touch more of it than I need to.

Can I get an STD like this?

To her credit, Ashley's face remains neutral, and when she nods, John seethes, "You fucking bitch. If you touch a hair on Ashley's head, I swear to God, I will slap a lawsuit on you so fast, your grandchildren's grandchildren will still be paying it off."

I smile brightly. "I think we're beyond lawsuits."

And Niccolaio, I kid you not, *slaps* John. Like an actual slap. Flat palm and everything. John opens his mouth, and Niccolaio slaps him again.

"You... You *slapped* me," John splutters, as if he can't believe it.

To be honest, neither can I.

Niccolaio shrugs. "You don't deserve my fists."

John lunges for Niccolaio, but it's a pathetic attempt, especially with his limbs all tied up. He ends up falling on Ashley, who groans under the weight. I wince sympathetically and move to push John off of her.

In the back of my mind, I register happiness at the fact that I no longer have to touch John, and other men like him, out of my warped sense of need. I no longer have to gold dig, and that makes my good mood even better.

Niccolaio says, "I met your friend David."

John replies, "I have no idea who you're referring to."

I lean back and watch the exchange, curious as to how Niccolaio will get John to talk but confident that he will.

"I found your number on his phone."

John's eyes flash. "Impossible! I blocke—" his voice falters as he realizes his mistake.

"You blocked it. Is that what you were going to say?" At John's silence, Niccolaio continues, "You know, at first I thought you used our cameras. But then I saw the picture of me on David's phone again and realized the quality was shit. You had someone hack into the city's CCTV cameras, didn't you?" He doesn't wait for a response. "Now the question is why."

"I didn't do anything."

"Your fiancé here is beautiful." Niccolaio winks at me before turning to Ashley. "Ashley, is it? This all started when she showed up that first time." He inches closer. "If it isn't you, John, was it your girl?"

I know Niccolaio won't hurt Ashley, but John doesn't, and Niccolaio is a pretty damn good actor.

John's nostrils flare, and he struggles against his binds, the rigor of the movement causing me to forget his age for a moment. "You fucker. Leave her alone. I did it. Okay? Is that what you want to hear?"

"Why?"

"Because Ashley came back into town, and we picked up where we left off. Because I was determined to make sure our relationship had no problems this time around, and you were a problem. Or you were going to be. I'm going straight, and I was just tying up loose ends. Nothing personal, okay? I didn't need you coming after me now or in the future, so I came after you first. Helps that there's a hit on your head. I saw an opportunity and I seized it. You can't fault me for that. You would have done the same."

"You're a fucking idiot."

"Excuse me?"

"I wouldn't have come after you. You're not important enough. Who the fuck do you think you are?"

John flinches, his face red with embarrassment. "I—you would have."

"Yeah? Why?"

"B-because we have past dealings."

"I have past dealings with a lot of people, and most of them are they're still alive."

"You live next door to me."

"And how often do you ever see me leave the brownstone?'

He sighs. Resigned. "Rarely."

"Exactly. You fucked up. I wouldn't have come after you. I don't give a shit about you. Now, on the other hand, I have to do something about you."

"I-I won't... It was a mistake. I won't come after you again."

"Are you familiar with the Syndicate?" Niccolaio asks, his tone ruthless.

John nods his head, dread filling his face. Before we came here, Niccolaio explained to me what the Syndicate is. No matter how often the five syndicates—De Luca, Andretti, Romano, Camerino, and Rossi—fight, they're still part of one larger Italian syndicate, run by one godfather and counseled by the five *capo famiglias* (bosses) of each individual family.

Like a normal company, the Syndicate has receptionists, and part of what they do is processing hit orders. Like the one out on Niccolaio, which was approved thanks to the blood debt. And like the one Niccolaio put out on John, which was approved because John came after him first.

"I put a hit out on you," Niccolaio says, causing John to pale. "Contingent on my death. If I die, you die."

"B-but what if you die before me, and it's not because of me?"

"You better pray to God that I don't die."

"Please. Call it off." John is begging now. "I won't do it again. It was a mistake. I just wanted to make everything safe for Ashley."

"And that would have worked if you had killed me, but you didn't. Now, look where we are. You stepped wrong, John. This is the consequence."

And then, Niccolaio and I exit John's brownstone, leaving him and Ashley tied up. As we walk past the door, Niccolaio gets a phone call from Asher, and the blood drains from his face, causing me to tense.

John is dealt with. That's one problem less. We should be feeling better, even though there's still a $5 million hit on Niccolaio's head. But his expression right now? It doesn't look like everything is going to be okay.

"What happened?" I ask, breathlessly waiting for a response.

"Vincent Romano is missing."

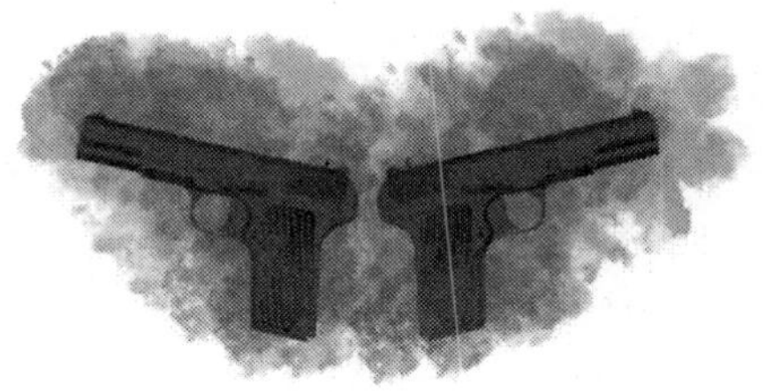

Fourteen days.

That's how long we tear apart the town, fruitlessly scouring the entire city for one man.

That's how long it's been since Vincent Romano's been missing.

And that's how long it's been before Niccolaio calls a meeting with Asher, Lucy and Bastian, Vincent's nephew. The five of us meet at Asher's penthouse, a lavish ten bedroom apartment close to Wilton, which is convenient for Lucy, since she's still in school.

The news of Vincent's disappearance came before Asher and Lucy left for their honeymoon, so when Niccolaio and I enter the penthouse, we find packed suitcases abandoned in the foyer. Niccolaio grabs my hand and leads me into the kitchen, where Lucy, Asher and Bastian are sitting on bar stools at the kitchen island.

When Asher sees us, he immediately springs up, saying, "What is it? Why did you call this meeting? Did you find him?"

Niccolaio runs a hand through his hair, which he's been doing a lot lately, the stress of what's happening getting to him. "No, but we need to talk. Dex tracked down that lead we've been following." He's referring to a burner number that Vincent has called almost twice daily for the past few months. "And... God, Vince didn't want me to tell you guys this, but given the situation, I think I should."

Asher grits his teeth. "Spit it the fuck out already."

"Vincent has cancer. Late stage. The number belongs to his oncologist. Fuck, Asher, he might even be dead already. I don't know how bad it is, but don't you see how he's been looking lately?"

When I found out that Vincent Romano has cancer, it didn't hit me like it does everyone else. I didn't know him like these people do, and even I knew through the grapevine the type of person he is. And for that, I mourned the impending loss.

I feel like I'm intruding on a private moment uninvited as I watch Asher, Lucy and Bastian react to the news. Bastian's face flits back and forth between sorrow and rage. Asher has a blank mask on, but his shoulders are tense and fists are clenched. Lucy is the strongest of them all, holding her head high, unashamed as fat tears drop down her wet cheeks.

I wait for someone to say something, but a ringing fills the air.

Niccolaio pulls his phone out, his eyes widening when he looks at the screen. "Holy shit, guys." He shows us the name on the screen. "It's Vincent."

We all spring into action, crowding around Niccolaio as he accepts the video call. But when a face comes onto the screen that isn't Vincent's, I take in a sharp intake of breath. Black hair. Chocolate brown eyes. The same strong jaw. I've never seen him before, but I know who he is.

And when he opens his mouth and says, "Hello, brother," my suspicions are confirmed.

This is Ranieri Andretti.

CHAPTER THIRTY-NINE

To be wronged is nothing,
unless you continue to remember it.
Confucius

Niccolaio Andretti

Ranie's face fills the screen, and I don't think I've ever hated it more.

"Why the fuck do you have Vincent Romano's phone, Ranie?" I snarl.

A scowl crosses his face. "It's Ranieri to you."

"Just answer the fucking question."

"You owe me a blood debt, and imagine my surprise when Vincent fucking Romano just offers himself as a sacrifice."

Oh, God.

Tell me you didn't, Vince.

"No. I don't accept his sacrifice," I protest.

Ranie smirks, and I wonder when he became this person, so eager for blood and death. Did I do this to him? Is it because of that goddamn night?

"Well, it's not really your decision. Is it, Niccolaio? And I most definitely do." He leans the phone against something and backs up, so we have a view of the room. Of *Vince*. "Any last words, Romano?"

Vince is sitting at the dining table. I recognize it immediately. There's a half-eaten steak dinner in front of him, and aside from the healing bruise my fists caused, it looks like he's been treated well.

At least there are small mercies.

Vince looks at the screen. "Is Asher there?"

I pass the phone to Asher, who answers with a guttural, "Vince."

The four of us clear the room to give Asher privacy, Lucy still crying silent tears for Vince—and probably for Asher's loss, too. Minka takes my hand and leads me onto the balcony.

She turns to face me. "This isn't your fault."

But that's the furthest thing from the truth.

"It's *my* blood debt. It's my fault."

"And Vincent *chose* to sacrifice himself for it. It was his decision. His choice. No one's fault but his."

I sigh, not wanting to argue with her today. "I don't know how I'll ever live with myself if he dies, Minka."

She looks at me with a stubborn expression on her beautiful face. "We're going to be happy, Niccolaio Cristiano Andretti. I think I deserve it, and I definitely know you do."

And for a wonderful moment, I believe her. I thought I needed the Andrettis—that they were my identity, my essence—but I was wrong… I need Minka.

It occurs to me that the motivation for my words and my actions are *her*. Since she came into my life, intruding on me like a bad case of lice, my world has been consumed by her. If I wash her off, she always comes back. If I brush her off of me, she flies back to me. And just when I finally think I've rid myself of her, I find she's still here, hidden beneath my skin.

She's looking at me like she doesn't want to fix me. Like she loves me just the way I am. Like she knows I'm a fucked up mess, but I'm her fucked up mess, and she wouldn't have it any other way.

And I hate to admit it, but I want her to stop hiding behind her anger. I want her to stop making these poor decisions. I want her to live her life for *her*. And I want to be the one to help her do all of that.

It's the worst time to come to this realization, but maybe in the wake of Vince's selfless sacrifice, this is exactly the right time for me to realize this.

Damn it, I love Minka Reynolds.

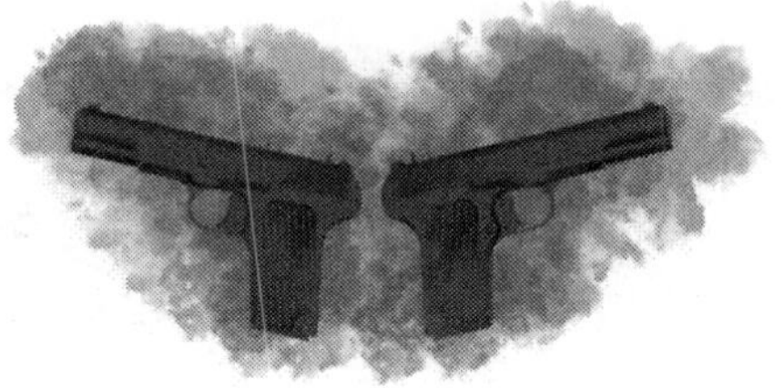

When the phone is finally handed back to me, I expect to find rage from Asher and Bastian. Maybe even from Lucy. What I don't expect to find is sympathy. Friendship. Family. And though I have no clue what Vince told them, I know he's behind it.

Has he always looked out for me? How hadn't I realized this?

I wish I wasn't so angry back then. That I could see past the fury and forgive all of the wrongs of my past. That I could move on. Maybe then would I have enjoyed Vince and Asher's company and appreciate that I found a family here.

And I did.

That's exactly what the Romanos are to me.

I make a mental vow to never take Minka for granted.

On the screen, Vince is still sitting at the dining table. Ranie sits on his right, and Luigi sits on his left, reminding me that Ranie still has not fulfilled the King's Will.

"Niccolaio, my boy," Vince greets. "You're blaming yourself, aren't you?"

"Who else is there to blame?"

"No one but fate, son."

I bark out a laugh despite the situation. "That's a load of crap if I've ever heard one."

Vince smiles at me. "Perhaps, but it made me sound wise, didn't it?"

I agree. "You're the wisest person I know." I sigh. "How did I never notice this? I had this family here, and I never even realized it. I never even appreciated it while I could."

"But you still can appreciate it. Asher, Lucy, Bastian—they'll be there when I'm gone. You were sifting through your own struggles. You would have figured it out eventually, once you healed."

"I just... You still had me scanned for bugs!"

"Because you *wanted* it. You wanted that distance."

Shame fills me. "And I regret that now."

"Well, don't. Don't you ever look back on me and feel regret. That's not what I want my memory to be associated with. You hear me?"

"But you're dying because of me."

"We all die eventually, Niccolaio. I was going to die anyway."

He's right. He said so himself last time I saw him... but I didn't think he'd go like this. Because of me.

"You don't have to sacrifice yourself for me."

"But that's the beauty of living with forgiveness in your heart. Of absolving your life of the anger and living with compassion. I *want* to do this, son. I'm happy to. If my last act on Earth can be for someone I love, then I've lived a privileged life." I open my mouth to protest, but he cuts me off, "When you made that choice all those years ago to save your brother over your uncle, did you regret it? Have you regretted it ever since?"

I open my mouth to say that I haven't, but I don't get the chance.

"Enough," Ranie says, cutting us off. His eyes focus on me, but they look uncertain before he steels himself and says, "Your blood debt has been paid."

Then, before I can even process his words, he lifts his gun and shoots Vincent right in his too big heart.

And with that, Vincent Romano, the greatest man I've ever known, is dead.

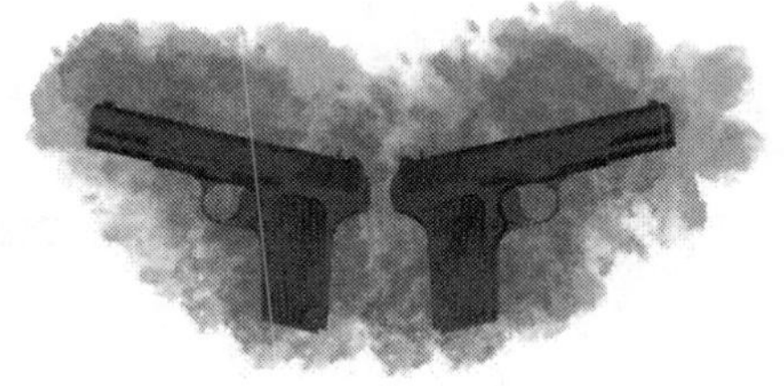

I always thought that the moment I stopped being on the run would be a happy one, but it isn't. Instead, I'm forcing the tears not to fall down my face. And I'm not the only one affected. The others heard the gunshot, too—Asher flinching, Bastian punching his fist through a wall, and Lucy squeezing Asher's hand with a death grip. But no one, not one of them, says a word to blame me.

Even in death, Vince is here.

Minka walks over to me. "He died a dignified death," she says. "One he found fulfilling."

And right now, that, and the fact that I no longer have to worry about the hit endangering Minka's life, are the only salvageable things about this moment.

I turn to Ranie on the screen, who even looks somber at the moment, which only reinforces my belief that Vincent Romano was an amazing man. One who left an impact on everyone he touched.

"Will you return his body to us?" I ask, begging him with my eyes to do so.

Ranie looks tired, of our fighting and perhaps fighting in general. He nods. "You'll have it by the end of the night. My men will fly it in. I—" he hesitates. "What did he mean about choosing between my life and Uncle Luca's?"

I finally, unencumbered by the anger and betrayal between us, get the opportunity to tell my brother what happened all those years ago, but it's too late to make a real difference. "That night, I was given the option to save you or Uncle Luca. I couldn't save you both… but I could save Uncle Luca from a painful death. So, before Asher could kill him, I shot Uncle Luca. It was quick. He died instantly and didn't suffer," I promise.

"All those letters..." his voice trails off. "Did you tell me that in them?"

I nod and let out a bitter laugh. "That and a bunch of fuck yous."

His fist clenches. "If I had just read one of them..."

"I forgive you," I say, because I know it's what Vince would want.

For me to live with forgiveness in my heart.

And I hope Ranie can do the same.

"I've canceled the hit on your head. You won't have a problem with the Andrettis anymore." He hesitates. "And if you want, you can come back home, brother."

"But the King's Will," I protest.

Ranie laughs a bitter laugh. "Dad's King's Will wasn't to kill you Niccolaio. It was to *forgive* you. I just... I was too damn angry to do it."

And I realize that Luigi is no longer sitting at the table. That, finally, after seven years of extended service, the former *consiglieri* can now retire in peace. Dad's King's Will really was to forgive me.

"All this time... I thought Dad hated me when he died, but he must have read my letter."

"I'm sorry, Niccolaio. I really am." His eyes beg of me, "Come home. We'll fix this."

"I *am* home, Ranie." And I am. With Asher, Bastian, Lucy. With *Minka.* "I met a girl, Ranie."

And for the first time in a long time, Ranie smiles in front of me. "Tell me about her."

And I do. For the rest of the night, I tell Ranie about Minka and how, in an odd, fucked up way, he brought us together. For the rest of the night, Ranie and I learn how to forgive each other. And ourselves.

And through it all, Minka is beside me, her hand in mine and a quick and witty retort always at the tip of her tongue for Ranie.

CHAPTER FORTY

Forgiveness is not about forgetting.
It is about letting go of another person's throat.
William Paul Young

Niccolaio Andretti

July 2013

Dear Dad,

I probably shouldn't tell you this, but I go by Nick now. Nick. Just Nick. I've dropped the last name, too, and it feels dirty. Like everything I think I am is just a figment of my imagination. Loyal. Strong. Brave. How could I have been so wrong? And is it fucked up that, despite my excommunication, I wish I was still Niccolaio Andretti?

I've told you this in previous letters (with a lot more cursing), but in case you didn't get those or you burned them or whatever, I'll say it again. I killed Uncle Luca. It tears me up at night. I replay the decision in my head, the chant *Ranie or Luca, Ranie or Luca, Ranie or Luca* on repeat until those are the only three words I seem to know. And God, I see all those times he cared for me and imparted his words of wisdom whenever I close my eyes at night...

But something's happened, Dad. I found someone who reminds me of him, and it feels like Uncle Luca is alive. His name is Vincent Romano, and I think he's a decent guy. If we weren't in this stupid fucking Romano-Andretti feud to the death, I think you'd like him. Hell, *I* like him a little, even though a part of me feels like it's wrong to. That I'm betraying my family just by associating with him.

But the Romano family isn't bad, Dad. I know you taught me to hate them, and your dad taught you that, too... but they're good people. They've taken me in, given me a job and a home. Don't let that piss you off too much. I'm not exactly living the good life. I kill people for a living, and I spend 99% of my time pissed the fuck off and hiding out in my home all day long. Not exactly how I used to live.

And fuck, Dad, wouldn't it be awesome if we could just forgive each other?

Love,

Niccolaio Andretti

True to his word, Ranie ships Vince's body back to New York. And imagine my surprise when I find that he escorted the body himself.

If you asked me a few months ago, I would have told you that it'd be a cold day in Hell when an Andretti *capo famiglia* steps foot onto Romano territory willingly (and without being shot down by a trigger happy Romano), but I'm not the same man that ran off to Nowhere, hiding from his little brother.

And everyone around me is different, too. The Romanos are no longer at war with the Andrettis. Vince did that. Even after his death, he has the power to sway people. It'll take some time for everyone to get used to, but Ranie sent out the decree to end the war, and apparently, the same was Vince's King's Will to Bastian, who will take over as the Romano head of enforcement.

Even though Vince wasn't a *capo famiglia* and technically can't invoke a King's Will, Vince's brother, the Romano *capo famiglia* honored the Will, and a decree ending the war on the Romano's side followed shortly after.

"Are you ready?" Minka asks, facing her back to me.

I zip up her black dress for her and take her hand. "As I'll ever be."

I drop Minka off at Lucy's and join Asher and Bastian in the car that will escort Vince's body to the cemetery, where thousands of people have gathered to pay their respects. When we get there, I see a sea of somber Romano faces, Andrettis, and De Lucas. Hell, even some of the Camerino and Rossi family members have put down their weapons long enough to give Vince the respect that he earned.

When it's my turn to speak, my eyes find Minka's warm ones in the crowd, sitting beside Ranieri, and I begin, "Vincen—" I pause, and the pain on my face evident. I don't even try to hide it. I want the world to know that Vince was a good man, the type of man that could make an Andretti mourn the loss of a Romano. "*Vince* was a good man. When I came to New York, I didn't understand how it was going to work. All I was taught was to hate the Romano family, and I assumed that was all the Romanos had been taught, too. But it turns out that all it takes is one person, one man that everyone is willing to follow, to change things. Vincent Romano was that man.

"He was tough but fair. Strong but gentle. And even in the darkest of times, he was always a guiding light. How he could live in this world and maintain that rigid moral compass of his, I'll never know. But he did, and for that, he will forever be an example of how we may hold ourselves, even in a world as dark as ours.

"There will never be another Vincent Romano, but if we all strive to act like him and honor his memory, I know the world will be a better place. And that's what Vince would have wanted from us."

CHAPTER FORTY-ONE

Forgiveness is giving up the hope that the past could have been any different.
Oprah Winfrey

Minka Reynolds

When I'm dressed, I find Niccolaio in the office of his brownstone, staring up at a stray fleck of paint on the ceiling.

"What are you looking at?" I ask him.

"Nothing," he says, a cute and carefree grin on his face. "I just... I used to be so angry."

I know what that feels like. Sometimes, I wonder—how had I been so angry? And how did that anger leave me? But standing next to Niccolaio, I realize that it was the calm that managed to extinguish the fury in me, and that calm I found in Niccolaio's arms, by intertwining my soul with his.

He turns to look at me, his gaze darkening as his takes in my curves under the tight Emerald green cocktail dress I'm wearing. "Ready to go?"

I nod, and together, we go to pick Mina up. When we enter the group home, I feel the stares of everyone around us. Parents, siblings, children, and staff all stop to stare at Niccolaio, some in interest but most in fear.

"Stop," I whisper out of the side of my mouth.

"Stop what?"

"That look. You're scaring people."

"What look?"

"The one that says you'll kill anyone who touches me."

If anything, his eyes darken further. "But I *will* kill anyone who touches you."

"They're children," I say, exasperated.

"Not all of them." At my look, he sighs and pastes an alarmingly handsome smile on his face. "Fine."

His smile is beautiful and attracting way too much female attention, so groan and say, "That's even worse."

"Jealous?" His eyes glint in amusement and satisfaction.

I sigh. "There's no winning with you."

He leans into my ear. "I beg to differ. You sounded quite victorious last night when you were coming around my cock and calling me your god."

I playfully shove him away from me with a laugh, opening the door to Mina's hall after we sign in.

When she sees us, Mina screams, "Niccolaio!", basically ignoring me completely.

I roll my eyes, a small smile on my face as Niccolaio goes to hug her. Mina is obsessed with him, and I think he's taken my place as her favorite person in the world, but I don't mind. As Mina talks animatedly with Niccolaio, Erica finds me and walks beside me, watching the scene with a smile on her face.

"She's been happy lately. Have you noticed?"

"Yeah," I sigh, watching Mina's bright smile.

It reaches her eyes, causing them to shine.

"You don't like me much, do you?" Erica asks, confronting me about this for the first time in our four years of knowing each other.

"I used to not like you."

"And now?"

"I'm learning to forgive."

There seems to be a lot of that going around lately.

"I'm not a bad person, you know."

I nod, because I do know that. Maybe not back then, but I see things more clearly now. I'm not as angry as I used to be. I've quit gold digging for good, and I've put a hiatus on law school until I'm sure that I know that becoming a lawyer is what I want to do with my life. Asher offered me an internship in any division of his company as a way to figure out what I like and dislike, and I think I'm going to take him up on that offer.

Beside me, Erica says, "I used to be in foster care."

My eyes widen at that tidbit of information, because I always assumed she came from money. As a social worker, she probably gets paid poorly, but she's always dressed well—with Hermès Birkin bags, Louboutin heels, designer clothing and diamond-embedded jewelry.

She continues, "But when I was your sister's age, a family took me in. They had money, but no amount of money in the world could get my adoptive mother pregnant, so they adopted me. And I was this girl who didn't care for it. Who was jaded from the world and hell-bent on pushing everyone away, even if they were trying to help me. It took a while for me to grow up, and I needed a lot of help from my parents and friends to do so, but I finally did. And now, I'm happy. Every day, I'm happier than the last." She turns to face me. "When I met you, Minka, you were just like the younger me. Jaded. Pissed off at the world. But now, I look at you and see that you're different. You're happy. Good for you."

And with that, she walks off.

The problem with raising yourself? You grow up fast, but you don't grow up completely. And as I stood there and listened to Erica talk, I confirmed what I already suspected—that maybe I've finally grown up. That maybe I'm finally evolving.

"What did she say?" Niccolaio asks, cautiously approaching me.

I smile at him. "Nothing I didn't already know."

With Niccolaio pushing Mina's wheelchair into the handicap-accessible van Niccolaio bought for when we take Mina out, which is every weekend, the three of us head towards Mina's school. Mina leaves us to head backstage, and Niccolaio and I find a seat in the front row beside Bastian; Asher; Lucy; and hell, even Aimee.

I was worried that I wouldn't be able to make the transition from mother slash sister duo to only being Mina's sister, but I have. And as the curtains pull back and Mina nails her first lines a few minutes later, I realize that I may not know what I'm going to do with my life, but I know that, whatever I do, I'll have my family—Niccolaio, Asher, Lucy, Aimee, Bastian, and Mina—by my side.

I lean into Niccolaio's ear and whisper, "I was right when I said we were going to be happy."

EPILOGUE

But we can't go back. We can only go forward.
Libba Bray

ADMISSIONS ESSAY #4

Question: In four hundred words or less, explain what has been the most significant day of your life and how it altered (or continues to alter) your perception of your future.

It's a Dream
by Mina Reynolds

Six years ago, I was cast in my middle school's production of Romeo and Juliet. For any other girl, that would be lauded. For me, it was like pigs suddenly sprouted Red Bull colored wings and began to explore the sky; purple rain was striking the unsuspecting New York pavement as a resurrected Prince sang notes at A5 that only dogs were able to hear; and a miracle had happened, and the Vatican had just received absolute, irrefutable confirmation that God exists, and we no longer needed faith to believe in Him.

You see, I have spina bifida, and I was told at a young age by a chorus of cynics that I wouldn't amount to anything. That for the

rest of my life, I would be nothing more than a girl stuck in a wheelchair, and I shouldn't aspire to be anything more than that. That I was nothing more than my disability, and we were one in the same. And for a dark moment, I believed them. For twelve years, I thought that I couldn't reach further than what my wheelchair would allow.

But as I opened my mouth and said as Juliet, "How now! Who calls?", my voice reverberating around the theater and reaching the loving ears of my family, a band of nonconformists that, though not all related to me by blood, have been the only family I've ever known in every sense of the word, I realized that I could be anyone. Not just a foster kid. Not just a cripple. Not just Juliet.

Anyone.

I am Mina Reynolds, and my hopes and dreams aren't bound by a stupid chair I've sat in for most of my life. They are the moon, the stars and the skies, and though they look so far out of reach, they are just as much mine as they are anyone else's. Being Juliet was a wakeup call. A much-needed eye-opener. And after that, everything else became much clearer.

My life isn't just the things that are arms reach from a wheelchair.

It's a dream.

WILTON UNIVERSITY
OFFICE OF ADMISSIONS

December 15, 2023

Dear Ms. Mina Reynolds,

We are delighted to inform you that the Committee on Admissions has admitted you to the Class of 2028 under the Early Action admissions program. Please accept our personal congratulations for your outstanding achievements.

In recent years, we have received an average of over thirty thousand student applications for the twelve hundred and fifty places available in each freshman class. Faced with an increasingly competitive selection of talented individuals to choose from each year, the Admissions Committee only chooses students that show great strength in academia, extracurricular activities, and personal areas.

With each decision, we are confident that we have chosen the best and brightest students this world has to offer. In voting to offer you admission, the Admissions Committee displays our firm belief that

you will make outstanding contributions to this university during your undergraduate years and the many that follow.

Should you choose to accept your admissions, you will receive an early orientation in May of 2024, where our faculty and your fellow student body have arranged a special welcome to help you choose your major. You will find the remainder of your application and steps to accept your admissions on the Wilton University admissions website. For more information, please visit the website.

We look forward to teaching you in the years to come.

Sincerely,
Wilton Admissions Committee
The Wilton University Office of Admissions

ACKNOWLEDGMENTS

Even after struggling to write tens of thousands of words, the acknowledgments portion always seems to be the hardest to complete. I want to thank everyone, and I want to do justice for their contributions to my success, my life, and my future as an author. Because everyone one of you guys deserve my thanks and more.

As always, I have to start with my family. L, you're an amazing boyfriend. It's crazy to think that we've been together for twenty-percent of my life—not because that's a long time, but because it doesn't feel long enough. You deal with me when I'm the biggest pain in the ass, and we both know it. I don't know how you do it, but I'm glad you do. (Also, thank you for being the first to read my books, even though you're so not a fan of romance. LOL.)

Bauer and Chloe, you guys are the best writing partners ever! I'm sure that if you guys could write with your paws, you'd be bestselling authors. Instead, you'll have to settle for writing gibberish on my Word docs every time one of you steps on my keyboard. (Thanks for that, by the way.)

Elan! You're kind of, sort of my best friend. I'd say it more affirmatively, but we wouldn't want your already bloated ego to expand. I'm already amazed that it can fit inside your body, and I'm sure that an ounce more of self-esteem would surely blow you up, and we can't have that, can we? Thanks for dealing with my sparse replies while I'm writing (which is always), and always replying when I manage to find the time to shoot a few texts here and there.

Emmanuel, I'm adding you to my acknowledgements, because you said you wouldn't read a book of mine unless you were included. (So, you can go ahead and say you're only reading a romance novel because you're acknowledged in it, but we all know the truth... You're reading it because you love me.)

Thank you, thank you, thank you to my author friends, who have helped me SO much! Kat Mizera, your advice has been invaluable. Silla Webb, you are the kindest, most talented soul I've encountered. Erin Trejo, you are an advice QUEEN! Odette Stone, if you ever decide to retire, I'll hire you as my rock. What that job description pertains, I have no clue. Knowing you, you'll figure it out for me. LOL.

Last but not least, thank you to my amazing readers! Without you all, none of this is possible. I want to give a special thanks to my Park-erettes, particularly the first ladies to join the group, who are always encouraging me to be my best. Carla, Krista, Aglipay, Joanne, Carrie, Pam, Brandi, Sarah and Heidi, this one is for you guys!

Oh, and before I forget, thank you to the bloggers, ARC readers, and reviewers for all that you do in spreading the word, writing reviews (which help more than you know!), and getting my work out there. Take the credit for any and all of my successes, because you guys are all a part of it. Hell, y'all are the reason for it.

ABOUT PARKER

Parker S. Huntington hates talking about herself, so bear with her as she awkwardly toots her own horn for a few sentences and then bids her readers adieu.

Parker S. Huntington is from Orange County, California. She graduated pre-med with a Bachelor's of Arts in Creative Writing from the University of California, Riverside. As of August 2018, the 21-years-old novelist is still pursuing a Master's in Liberal Arts (ALM) in Literature and Creative Writing from Harvard University. *Go Crimson!*

She was the proud mom of Chloe and will always look back on her moments with Chlo as the best moments of her life. She has 2 puppies—a Carolina dog named Bauer and a Dutch Shepherd and lab mix named Rose. She also lives with her boyfriend of five (going on six!) years—a real life alpha male, book boyfriend worthy hunk of a man.

For more information:
www.parkershuntington.com
parkershuntington@gmail.com

36363630R00179

Made in the USA
Middletown, DE
13 February 2019